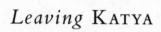

Leaving KATYA

Leaving KATYA

ও

Paul Greenberg

G. P. PUTNAM'S SONS

New York

Song lyrics from the musical *The Overcoat* are used by permission of Vail Reese, author of the book and lyrics.

G. P. Putnam's Sons
Publishers Since 1838
a member of
Penguin Putnam Inc.
375 Hudson Street
New York, NY 10014

Library of Congress Cataloging-in-Publication Data

Greenberg, Paul, date.
Leaving Katya / by Paul Greenberg.
p.   cm.
ISBN 0-399-14835-3
1. Men—United States—Fiction. 2. Women—Russia—
Fiction. I. Title.
PS3607.R45 L4   2002   2001034920
813'.6—dc21

Printed in the United States of America

1   3   5   7   9   10   8   6   4   2

This book is printed on acid-free paper. ∞

Book design by Amanda Dewey

For my mother, Ruth

The streets of St. Petersburg possess one indubitable quality:
they transform the figures of passersby into shadows.

ANDREY BELY, *St. Petersburg*

Contents

Part One

One White Night

The more I undressed her, the more foreign Katya seemed. Beneath her clothes was a whole parallel universe of underwear. Garters and stockings made of an industrial material I'd never felt before snapped together and intertwined and were somehow caught up in a bra that appeared to want to come undone by releasing not one, not two, but three different catches on the front and the back.

Was this sexy or just Soviet?

I didn't know, but I fought with the stuff uselessly until she said in English:

"Oh, please. Just destroy all that."

The catches were poorly made and they popped off when I took a good pull at them. By the time I had undressed her completely, there was a mound of ruined fabric lying on the floor just below her giant Bob Dylan poster.

Katya rolled under the covers and wrapped the blanket tightly around her, concealing her breasts like a lover in a PG-rated movie. She reached over and drew up a corner of the sheet, and for some reason I had the thought that unless I hurried she would seal the bedding up around her once more and order me to leave. I rolled in. I didn't manage to see her body before she flicked off the light. She took my far hand and pulled me around, over, and in.

Katya barely stirred under me. Inside the glass curio cabinet in front of us a night-light illuminated an advertisement for a Finnish shipping company. The ad was one of those shifting, optical illusion things, and as I rocked back and forth on top of her, the oil tanker in the picture passed backward and forward across the Finnish Gulf between Helsinki and Leningrad.

I listened to Katya, my ear against her mouth, trying to detect some quickening, but her breath remained constant and her arms stayed fixed in an X across my back. When I tried to move us into a different position, she caught her foot between the bedstead and the wall and locked us in place. And before long the correctness of the angle, the blanket wrapped around us like a sheath, the whole grinding closeness of it all produced that familiar welling up.

"The oil tanker belongs to Finland," a nonsense voice in my head said, and I looked at the shipping company ad one more time. Katya sensed the change and locked her arms even more tightly around me. I opened my mouth and just as I did, she stuck one hand between my teeth and said—as I had heard other Russian women say to dogs and children—*"Tiho!"* Quiet!

I stayed there a moment and had another nonsense thought—that I was now as far inside the Soviet Union as I had ever been. The colors in the room seemed to fade. Gray light came in through the drawn lace curtains. The blood in my ears quelled and I began to make out the rumble of Katya's father snoring on the other side of the wall.

"Did you finish?" Katya asked in English.

"Finish?"

"Yes, finish. Are you satisfied?"

"Yes. I did. I am. Did you . . . finish?"

"In some way. Actually, it doesn't matter."

"Well—"

"Well, well," she said. "Time to go."

She turned back a corner of the blanket and let me out. Then she rolled on her side, away from me, and lay her body flat against the wall.

I pulled on my jeans. I put on a Soviet army shirt I'd got from a black marketeer in a swap. I reached in my pocket for my passport and my exit visa. Both documents were gone. Probably stolen. I checked again. Stolen. Definitely. I opened all the drawers. I lifted the carpet. I started sweating. I looked in the curio cabinet. I checked her bookshelves. I put my hand in the gap between her Russian authors and *More Knots by Houdini,* the first in her small collection of American books. Nothing. I felt hot tears in my eyes. I shook my slippers. The passport and the exit visa fell out of the right slipper onto the floor. The flutter passed. I sat back down on the bed and touched Katya's shoulder.

"*Ty spyesh,* Katya?" I asked her.

"*Spish,* not *spyesh.* Your Russian is a catastrophe. How long did you study it?"

"Until last year. All through college."

"*Katastrofa.*"

"So," I said, *"ty spish?"*

"No, I'm not sleeping."

"Should I call you?"

"That would be the honorable thing to do. A man should always call. But now it's time to go. Bye, bye." She closed her eyes and yawned. I gathered up her underwear, hid it in one of the open drawers, and walked out into the corridor.

Only after I left Katya's room that night did I start to understand how her apartment was laid out. The week before, when I'd first visited, I'd had the impression that there were more rooms; that in addition to the dining room, living room, and kitchen, the main corridor went on further and led to three or four other rooms. But now, as I closed Katya's door, I took a false step to the right and realized that what I'd assumed was the living room was actually Katya's bedroom. Katya's parents and her toddler-aged niece were sleeping in the dining room where we'd all gathered for last week's party. Even the kitchen had a small bed in it and Katya's sister appeared to be sleeping there. As for the corridor that I had thought led to other rooms—actually, it led nowhere at all. Around the corner it stopped short at an obtusely angled wall. The wall must have been put in after the Revolution, when this old Petersburg mansion was subdivided into single family units. Well, it wasn't as big as I'd thought, but it was definitely from a better, more classical era. And at least it wasn't a communal apartment. Unlike poorer Soviets, the Konstantinovs had their own space, completely separate from other families, and Katya had an almost Western sense of pride that comes with that kind of privacy.

I tiptoed to the foyer and put on my hiking boots. I walked down the poured-concrete staircase and out onto the Griboyedov Embankment. It was only four in the morning but the light angling down along the canal already had a worn-out look. Actually the sun had barely set—mostly it had spun a wide circle in the northern summer sky.

The metro wasn't due to open for another two hours and the bridges over the Neva were still up so there was no getting back to my dormitory over on the island in the middle of the city. There were no taxis or buses. The streets were so quiet I could hear the gears working inside the traffic lights.

I walked in the direction of the Winter Palace and the city's central square. I passed empty grocery stores, burnt-out neon signs, and too many shops that repaired shoes. I cut through narrow alleys that ran between rummy old townhouses—everything dimmed down a notch by a layer of industrial grime. Military trucks were parked here and there. Some had a few kilos of sprouted potatoes, others had a bushel or two of dirty, withered carrots. Even at this hour, women lined up for blocks behind them, holding out empty plastic bags and tin buckets. One of these women, I thought, was probably Katya's mother.

I could still feel the warm, pleasant abrasion where Katya had crushed up against me, and I couldn't stifle a guilty smile thinking of what I might later describe as a conquest. But I also sensed a growing twinge of unpleasantness over what had just happened. In this city, where a gray melancholy rose up daily and washed over the population like a flood tide, Russian women were a kind of breakwater. Peter the Great's buildings might peel and fade, Empress Catherine's parks might grow tired and weedy, but every morning thousands of young Leningrad women made up their faces, their hair, their clothes miraculously out of nothing, with nothing, and for no other reason, it seemed, than to restore beauty to the world. And the men were awed. "Can you believe our Russian girls?" they would ask, raising their eyebrows incredulously at this rare bit of good luck. In the end, I thought, it certainly wasn't Gorbachev or *perestroika* or the new "openness" that made the average Soviet man look forward to the future; it was a Russian woman, with a fresh, smooth face, laughing in the Summer Garden at twilight.

And now I had gone and just taken one of them for my own pleasure; I had violated her neckline, which had been positioned just so to show a small V-shaped birthmark in that no-man's-land between her collarbone and breast. I had seduced her, taken her, invaded her—all those things that a local boy should have been allowed to do as compensation for enduring a cruddy Soviet life.

But on the other hand, I thought when I reached Nevsky Prospect and turned toward the river, hadn't I fought the good fight? And hadn't she, in a way, put the thing in motion? At that silly tea party the week before there had been other men. One of them had grabbed the guitar from her hands and sung a lugubrious Russian ballad looking into her eyes:

Zahodite k nam na ogonyok . . .

He'd sung the whole song and then a second and a third.

And when they'd passed the guitar to me and said, "*Davay,* Daniel, play something," I'd said very firmly that I didn't play.

"*Nu,* don't be shy," Katya'd said. "Of course you know something. *Davay, davay.*"

And even though I'd taken the guitar I'd refused a third time.

"Danochka, *davay,* we're not gonna eat you."

I sat up straight and cleared my throat. I strummed and sang a song someone had taught me in college:

Baby let me follow you down,
Baby let me follow you down,
Well, I'll do anything in this God Almighty world,
If you'll just let me follow you down.

I struggled with the instrumental bit meant to cover for the har-
monica solo. When I finally got through it, Katya burst out with the
next verse:

Can I come home with you?
Baby, can I come home with you?

And then both of us laughed and sang together:

Well, I'll do anything in this God Almighty world,
If you'll just let me come home with you.

They had me play the song again and again and I played it worse
and worse each time. The color rose in Katya's face. The guy who'd
sung the Russian ballads tried to follow along, but he couldn't pronounce the words and he shot angry glances at me, trying to get me
to knock it off.

Yes, Katya had tested me then and it seemed I possessed whatever
it was she'd been testing for. Why else would she have called me a
week later, invited me to her home, and ordered me to destroy her
underwear?

I smiled again—this time without any shame or self-consciousness.
I whistled *Baby Let Me Follow You Down,* all the way down Nevsky
Prospect. I stopped only when an old woman glared at me and
I remembered that the Russians had an odd superstition about
whistling. I reached the Winter Palace and crossed over to the Neva.
I looked downstream toward the delta. It was almost five o'clock.
The mist had burned away, the light grew, and the morning clouds
brightened until they were as pink as the stonework along the river.
The bridges lowered one by one while the night's last tanker slipped
beneath them, eastward into the country's interior.

And all at once I felt a comfort with Leningrad that I hadn't felt before. The pointless disorder of the streets, the toxic stink of cheap gas, the unfair rules that kept people panicking—all of that seemed to burn away with the mist. I smelled Katya on my clothes. My fingertips tingled with the phantom of her figure—a figure that had something to it, that curved and tucked like a 1940s pinup. I remembered the last glimpse I'd had of her face, her slightly upturned nose peeking outside the covers, her cinnamon hair shielding her eyes like a veil.

And I wished I could somehow save it all, arrange it exactly as I was perceiving it into a kind of multimedia presentation that I could mail back to my father. "Dad," I would write on an attached note, "enclosed please find 'The Russia Phase.'" And when he received it he would project it or boot it up or do whatever you were supposed to do with such things and he would pause. Maybe he would admit that he might have been too hasty in labeling another part of my life as a phase. Maybe he'd suspend his professional training just for a moment and stop picking apart what I was saying even as I was saying it. He might even think back to the argument we'd had in his office just before my leaving—me sitting, as usual, on the patient's couch; him swiveling anxiously back and forth in the shrink-chair-of-power, reminding me that we weren't in the 1980s anymore: the recession was deepening, he was losing patients, the new HMOs were killing him, and with his new family situation he could offer no more support from his end.

Now with just a week left of my time in Russia, the diagnoses Dad had written out on the air lost all their power. The troika of words he'd branded me with—"rash," "impulsive," "depressive"— were meaningless in this country. If I was rash and impulsive, then so was Katya. And actually, without rashness and impulsiveness there would have only been those halting American phrases that had always tripped me up in high school and college—"Do you like me?" "Can I kiss you?" "Will I see you again?" There was none of that with Katya. Just attraction and motion.

And if Katya and I were both a little on the sad side, "tending toward depression" as my dad might say, well that was okay with me too. I liked Katya's melancholy abruptness. I liked the whole direct-but-gentle sadness of the Soviet Union. I liked how nobody here went to a shrink and how people stayed away from shrink words like "depressed," "depressive," and "depression." Russians somehow seemed to understand that depression was just sadness and that sadness was just a mood. One of many lenses through which you can take in life's light. Moods colored life, sometimes darkly, but they also gave life immediacy and freshness, allowing you to react sincerely to every new thing that came your way.

The bridge ahead locked into place and I crossed over the Neva to Vasilevski Island. The seagulls chattered overhead and in another half-hour I was back at my dormitory. The corridor going down to my room was strangely alight and I heard Soviet television muttering from my room. I opened the door. A TV had been moved into the common area and a dozen Russian students crowded around it.

"What's this?" I asked.

"Some kind of coup," my roommate said between cigarette drags. "They got rid of Gorbachev. They're closing the borders."

He saw the color drain from my face and laughed.

"Don't worry," he sang in English, "be happy."

Emergency Committee

The Government Committee for Emergency Situations looked like an American parody of Soviet Communism. Eight drab men, two of them in military uniform, sat at a table with plastic flowers and stared out at the cameras. Everything about the scene was gray: gray suits, gray faces, gray prospects. There was no escaping the Committee's dreary proclamation. They were on every channel.

I couldn't follow the speeches—it was Soviet bureaucratic terminology—subordinate clauses hanging down like twisted rope-ladders from every verb. My Russian friends had difficulty translating. Occasionally a loud whoop of laughter sounded from one of the students around the television.

"Now they saying our moral level has gone too low 'cause of the Gorbachev," someone hurriedly translated. "Now they saying influence of American people is catastrophic problem." After a while I started to relax. I laughed with them when they laughed, even though I didn't understand. A bottle appeared and made its way around the circle. I drank some and everybody seemed to be lightening up.

We watched for two hours and near the end of the broadcast a little party had broken out. A rare baton of good sausage was brought out and evenly distributed. Toasts were made.

By nine, people started pulling themselves together for class. One by one they filed out and shook my hand. I turned to one of my dorm-mates and asked him jokingly, "So Kolya, seriously, when will this be over?"

The smile left Kolya's face and he stared at me blankly. "What does it mean, 'over'? Next comes the civil war. Then a lot of blood. You'll see. Like the Great October Revolution all over again."

I skipped language class and slept off the long white night. It was a complicated nap, with nagging characters worming their way back and forth between sleeping and waking. Some time in the early afternoon I felt Katya move up close to me. We were still in her bed and we were trying to have sex again. The bed had decreased in width and I kept sliding off. I seemed to hold her but she kept slipping through my fingers and I started to tell her in a jumble of Russian and English about the bridges being up on the river and the coup and the Emergency Committee. I felt a weight across my leg and reached down to gather up her thigh, but my hand came up empty. I heard my Russian textbook fall off the bed. I made out the sound of the television in the next room and the clanging of the crane outside the window.

I opened my eyes and looked out my dormitory window at the Finnish Gulf. A wave of anxious nausea seemed to roll out of the gray sea up through the window.

Could they really just close the borders? I thought. Would they just tear up my exit visa and "retain me for questioning"? I saw myself in that gray room we all know, a Soviet KGB officer with a hammer-and-sickle pin on his lapel looking through the diary I'd kept over the last few months saying, "Now, let's talk about this woman you call Katya. . . ."

It all seemed so unfairly arbitrary. Could the Communists just get rid of Gorbachev, cancel *glasnost,* and declare a "do over" to the world? Actually, it appeared as though they could. What would the world do? And what about people my age? Would it be like Stalin's time for them? Would they be sorted out according to their usefulness and then shipped off to Central Asia or summarily executed? Which category would Katya fall into? She came from solid, upper-middle-class *nomenklatura.* Katya's father had stayed a devoted Party member throughout. It was comforting to think that the Emergency Committee needed people like him and his family.

Then with a groan I remembered a moment from Katya's tea party the week before. At the time it had seemed so charming and new. The guitar playing and drinking and joking had stopped and Katya had stood up and sauntered across the room to the piano.

"And now," she'd said, "I have something very important I want to do. I want to make an announcement." She flexed her fingers and banged out the opening cadenza of Chopin's *Polonaise Militaire* while standing up. Then she picked up her purse.

"Dear friends," she said rifling around in it, "I have some complaints. I have some real complaints. Nothing is made up here. Lena," she called out, "help me please."

Lena handed her a box that was labeled "ordinary matches." Katya reached into her purse and pulled out a card.

"For fifteen years I did all that was right," Katya said. "I was a Child of October, I was a Young Pioneer."

"And the head of your unit," Lena said. "Always prepared."

"Yes, the head of my unit," Katya did the Young Pioneer salute, her right arm angled across her forehead. *"Vsegda gotova!"* she said—Always prepared.

Lena saluted her back and they both laughed.

"No, but this is serious. Listen. So where was I?"

"You were a Young Pioneer of the first class," I said.

"Of the first class," Katya said, holding up her pinkie. "I had respect. I held the line. You all went your own way when Gorbachev, that goat, came along. But I didn't listen. I held on throughout this stupid time of ours. 'You're just obsessed with the West,' I warned you. 'It's just an American Phase,' I said. And then Dad helped me move up in the Young Communist League. 'Great,' I said, 'let's go!' I marched around in a circle. I marched and filled out forms. I wore a stupid badge. And today, my mum is outside waiting in line for potatoes. Tell me friends, what is there for me in this?"

"Nothing," Lena said.

"Exactly nothing at all. So that's that. I'm finished."

Katya struck a match, held up her Young Communist League card and lit it. She burned it until the fire licked her fingers. She threw what was left of it into an ashtray, walked back over to the piano and finished the Polonaise.

Lying on my thin dormitory mattress, thinking back through this scene I decided I had to call her. Not only because of the coup, but because I had said I would and if there was one thing I'd learned during my time in the USSR it was that giving your word to an intimate was a serious thing. I went out into the street to the nearest pay phone. I put in a rare two-kopek piece that I kept in reserve and dialed her number. The line crunched and whirred and went dead. My two-kopek piece disappeared into the gray metal box.

It took an hour to find another coin. I asked sales clerks and street vendors, but no one had one. I heard my heavy accent and the messiness of my Russian verb conjugations. People looked at me cockeyed when I spoke to them and I wondered whether it was because they didn't understand me or because now they feared the worst from any interaction with a foreigner.

In the end a black marketeer sold me a two-kopek coin for five dollars. This time the call went through and Katya answered.

"Katya," I said in English, "it's me."

"Hello, you," she said.

"Are you all right?" I asked.

"I'm magnificent." She laughed.

"No, seriously."

"Seriously?" she said. "Seriously, you shouldn't call me. There will be all sorts of questions."

"But do you want to see me?"

"When do you leave?"

"Saturday."

"Then it's possible we could meet on Friday when this is all over. Maybe at the Metropol Restaurant—you said you like those old places, didn't you? We could meet at seven." And she hung up.

۶۵

The next few days began with the same waves of anxiety followed by bursts of pointless activity. The students in the dormitory took me from meeting to meeting. They took me to apartments where different people wanted me to "take down their testimony" in English. We went to a bread factory. We went to a cafeteria. We went and looked at some sick bears at the zoo. We drove out to the island of Kronstadt in the middle of the Finnish Gulf where we took photographs of hulks of concrete and dirty water.

I tried to book calls home, but the international lines were jammed.

A queue in front of the American Consulate went around the block twice.

The television and the radio were useless. Every day more proclamations came from the Committee. The old newsmen from Brezhnev's time were brought out of retirement and given prime-time slots. Here and there a pirate signal would break through the state channels and we'd get a glimpse of murky images of barricades and fires. There were rumors of fights in the streets of Moscow and talk of an opposition leader rallying the protesters. I sent a telegram to my mother and my brother Cam, telling them I was okay, telling them that I missed them terribly, that all I could think of was home, and that if I was able to get out, maybe through Finland, I would come back and live with them in Connecticut. . . .

And then, as quickly as he had vanished, Gorbachev reappeared. He showed up on Friday morning, hand-in-hand with the opposition leader, who was called Boris Yeltsin. They posed for photo-ops in front of a tank. American correspondents arrived and soon everyone on television was calling the last few days "historic." The army turned against the Emergency Committee. The tanks went back to their barracks and beautiful girls kissed soldiers open-mouthed and put flowers in their gun turrets. One of the Emergency Committee members blew his own head off and the rest of the group was taken into custody where they continue to cause a legal problem to this day.

I tried to call Katya, but the shuffling of regimes seemed to have affected her phone line. I tried from different booths all around town thinking that a path might be found through the old copper circuits and the resentful switchboard operators. But no matter whether I was in the center of the city or far out by the Pioneer

Metro Station, when I dialed her number I got an erratic beeping that gradually faded away into the dull chatter of other conversations muttering over faraway crossed lines.

I thought again of the night we'd spent together. I retraced the relatively few steps it had taken to get her from sitting inviolably across from me at her tea table to lying diagonally across her bed, one leg bent, her dress sliding recklessly off her thigh. The attraction had been very strong then, and yet the elements that had brought us together were so arbitrary—a common acquaintance, a guitar, a song that we both happened to know. A few arbitrary events working against us—a coup, a damaged phone line—were equally effective at separating us. The only thing preventing our losing each other completely was a vague plan she'd suggested over the phone, that we meet at the Metropol Restaurant.

But now, without any kind of confirmation, that last conversation and the rendezvous she'd hinted at felt intentionally vague. The hurried, offhanded way she'd mentioned it might easily have been an excuse to get off the phone. When she'd said we could meet on Friday night "after all this was over," how had she known that "all this" would be over so soon? I clenched my teeth and realized that there might be little difference between how women saw me in Leningrad and how they saw me in high school and college. I was still an over-aggressive adolescent, fruitlessly badgering girls to go out for a walk, over to the parking lot, back to the dorm, out behind the Winter Palace.

So I decided that this one time I would not play the idiot, teenage hanger-on. I would not go to the Metropol Restaurant. Instead I would sit and drink into the night with my dorm-mates. I would make toasts to our never-ending friendship and then I would slip away onto my Aeroflot flight and disappear into the West.

༄

In fact I arrived at the restaurant at seven, just as she'd suggested. All I found was a gray, hungover crowd swirling around the building's raised portico. An imbecile with a patchy beard yelled at me for no reason at all. An old man selling puppies from a plastic bag walked over and offered me a dog. *"Nyet, nyet,"* I said, and waved him off.

A prim figure in an emerald-green parka hurried away from me. The girl's bright coat matched her shoes exactly and she stood out from the scene like an animated character painted over a black-and-white film. I watched the brisk way her hips moved in her dress and thought again how well Russian women understood their beauty. I wanted to see this particular girl's face. I imagined her naked. I wondered if she would "finish" in the same way Katya had. I turned the other way and stifled the thought.

I swept my eyes back and forth over the crowd. Nothing. Fifteen minutes went by. Still no sign. Another fifteen minutes. It was now seven-thirty. The familiar high school humiliation burned in my forehead. I blinked away a tear. Someone tapped my shoulder and I turned angrily to ward off either the imbecile or the puppy man. But it was the girl in the green parka who faced me. She smiled with bright green eyes and green eye shadow, all the same shade as her emerald shoes.

"There you are," Katya said lightly, "I thought I'd lost you."

Inside the Metropol thirty or forty waiters lurked in the sepia shadows and avoided the responsibility of the grand dining hall as much as possible. Only a few other couples shared the restaurant with us and the empty space bounced our words around so that we were all aware of one another's conversations.

Katya picked at a pink-and-white-striped platter of salmon and sturgeon. She took a forkful of red caviar and rolled one of the eggs around on her plate until it punctured and caved in. I reached across the table and took her hand.

"Is there something wrong?" I asked.

She looked up miserably. Her lips flattened out and the arrogant hint of a smile she usually wore disappeared. Her face, which I remembered as accusing in its sharp, angular beauty, softened into a lovely weariness.

"What could be wrong?" she said quietly, almost to herself.

I put my other hand over hers. Her palm felt like a hot, small animal trapped between my hands.

"You're not even a little excited?" I asked after a few moments.

"For what?"

"I don't know. Everything's sort of open now, don't you think? There are possibilities now."

"Possibilities for what?"

I tried to think of some way to describe the kind of possibilities that I felt lay ahead. What I wanted to say was that now, with the Communists out of power, there was the possibility to live life without a label. The nuclear bogey that had circled over us had been erased from the sky, and soon our generation would have its own name—a name that we ourselves hadn't even thought of yet. Our decisions would be brighter and more airy—free of the dark Second World War gravitas that weighed down our parents and their parents.

Those were the kind of possibilities I meant. But when I tried to translate all this into either bad Russian or simple English, the meaning was stripped away and the only word that came out of my mouth was,

"Democracy."

"Democracy?" Katya answered with a bitter laugh, raising her eyebrows high. Then she made a "ts-ts-ts" disappointed sound and looked down. She pulled her hand away and smoothed the table-cloth in front of her. She turned her head and flashed a tract of her strong ivory neck, eyeing me suspiciously from an angle.

"Democracy has nothing to do with you and me," she said. "Democracy is just a label that someone puts on something. It's like a sign that says 'this should cost thirty rubles' even though you know it's only worth ten. What does democracy have to do with you or me or the strong way we're feeling about each other right now at this special moment in time?"

A keyboard player and a singer came onstage. They played *Yesterday* and then *Feelings*. I offered Katya my arm and we walked out onto the dance floor. One of her fingers brushed the bare space between my sweater and my trousers as she put her arms around me. I kissed the birthmark just below her collarbone. A drunk ran into a woman dancing next to us. Her date balled up his fist and rammed it into the drunk's mouth. Two teeth flew out onto the floor. The drunk stared down at his teeth for a moment and then kicked the other guy in the stomach. Four waiters came over from their columns, seized them, and threw them outside into the street. The band started up again. Katya pulled close to me.

"Did you ever think of killing yourself?" she whispered in my ear.

"I don't know," I said. "Maybe."

"I do all the time. One friend of mine, he wanted to do it but he only could find a butter knife. He cut and cut away at his arm like it was wood. Then he fainted."

"That's terrible."

"We all thought it was funny."

We were the only couple dancing now, the rest had retreated back to their tables. Men were sliding their hands between the buttons at the backs of their dates' old-fashioned dresses. A musky smell of sweat and perfume rose up and covered over the cognac fumes.

"You know what's not funny?" Katya said suddenly.

"What?"

"That after tonight you will go back to New York, slip out of here like Houdini cheating his way out of a knot. And I'll go back to my apartment and they'll close up this box with real chains and real locks and then it will all be over. And we'll just lose each other."

"We'll see each other again. It won't be so hard to come to Russia now. I'll come again."

"Of course you won't. It's clear how it will go," she said. "Once some Mormons came here, from Utah. Oh, they *loved* Russia! They made toasts. They made promises. Then they all left. And they never even sent a postcard."

We caught the last metro of the night and headed toward her apartment. I convinced myself that I was being gracious and chivalrous in accompanying her home. But I was also calculating the amount of time I could spend in her bed before I'd have to sprint to my dorm room, gather my things, and make the morning flight back to New York.

The seats in the train had all been taken by old women carrying sacks of food. I held one of the straps while Katya hung loosely from my arm. A couple of times she turned her head up as if to inspect the ceiling vents or read the posted rules and regulations for behavior on the metro. Then she'd look coyly over at me and wait for me to kiss her. The old women stared at us, scandalized. I smelled Katya's shampoo and perfume, and underneath those smells I detected her given smell, a deep pheromonal thing that I find hard to describe because I seemed to perceive it through another, indefinite sense. I imagined tracking this smell under her arms and down her sides. I thought about her embroidered sheets. I wondered what kind of underwear she was wearing beneath this particular dress. I kissed her neck and pushed the shoulder of her dress back, revealing a thick, black bra strap. I pushed back the strap with my nose and saw the birch-leaf pattern the elastic had pressed into her skin. I started to raise my hand to run my fingers over the relief. The train slowed, the lights flickered, and all at once Katya stood up straight.

"Oi!" she said, "it's my station." She pulled her arm out from mine, adjusted her dress, and disappeared out the door of the train.

"Careful," the automated metro voice said, "the doors are closing." I stopped short and felt for my passport. I looked up. Katya zoomed away up the escalator. The doors of the metro slammed in front of me, bounced once, and closed tight, and the train carried me off under the river.

Temporary

It really didn't occur to me that I could stay longer in the Soviet Union. My exit visa had an expiration date stamped on it and I imagined that if I exceeded the length of stay, someone would rule that I had irrevocably waved my right to exit. And when I went into the passport control booth at Pulkovo Airport, the border guard's behavior was in line with my suspicions. He checked my face against the photo on the flimsy lavender document half a dozen times. He passed it under an ultraviolet lamp that detected the presence of a symbol that was invisible in natural light. Then he slipped the exit visa into a slot where it disappeared into what might have been a vast, cross-referenced archive of the movements of American travelers. He continued to stare at me. I smiled. He didn't. Finally with a tilt of his head he signaled me to go on to departures. He didn't even stamp my passport. In fact there was no official evidence I had been in the Soviet Union at all.

And eighteen hours later, when I came out through the arrivals chute at Kennedy Airport and took in the blocky brown signs, the Clorox smell, and the dull faces of uniformed men patiently riding their floor buffers, the existence of the Soviet Union grew improbable. Katya's birch-leaf underwear, the Emergency Committee, even the paranoid border guard at Pulkovo Airport had no credibility in the "real" world opening up beyond the rental car desk. I stepped out onto the curb and I saw my mother's 1979 champagne-edition Chrysler Cordoba take shape out of the rain. I saw that my brother Cam was at the wheel of the car, smoking, while my mother sat in the backseat puffing away on a cigarette of her own. The front passenger seat had been left empty, just for me—my own special slot as the prodigal older son in the divorced family unit.

I remembered now the frantic telegram I'd sent during the coup—how I'd promised to come back and live with them in Connecticut. At that time home had seemed a miraculously safe place. The center of good at a terribly bad moment. But seeing Cam and Mom splitting a pack of Virginia Slims I felt the center of good slide eastward. I remembered now how Cam had decided not to return to college for his senior year and how Mom had lost another paralegal job after a nit-picking squabble with a toady old lawyer. And I was planless and jobless. The only money I had was a wad of rubles I'd been unable to change back into dollars. The life ahead wracked into focus. The three of us would live as we had lived back when Cam and I were in high school—tucked away in Mom's liveryman's cottage in Connecticut. We would bicker over breakfast, check the want ads, and eat at Hunan Taste once a week.

Cam spied me first and tooted out shave-and-a-haircut on the

Cordoba's bossy horn. He barreled up onto the curb and almost hit a garbage can. He powered down the window and looked dully through his mussed-up sandy hair.

"I see you have completed your mission, comrade," he said in a kind of spooky KGB voice. "Have you brought zee documents?"

"We were so worried," my mother blurted out and then choked back a sob.

Before we could properly greet each other, a taxi behind honked and forced us to drive away up toward the airport thoroughfare. Then we stopped dead while a hundred cabs and shuttles flashed their brake lights and converged on a single lane. The smell of our old German shepherd, Lucky, wafted up from the upholstery. Two signs ahead warned "roadwork next ten miles" and the sluggish day that was now in its twenty-fifth, jetlagged hour seemed permanently stuck in a deep, gray groove.

"Some girl from college called this morning," Cam said, and then coughed a long smoker's cough, just like my mother's.

"Anne?"

"Yeah, Anne. She said to tell you that she and that Elizabeth girl rented an apartment in the City, on Henry Street. They invited you for dinner."

"What did you tell her?"

"Told her you couldn't. Too tired. Jetlag, right?"

I glared angrily ahead. "Right," I said.

"Anyway, you don't even know where Henry Street is, do you?"

"No, I don't. Where's Henry Street, Cameron?"

Cam took a long drag on his ultra-slim and paused for effect. "It's Chinatown, Daniel," he said.

Cam made a wrong turn and instead of cutting through on the Van Wyck he put us way out on the Belt Parkway. We made an ex-

cruciatingly wide arc and traced the entire southern shoreline of
Queens and Brooklyn. The rain hammered away at the roof, and the
worn-out windshield wipers only shunted the water back and forth.
Dirty puddles sprayed up from the tires onto the windows and then
sloughed off into the murk of Jamaica Bay. We passed the cemetery
where my grandfather and my aunt are buried. We passed the projects at Coney Island—projects that stood high and bleak like the
novostroika towers in Leningrad's newer neighborhoods. Off in the
distance a sign in Cyrillic advertised "M. P. Klimov, Shoe Repair."
My head fell against the window and through the raindrops it all
merged into a kind of gray New York/Leningrad blur. My eyelids
had started to droop when Cam burst out suddenly:

"I found an awesome temp agency."

"Great," I said.

"They pay fifteen an hour for word processing."

I tried to multiply fifteen dollars times forty hours a week times
four and a half weeks a month.

"That's almost three thousand dollars a month before taxes,"
Cam said.

"Wow."

"You have to know Wang, though."

"Oh."

"You don't know Wang, do you?"

"It's an obsolete computer program. No one knows Wang."

"I know Wang," Mom ventured from the back.

We were all silent for the next fifteen minutes.

Cam missed the turnoffs to the Battery Tunnel, the Williamsburg
Bridge, the Midtown Tunnel, and the Queensboro. It was as if some
force field was keeping him from cutting through Manhattan. He
was in fact making a complete circle of the Outer Boroughs, taking

us around and almost back to JFK. A giant, goddamn do-over. Somehow in Astoria, though, he managed to find the Triborough turnoff and we crossed over the first leg of the bridge. But then I could see him grow confused as the signs ahead suggested either north or south, the Bronx or Manhattan. I realized that he was so turned around he didn't know which way was which. He warbled the wheel and the big silver car rolled back and forth over the watery lanes like a great, wounded fish. A truck blasted its horn blowing us all the way to the right. I couldn't stand it any more.

"Jesus, Cam, what the fuck?" I shouted. "Is this the frigging Circle Line?"

"What the hell do you want me to do?" Cam shouted back. "We drive all the way out to Kennedy, pick you up like you're the goddamn tsar or something, and then you sit there like a rock. I give up. I'm just following the traffic."

Cam turned and looked over his shoulder at Mom, silently imploring her to make a judgment on all this. The car was straddling two lanes now and we were headed directly for a neat row of orange construction barrels.

"Cameron, you have to watch the *road!*" Mom screamed.

Cam snapped his head forward. He jammed the wheel to the right and before anyone could say anything, we headed unstoppably downtown on the FDR Drive to Chinatown.

At the very end of Manhattan Cam started to try to round the horn of the Battery. He headed for the West Side Highway but he was buffeted by waves of Asian shoppers pulsing through the Chinatown markets. We came to a complete stop at the corner of Henry Street and East Broadway.

"You know what, Cam," I said, my hand on the door handle. "You guys go on home. I'll stay at Anne's tonight."

Temporary

❦

Anne and Elizabeth's place was a railroad apartment in a gray brick tenement on the border between Chinatown and the Lower East Side. It was just temporary, they said, but they were having trouble making the rent and there was something between a room and a hallway that they offered me for $200 a month. They'd already paid for September, so I had more than three weeks to earn my security deposit and the first month's rent.

At first the dark windowless room suited me perfectly. The previous tenant had built a clever loft bed, and once inside this sleeping slot, it was impossible to tell whether it was day or night. I could sleep at will, whenever my jetlagged mind demanded it.

But in time the lack of light compounded and extended what should have been only a few days' displacement. I fell asleep too early and woke at odd times with an air-raid alertness. Every night became a series of interrupted naps; every dream a repeating slide show of difficult pictures and phrases. I did not get to see Katya's face in all this. Instead I got a string of arbitrary Russian words: *nezhny*—tender, *myagki*—soft, *tyomny*—dark. My dream mind correctly conjugated the perfective and imperfective aspects of the Russian verb *teryat*—to lose—something my conscious mind had never been quite able to do. And just as I was better at Russian in my sleep, so too was that ballad singer at Katya's tea party better at his English. He fluently sang *Baby Let Me Follow You Down* in a flat monotone while the sound of Katya chanting *"Nu, nu, nu"*—Well, well, well—chortled everywhere.

The jetlag worsened. It was as if the room had become a kind of decompression chamber where the people in charge had forgotten to adjust the pressure to normal and allow for the victim's release. I would return home at six o'clock after searching uselessly for a job, my head aching from the previous night's sleeplessness. I would climb up to the loft, lay my head down on the pillow, and say to myself: "Just a little nap, just a little break." Then there would be Katya's hair, her verbs, and the singing. I would open my eyes and it would be seventeen minutes before midnight. I'd fold the pillow into halves and quarters and bunch the whole world around my ears in a sleepless panic until Anne or Elizabeth passed through my corridor to the shower and I knew that morning had come again.

It went on and on like this for almost two weeks. Finally I decided I had to recalibrate. On the second Monday after I'd returned I stayed up for an entire night. In the morning I jogged to the Battery and back three times. I stayed on my feet all day. When Elizabeth came home at seven I sat facing her in an uncomfortable folding chair and demanded that she engage me in a conversation about applying to medical school. And when Elizabeth started to yawn, I yawned back and saw that eleven o'clock had come. I mounted the platform and lay myself out. At last I could feel sleep, the Real Sleep rising up and rolling over me like a powerful blue Hawaiian swell. The Russian words were drowned, the slide show of Katya's suitors flooded, and the blue before my eyes deepened to azure, to violet, and then to black.

"Daniel," Elizabeth shouted, "From Russia with love."

She threw the cordless phone into the loft-slot and slammed the door to her room.

I looked at the clock. It was two-thirty-three A.M.

"Hello?" I said into the phone.

Nothing in response. Nothing, that is, except for the white noise of a distant Russian phone circuit.

"Katya, is that you?" I called out in English.

A chatter of ghostly, unrelated Russian conversations answered back. A hundred crossed lines. A woman called Tanya was asking Vladimir Petrovich if he had received her parcel. On another crossed circuit Sasha was shouting, "Milk! Milk! Milk!" to which Maria was answering, "What? What? What?" "Who's speaking English?" an unidentified person asked. And then underneath it all the faintest whisper, a Who on a dust speck, Katya's voice.

"Alloooo?" she called.

"Katya?" I answered back.

"Milk!" demanded a voice.

"Parcel!" shouted another.

And then Katya: "This is completely useless."

And the line went dead.

I sat up in the loft bed and banged my head on the ceiling. I was once again fully awake at the wrong time. The deep blue wave of sleep was gone and I floated, motionless like a boat without a breeze.

I climbed down the ladder and dug Katya's number out of my backpack. I dialed all the digits, save one, and then finally punched the last number. I held my breath. The phone choked and beeped in protest. I hung up and tried again. The same result. I called the operator. She told me that a call to the Soviet Union had to be placed person-to-person. I asked her to book the call. I waited on the line. In a few minutes she returned. "I'm sorry," she said, "but it's impossible to get through these days. There are simply not enough circuits to the Soviet Union."

I tried to get back to sleep but it was useless. I kept hearing the beeping of the rejected phone call. At five I got up again. I had three more hours to kill until I could register at Cam's temp agency but I put on my only jacket and tie anyway and wandered out into the city—up along East Broadway where the first delivery men were unloading pallets of spoiled weakfish and flounder, up through the remains of the routed tent city in Tompkins Square Park, past the Pakistani food stalls along Lexington where the cab drivers were changing shifts or merely taking a break before logging another twelve fruitless hours in this time of thin fares and stingy tips.

The Maplewood Temporary Agency had come up with a scheme to make use of the recession's dead wood. New temps were told to show up at Maplewood's offices at eight in the morning and go standby while the dispatcher filed her nails and looked over the day's crop. There were five standby candidates for every possible job but for going standby you were paid six dollars—breakfast and a round-trip subway ride—if no one bought you for the day.

I was eavesdropping on a conversation two heavyset women were having about the shape of a boyfriend's butt, when my brother marched in wearing a neatly pressed suit and carrying a briefcase. He pretended not to notice me. He opened his briefcase and took out a comic book and read it studiously as if it were *The Wall Street Journal*.

In a little while an Asian woman appeared from the back of the agency and smiled when she saw Cam.

"Cameron, you're back, thank God!"

"Yeah," Cameron said bashfully, "there just wasn't enough data for me at Morgan."

"Well," she said, "I have a *wonderful* assignment for you. We're talking long-term."

"Oh, really?" Cam said coyly. "What exactly are we talking about?"

"We're talking Radio City. We're talking legal."

"Sounds interesting. What's it pay?"

"I think I could get you thirteen."

"You're better than that. Try for fourteen."

The dispatcher smiled but then a worried expression came across her face.

"Wait though, you know Wang, don't you?"

Cam's face broke into a big smile.

"Of course I know Wang," he said. "It's the language of our world." He winked at me and then in an instant he was whisked away to midtown.

It took a week of going standby for Maplewood to find me something. I knew lots of computer stuff—probably more than Cam. My college computer center had all the new programs. The problem was that the big old companies that were hiring had never bothered to upgrade. They needed steady, retrograde drones to operate their old machinery—WordPerfect pros, Wang aficionados.

So I got no promises of long-term or fourteen dollars an hour. I got two weeks at half that rate for telemarketing. Maybe if I out-performed, the dispatcher said, I might be able to stretch it out into a month and get a raise. I reported to a tired-out guy in human resources who set me up at a desk in a long field of desks. A sign mounted on a placard at the front of the room, like some kind of communist factory workers' slogan, declared:

The phones have been cleaned and disinfected.
DON'T DO IT AGAIN.

I was given a list of potential subscribers and then told to cold call my way down it. Nobody was buying. Not in New York, not in California, not in Canada. By the end of the second week it was clear I wasn't going to meet my quota. On Friday I waited until my supervisor went to a late lunch at which point I dialed the operator and said that I would like to book a call to the Union of Soviet Socialist Republics.

❧

Maybe it was the high quality of the telemarketing company's lines. Maybe it was some backdoor deal they'd struck with NYNEX or maybe it was the fact that it was almost midnight in Russia; whatever it was, this time the American operator told me that a circuit was available and that she would put me through to a Soviet operator. From there it was "up to me" how to get further. The domestic operator left the line. I heard the boring old hum of the American switchboard through the receiver. I stared out blankly over this most American office and sighed with tempish, untired exhaustion.

And then, suddenly, there was a shift. The circuit jumped from fiber to copper. I heard the cluttered whisper of the USSR's patchwork phone system. Different voices muttered over the crossed lines, and after a short buzz an impatient woman's voice blurted out in Russian, "This is Moscow. I'm listening to you."

"Yes," I said, the Russian coming flooding out of me like steam from a forgotten valve, "I want to call someone in Leningrad." A Maplewood temp stared at me from the next desk and I cupped the phone.

"Who do you want to call?" the operator demanded.

"Her name is—"

"No, no," the operator shouted impatiently. "What number? You must give me the number. The number. Zee numberrr of ziss person," she said finally in badly accented English.

I gave her the number and she warned me that the lines to Leningrad weren't working well but that she would try. A few moments later another woman picked up the phone and I felt a gleeful rush.

"Katya?" I blurted out.

"*Tiho*—quiet!" shouted the Moscow operator. "That's not your Katya. That's the Leningrad operator. It's not your time to talk yet."

"Oh, please excuse me."

"It's okay," the Moscow operator said. "Just stay out of this." And then she spoke to the Leningrad operator with the authority of Moscow back in her voice.

"Leningrad?" she said.

"Yes?" said Leningrad.

"This is Moscow. I have New York here. He's looking for a number in the Admiralteyski District."

"Admiralteyski's down," Leningrad said dismissively.

"Try through Kirovski then. This man is looking for a girl. A very special girl."

"Gospodi," said Leningrad, and rang off to give it a try.

Moscow and I waited on the phone. The electric wind whistled in the circuits and I could hear the operator breathing patiently.

"You're crazy," she said after a minute had gone by. "Spending so much money on a phone call. How much does it cost you?"

I was going to tell her it cost nothing, since I was calling from work, but for some reason I wanted to boast, to show off that this call cost as much as the operator's monthly salary.

"It costs five dollars a minute," I said.

"That's a fortune," she said. "You must love her very much."

I tried to think of the Russian phrase for "I guess" or "I suppose so," but I didn't have those idioms, so instead I said, *"Da, ochen"*— Yes, very.

The operator sighed. Then with a new lightness in her voice she asked: "Where will you take her in America? Why not Miami?"

Just then the phone popped and squealed and the background wind grew into a gale.

"Go ahead, New York," Leningrad said, "I've got your girl."

I was expecting Katya to say something wry and nonchalant, like "Hello, New York" or "Calling so late?" but instead all I heard was a faint and ghostly murmur. "Allo?" she said.

The electronic storm blew harder and harder and the voice was so tiny and weak that it seemed it might blow away altogether. I stayed perfectly still and tried not to move the phone, as if staying still would somehow keep the line open.

"Katya, it's me, Daniel," I said.

"Oh," she said, genuine surprise in her voice. "How are you?" she asked.

"Okay, sure, yeah, pretty well. How is it there?"

"It's okay."

"I've heard after the coup . . . the prices . . . the cost of living is . . ."

"This subject is not for the telephone."

"Okay," I said, wondering which subjects were for the telephone.

"What about you?" she said after a pause. "Did you receive my telegram?"

"No."

"I see. So nothing is working then."

"What did it say?"

"It doesn't matter. It won't come," the whistling of the static-wind became a loud buzz. "And something very bad will happen here."

"Bad? What do you mean?"

"I dunno. Maybe another coup. Maybe a war. And when that happens, we'll just lose each other."

And then, as if on cue, the line went dead.

On my way home from work, Katya's words tumbled around in my head. It's not as if I thought that we had actually "found" each other, but the way she had said "lose" seemed so irrevocable. And as I thought more of losing her, all of the bludgeoning facts from Russian history started to come to mind: the fact that the USSR was so large that seven United States would fit inside it; that sixty million people had just disappeared in the twenty years between the Revolution and World War II; that the average life span of a Soviet citizen was decreasing every year. Worst of all, I realized that the hypothesis I'd read many times—that Russia opens its vault door briefly only a few times each century and then slams it shut again—that this was not a hypothesis at all, but an observable phenomenon. It had occurred from the time of Peter the Great all the way through the Khrushchev "thaw" on up to Gorbachev's "openness" and last month's Emergency Committee coup. The coup had failed, but the door of the vault was closing. You could hear its hinges creaking.

I did not meet my cold-calling quota and I was sent back to Maplewood standby and I could not get back through to Katya on any other phone line. For the first time in my life I had a strong desire to work in telemarketing. I kept calling from home and from the other offices where Maplewood temporarily placed me. I tried again and again, but each time along the way, either in America or Moscow or Leningrad, the call would fall flat. And when I finally did get through it was only for a brief few seconds and there was no time for emotional pussyfooting. Katya barely managed to dictate her passport information to me before the line broke again and stayed blocked, for good, it seemed. I went to a notary, made the letter of invitation, and went to the post office. I dropped the letter into the mailbox even though I had the impression that I might as well be dropping it into a garbage can. If I couldn't get through on the phone, how would a letter, a physical piece of paper, make it to her?

And as the weeks passed, the concrete procession of workdays and time sheets and weekends droned out any vague Katya possibilities. Russia disappeared from the headlines of *The New York Times* and the Russian started to disappear from my dreams. I was even getting ready for a sort of half-date–half-friend thing with a girl I used to sleep with in college when I received a telegram from Katya. Yes, she'd received my letter, and the American consulate had given her a visa. Her par-

ents had given her some of their savings and she had bought a ticket
that would put her in New York on Thanksgiving Day.

The Aeroflot arrivals gate at JFK was crowded and the air was thick
with cheap brandy, rose perfume, and the peculiar sweet-and-sour
smell of Soviet plastic. A man with a bouquet crushed in next to me.
He asked me in Russian when "the Leningrad flight" was coming in.

"I think they're calling it St. Petersburg now," I corrected him.

"For the moment," he said.

Two hours later the passengers started to come through, pale,
tired, and confused. Huge hugs smothered many of them and the
restrained chokes of weeping built to a wail. Near the end of another hour I saw Katya's cinnamon hair piled atop her head in loose
curls. She was turned away from me and she was saying something
to a passenger I couldn't see. Then she faced me, smiled, and
shrugged her shoulders slightly as if to say, "Well, why not?" Her
round, ivory face was nestled in the upturned collar of her fur coat.
The only bag she carried was a dainty little Louis Vuitton knock-off.

I walked to meet her and she kissed me lightly on the mouth. Just
lips. A baggage cart banged me on the backs of my ankles and a man
rushed forward.

"Oh, forgive me," the stranger said in Russian. "So, she belongs
to you. I didn't know that . . . I mean . . . I wasn't sure how she was
going to manage . . ." He turned to Katya and took her hand. "It
was wonderful traveling with you. Maybe we'll meet again someday,
in New York, yes?"

"In New York, Misha," she answered.

He backed away and was welcomed by two heavy women who
wiped their wet faces on his lapels and petted and squeezed him
all over.

"Katya," he called back, "if you want I can drive you and your friend," he held up a set of keys. "They've brought me a car. A big black one!"

"We have a taxi," I said.

"Forget it then," the man shrugged. "There's your luggage." I turned around to see the baggage cart he'd left for us. It was piled high with Katya's things—four large suitcases, all of them missing their handles.

During the taxi ride back to Manhattan we talked haltingly. My Russian was forced and inexact and finally we switched to English. When the communication between us became too mixed up and confusing, I held her hand and we both looked ahead into the Manhattan skyline.

"Who was that guy at the airport?" I asked her.

"I don't know, I met him on the plane," she said. "He's just some disgusting man from the black market."

The cab left us off in front of the tenement. Katya waited on the landing while I went up and down the stairs with the luggage. We finally came up together and I opened the door to the apartment. She didn't say a word. I set up the fan to blow the smell of the restaurant next door out the back window. I showed her my room and then pointed down the hall where Anne and Elizabeth lived. She stood by the bed and looked out the window at the laundry on the line across the street. We had a few hours before we'd have to leave for my mother's house for Thanksgiving dinner. She smiled briefly, kissed me, and then walked over to the cracked wardrobe. She hung her fur on a wire hanger.

"You didn't tell me," she said into the back of the wardrobe, "you didn't tell me that you lived in a communal apartment."

Communal

Katya was up early—getting ready to go to the Bronx and drop off some letters with an émigré friend of her parents. It would be the first morning we'd spend apart since her arrival, but we'd make it up by meeting again in the afternoon. I worried about her, though, riding the subway alone all the way to 145th Street. She was confident and dismissive of my concerns. "We have worse things in Russia than the Bronx," she'd said.

Anne and Elizabeth were also up early. They'd had word from their temp agencies. With the holidays coming, they were hard up for cash and there was a desperate sound to their goings back and forth along the corridor running through my room. I was only partly awake and I couldn't fully make out the conversation going on between Katya and Anne. I heard Katya say something about her interest in "antroposophian movements." Then I heard Katya leave—

heard her say "Bye, bye"—and after that I thought I heard Anne and Elizabeth laughing. When I woke up for good I climbed down the ladder and walked into the front foyer that served as our living room, kitchen, and dining room. I was alone for the first time in three weeks.

I decided to take advantage of all this privacy. Since the tub was positioned tenement-style in the middle of the kitchen, a bath seemed the most indulgently private thing I could do. The water ran brown at first but then gradually became an acceptable beige. I pulled the dirty shower curtain around me, slipped down into the tub, and started adding things up.

Back in October, when I'd found out Katya was coming, I'd cut expenses down to rice and beans. From temping and the occasional production assistant jobs I got through a friend of Anne's, I'd managed to put away about nine hundred dollars, which I figured would just about last the month that Katya was supposed to be here. But not a single day went by with her where we managed to stay within my twenty-six-dollar-a-day budget. Adding up the last three weeks now I realized we were coming in at an average of forty dollars a day, which meant that the final week of her visit was going to have to ride entirely on the back of my overdraft protection.

Still, I couldn't bring myself to talk to Katya about economizing. I liked her look of surprise when I inserted my card into the automatic teller and dollars—real hard currency—came out. And I also had come to understand that money was a strange and embarrassing talisman for Russians. When it was mentioned, the soft, delicate melody of a pleasant conversation grew dissonant and sad.

Above all, though, I believed that Katya had a sense of pride and self-worth that made money irrelevant. This had been clear from the day of her arrival when we'd gathered around the table at Thanksgiving in Connecticut. She'd sat there, patiently bearing all of

Mom's questions about poverty and starvation in Russia while Cam mangled a turkey way too big for the four of us to eat. Katya waved the whole holiday away and even claimed that yes, she had seen a turkey before, in fact there were millions of them, gobbling away along the Moscow–Leningrad highway, and that Thanksgiving in no way compared to the size or extent of a good Russian New Year's Eve feast.

"Well," Mom said, trying to equivocate, "the Pilgrims were very poor and very hungry when they first arrived in America."

"Yes, I know that," Katya said.

"Yeah," Cam said flipping the turkey with his hands, trying to get at the thing from a different angle, "and the Indians saved our ass."

"And then you murdered them," Katya said.

The ice in Mom's third scotch tinkled. I looked up at Cam. I had the feeling that she'd won him over with this little remark.

"Well, actually," Mom said hesitantly, "I heard an interesting thing on Channel Thirteen the other day. Apparently, there are more Native Americans alive now than when the Pilgrims arrived."

"Yeah, but Mom—" Cam started to say.

"Oh," Katya said smiling, "I do not criticize your Pilgrims. They did the right thing. The Indians were weak, you were strong. It was the inevitable and necessary process of history. The Indians owned this continent for thirty thousand years and all they did was chase buffalo. It was time for them to go."

Cam eyed her suspiciously over the carving knife.

"Here, Katya, take the wing," he said. "It's the best part."

I laughed now, thinking back to the confusion she'd wrought just for the sake of confusion. Hard to pin down, my Katya. I finally got out of the bathtub and looked around for something to eat. All I found in the cabinet was a crushed cereal box and in the fridge there was just an empty milk carton. There was a dirty pan sitting square in the middle of the table. I cursed my roommates under my breath and picked the pan up to wash it. When I grabbed it, though, I noticed the handle was warm and that there was a note on the table next to where it had been resting. The note was written in easy-to-read block Cyrillic letters. *"DLYA TEBYA,"* it said—"For you." Inside the pan were a dozen neatly arranged *syrniki*. Katya had found some old flour, sugar, and cream cheese, shaped the mixture into patties, and fried them in butter. They were delicious.

After breakfast, when I went to wash the dishes, I found a second note, this one from Anne. "My pots and pans are made out of Teflon and cost twenty dollars apiece," Anne's note said. "If you use metal on them, they scratch and then they are ruined. Things will stick to them. Your girlfriend has ruined all of these pots and pans." I crumpled up the note and threw it away. I made out a check for a hundred dollars and before taping it back to the faucet I wrote a reference in the lower left-hand corner of the check: "For the goddamned pots." I was over budget for the day and I hadn't even left the house.

It was one of those global-warming winter days. The leaves were on the trees later than they should have been and everyone in the park was in shorts. Katya met me for lunch in the chess pavilion. We sat across from each other at a table next to the outdoor theater. She set up the board and held out her hands. I picked the left. I was right. The first move was mine. She took out a plastic container from her bag and handed it to me. I lifted up the lid. Inside it was all purple.

"What's this?"

"Herring in a blanket," she said.

I took a spoonful and moved my knight over the front row of

pawns. Katya went *"ts, ts, ts,"* moved a pawn a double space and opened a book of Zen parables she'd checked out of the library on my card.

"How was it in the Bronx?" I asked.

"Beautiful," she said with her eyes still in the book. "Zhenya's apartment is so big."

"That must be nice."

"Yes." She looked up from the book for a moment and pushed a wisp of hair from her eyes. Once exposed, her irises seemed to pick up the green of the grass and throw it right back with doubled intensity. "What does it mean—'transcendental'?" she asked.

I swallowed the herring and moved a pawn. Katya captured it with a knight.

"Um," I said, "I'm not sure how to explain that to you."

"Oh, well."

I considered my bishop, moved it one diagonal to the left, then reconsidered and moved it two to the right instead. "Anne left another note this morning," I said when my move was final.

Katya sighed and darkened. "What did I do this time?"

"Remember how I told you about metal on her pots?"

"Oh," Katya said.

She started a march down the left side of the board and my pieces began to have a herded-up look. I stared at the board for five minutes trying to think of my next move. Katya then said in a measured voice:

"Well, I'm sorry. Can you tell Anne I'm sorry?"

"I'll tell her. It'll be all right."

Katya concentrated harder on the board and didn't look at me. "Actually, I don't think it will be all right," she said. "Three girls in one apartment! Things always turn out badly in a *kommunalka.*"

"Katya, it's not exactly a *communal* apartment. We live together but it's not . . . See, Anne and Elizabeth are old friends. Anne and I met my first year of college in an art class. And Elizabeth, she's known Anne since high school—"

"I don't disagree with you. They are good people," Katya interrupted. "But it's not really different. A *kommunalka,* excuse me, a 'communal apartment' is always a problem. You know how many of *my* things have been ruined in that apartment already?"

"Really?"

"Yes," she said. "People never respect your things in a communal apartment. They destroy them. They can't stop themselves. What is it your poet says? Good walls make good neighbors, yes?"

"Good *fences* make good neighbors," I corrected her.

"Exactly," she said.

We played without a word as she slowly riddled my line of pawns, advancing and retreating nimbly and nixing my feeble juggernauts almost as an afterthought. I tried to picture the real communal apartments I'd seen in Leningrad—those tight old flats where multiple families were jammed unfairly together by Communist fiat, their toilets shit-caked and urine-soaked and usually without seats, everyone and no one responsible for their upkeep. No, mine was not a communal apartment. My roommates were my friends. We had chosen to live together now just as we'd chosen to live together back in college. I thought about Anne with her big boots and the weird row of rings in her upper ears, always trying to look the formidable tough customer but always failing. No matter what her disguise, it was Anne's Wisconsin-bred decency and sense of fair play that people always noticed first about her. I thought about the check I'd left for her with its mean-spirited note. I shouldn't have been so harsh. I looked up at Katya.

"I'm sorry, but it's true," she said suddenly, giving voice to our silent conversation. "Anne is a very aggressive person."

"I'm sorry?"

"It's nothing serious. It's just that she is aggressive."

"She's had her problems over the years," I said. "But she's trying."

"How is she trying?"

"She's more careful with her temper. She sees a psychiatrist now."

"A psychiatrist?" This made Katya look at me at last.

"Yes," I said.

"A psychiatrist. I see. Do you know what Nabokov called that psychiatrist Sigmund Freud?"

"No."

"He called him a duck from Vienna."

"A duck?"

"I don't know the right word," Katya said. "But that's what Anne's psychiatrist is—a duck. Anne has an aggressive character. Nothing will change that."

"Well, what do you do with someone in Russia if they're upset, or angry, or depressed?"

"It's a personal problem. But if it is serious enough for a psychiatrist then they get some pharmaceuticals or some electrical intervention. Then the problem is finished. The psychiatrist does nothing. He just gives the medicine."

"You know," I said glaring at her, "my father is a psychiatrist."

"I know."

"And you think he just does nothing?"

"How do I know what he does? You never introduce me to him. You're too ashamed."

"No, Katya, that's not true. That has nothing to do with you. That's something else."

"What else could it be?"

Katya lay her king down on its side and pinged her queen off the table with her finger. She sighed and put her head on the table. "I dunno," she said, "maybe I should just leave on the twenty-seventh, like my ticket says."

I thought for a moment, trying to remember when it was exactly that we had discussed her *not* leaving on December twenty-seventh. True, she had a six-month visa, but the consulate gave out six-month visas from time to time, just for the hell of it, if they liked the person.

I looked at Katya's hair spread out over the chessboard and at the graceful way her shoulders sloped up into her neck. I held my hand up to touch her but then pulled it back when she shook her head and a dark expression played across her face. What was she thinking about? I waited until I saw her breath rise and fall more slowly. I reached back out and slipped my hand under her hair and rubbed her neck. I felt down and around for the birthmark near her collarbone. She kept her eyes closed, and smiled. A wave of tension seemed to pass out of her body. Amazing, how just my touch could transform her mood. And though I tried to fight it, it was undeniably true that the very texture of her skin and the way it seemed to rise to meet my hand overwhelmed any discord between us. I remembered how early that morning she had woken quietly. I had been half-asleep worrying about money in some dream of figures, but before leaving for the Bronx Katya had pulled up her nightgown, dug up into my shirt, and pressed her whole body against me— thigh against thigh, chest against chest. "This is yours," she'd whispered. She'd stayed there, frozen like that for just a moment and then in the darkness she'd pulled away and slid down the ladder. The heat was still off in the building. In the loft-slot it had felt cold and dark after she'd left and all I could think about was seeing her that afternoon in the park—about this very moment, in fact. I don't know, I guess maybe we had spoken of changing her ticket. Probably we'd talked about it in Russian and I had just kind of gone along with the

musical flow of her complicated subjunctives. Probably it had been
late at night.

"I don't want to be a stone around your neck," she murmured to
me from the chessboard.

"Oh, c'mon," I said gathering her hair into a bun and pulling on it.

"Oh, c'mon, *c'mon,*" she said.

I looped us in and out of the park, pointing out brownstones and
showing off ponds and bridges. She fit perfectly underneath my arm
and she synched her steps up with mine as we walked. It was one in
the afternoon and a fair amount of no-cost sightseeing could still be
done before sunset. And in the evening we would go home and I
would cook her dinner and we would return to our loft-slot and I
would finally get at all of her. I felt light with expectation. She
seemed to be enjoying herself and we had yet to spend a cent. Then,
at the bottom of the park, just as the sky was clouding up, we ran
directly into Christmas.

Katya looked east toward the expensive avenues. We started down
Fifth, past the Plaza, and I could see her eye drift over the outra-
geous displays in FAO Schwarz and on to Saks. I tried to think of
something that could turn us west. I thought of my brother Cam
and remembered that he was temping nearby.

"Hey," I said. "Wanna go see my brother?"

"Yes," she said, "that would be nice."

"He's over at Radio City."

"Which city?"

"It's a . . . Well, I'll show you."

I walked us briskly toward Rockefeller Center. The store windows on either side seemed to be laughing at me. We passed the
Aeroflot office. Katya looked away. I did, too. Then we crossed over
and walked by the big Christmas tree and the chicken-wire angels.

I tried to remember where in Radio City my brother had said he was temping. It was something to do with contracts. We went in through the Art Deco entrance catty-corner from the skating rink and found the legal department on the twenty-eighth floor. Cam was sitting Bob Cratchit–like at the corner desk in a huge grid of desks. He was looking wide-eyed into a computer and twisting one scraggly lock of hair. I tapped my keys on the glass doors. He looked up, startled. He squinted at us and buzzed us in.

"Oh, it's you," he said, glancing up from the green glow of his computer as we approached the desk. "I didn't recognize you. My eyes are shot from looking at this thing." He motioned for us to sit down around him as he continued typing. I picked up a picture of a woman and her kids in a gold frame from the corner of his work station. "That's Trudy. She's divorced," Cam said, thumbing the photo. "They're all in Boca Raton with some sailor guy." There were different documents pushed up on either side of Cam's monitor. Other papers were piled on chairs around him with Post-its all marked "urgent," "extremely urgent," and "critical." A half-dozen vintage comic books with names like *Shapeshifter* and *The Metamorphs* were spread around an open box of Entenmann's doughnuts. Cam was eating a doughnut and had another one going in the box. Powdered sugar had got into everything.

"You start looking for an apartment yet?" I asked him.

"Nah," Cam said as he swallowed, "No time. Radio City, you know. Show biz."

"Oh, well."

"Yeah, well, whatever," he said. "You seen Dad?"

"No. I haven't called him since I got back from Russia."

"Good man. We'll teach the old guy a lesson with this Noah nonsense."

"What is 'the Noah nonsense'?" Katya asked.

"New family. Stepmother. Half brother. Boy genius. Wanna doughnut?"

"Yes, please."

Katya dipped daintily into the Entenmann's box. She bit into the doughnut. She chewed carefully with her mouth closed and seemed to be thinking through what Cam had just said. Then she made a sour face and returned the rest of the doughnut to the box. Cam ri-fled off the end of a memo, showing off how fast he could type, and then turned back to us.

"Yeah, well, anyway," he said finally, "I guess you guys wanna see the Christmas Show. The matinée just started."

"Aren't you working?" I asked.

"Work, shmerk, it's the holidays. They're not *watching* me," he said, making quotes in the air and doing his ersatz Russian accent. He produced a janitor's ring of keys from his natty olive parka and took us down to the back freight elevator. It was dark and cav-ernous. There were no doors on the front and we could see the dif-ferent levels disappearing above us.

"What's that strong, bad smell?" Katya asked.

"Elephants," Cam said and held his arms out wide.

The elevator bottomed out and we heard, "Here comes Santa Claus! Here comes Santa Claus!" A mob of extras ran past. A flat flew down from the rafters carrying a row of women. Katya gasped, as the lights brightened and from behind we saw sixty legs kicking in the most perfect unison. Kicking, kicking, kicking.

"Are those the Rockettes?" I asked Cam.

"You bet," he said.

"Do you know any of them?"

He looked at me darkly and did his creepy, sci-fi-movie–narrator voice. "No. I don't know them. But I admire their purity."

The Rockettes finished their number. The elves circled around them with garlands. Then the whole entourage ran offstage for a costume change. One of the little people noticed Cam in the wings and fingered him.

"Hey, you work with Trudy, in legal, right?" the dwarf said.

"Trudy's on vacation."

"Yeah, well, tell that cunt she forgot to put the overtime clause in my contract."

"What does it mean, 'cunt'?" Katya whispered.

❦

We left Radio City and started home down through Times Square. I pointed out some 3-D ads above, trying to steer her away from a horrible dog-on-girl pornography ad at ground level. Katya looked up and smiled—then gasped. She was staring at the news ticker looping around the building on Forty-first street: "IT'S OFFICIAL: YELTSIN CALLS FOR END OF COMMUNISM," it read. "TELLS WORLD THAT USSR 'MUST GO.' COUNTRY TO BE DISSOLVED . . ."

"Oh, no," Katya murmured.

"It doesn't mean anything, Katya. It was bound to happen after the coup. Russia's still Russia. Your family will be all—"

"Oh no, no, no—" Katya said. She was rifling through her purse. She pulled out a billfold and produced $800 worth of traveler's checks.

"Katya, don't worry, I have—"

"No, no," Katya said. "What is the time? Look at these checks. It's all of my money. It's all my father's money."

"But you still have it, no?"

"These checks. They're from the Central Bank of the Soviet Union. How can I get the money for them if there's no Soviet Union? What time is it?"

"Three-thirty," I said.

"Oh, *Gospodi*."

We headed down Seventh Avenue looking for an open bank. Katya's face reddened, her eyes seemed watery. But she wouldn't run; she only increased her smart gait every time we found another closed bank. I didn't know what to make of her distress. When I had been in Russia I really couldn't tell how her family was doing. Katya's father still held a high position at the State Planning Commission. The family had traveled to East Germany and the Balkan states. Surely they had some connections, some money . . .

"Katya, what's the story with this $800 anyway?" I said. "If your father needs it, why don't you just save it? You can convert the traveler's checks back in Russia. I have money."

"How do I know there will be a bank when I go back? My father—he gave this to *me*. It was the last thing for *me*," she said. "Let's stop talking about it. I need cash money. Immediately!"

When we got back to my apartment it was after six. It had taken us two hours to locate an open exchange. We had finally found one near Fourteenth Street, open late for holiday shoppers. The Indian clerk took the traveler's checks and didn't even notice their hammer-and-sickle watermarks. He gave Katya eight crisp hundred-dollar bills, which she quickly squirreled away in a secret inner pocket of her coat. We were barely speaking to each other by the time we reached Chinatown.

We walked into my apartment and I could see Elizabeth's door was open at the back. I was about to walk in and say hi but I heard her breathing irregularly as if she were gulping a glass of water. A strange man's voice answered her breaths in a low, pulsing drone. Katya made a sour face.

"Sex," she whispered to me.

"I know."

"Foo."

"Katya, I know. But it's not—"

"I know," she said. "It's not a communal apartment. It's just a place where people live with no food or dishes and have sex with all the doors open."

I led her out of our building to a restaurant several blocks away. It was a deep, football field–sized dim sum hall that had peeling golden dragons on every wall. The restaurant was full with an after-work crowd of Asian garment workers. The maître d' squeezed us in around a large common table. Another family came and somehow managed to wedge themselves in on either side of us. They talked across us to one another. A toddler sat next to Katya and poked a pile of rice with his finger.

"Is the food here clean?" she asked me in Russian.

"Of course, it must be," I answered, also in Russian.

One of the men across the table overheard us and pointed at us. "Look! Look!" he said in Chinese-accented Russian. "Soviet people! Soviet people! How are you living these days dear comrades, dear neighbors?"

Katya smiled dismally. "It doesn't look clean here," she whispered. "It's so crowded."

The little boy to Katya's right suddenly darted forward and grabbed one of the dumplings off her plate. The mother saw this and slapped the boy's hand fiercely. The boy cried. The mother raised her hand again and the child was quickly silent.

"Not even my own plate is my own," said Katya. She was suddenly as close to crying as I had ever seen her. "We move from place to place, with no place that's really ours. We walk all day long, like Gypsies. What am I doing here? I'm already twenty-three years old. In St. Petersburg people my age don't behave like this. They're adults. They have children, and families, and, and . . . a life! But for me it's always like this."

"Well," I murmured almost to myself, "you'll be home soon in your own nice room, on the Griboyedov Canal." A woman pushing a cart rapped me on the shoulder. "Shu mai?" she asked.

Katya squinted meanly at the dumpling lady. The cart was pushed away. She took a long breath, steadied herself and said: "I don't have a room anymore."

"Katya, c'mon. Of course you do."

"No, I don't. It's just like with you and 'the Noah nonsense.' Your father has his new family, my sister has hers."

"But you're very close—"

"Oh, we're close. That's true. We're so close there's no room for me. It's my sister and that daughter of hers. My parents gave her my room. That little girl—it's like she has the whole place now. There's no room for me."

I reached over and stroked her forehead. She turned away from me and kissed the palm of my hand. She looked out over the wide expanse of the dining hall. Then she took out the eight hundred-dollar bills from the inner pocket of her coat. "Is this," she choked, "is this enough for you to get your own apartment? Is it? Will this pay for it? If you take this money, what kind of apartment can we have?"

The Promise

Money grew tighter and work was hard to find. Katya's $800 paid the security deposit on an apartment I'd found next to a homeless shelter in Chelsea. I had covered the last month's rent with a check I'd got when I signed up for a Discover card. But that still left us the short month of February to come up with another $800.

About this time, Katya reconnected with her friend Lena Netkacheva. Lena had come to America a little bit earlier than Katya. She worked as a baby-sitter on the East Side and she told Katya that another young couple in the building was looking for help. On a bright winter day midway through the month, I took Katya uptown to meet the prospective employers.

The couple's baby was unusually large and completely hairless with a broad blue vein zigzagging across its head, like a worm. He pointed his little pinkie down at a toy car and said, "gna, gna." Katya crouched on the floor in front of it. She reached out and rolled the car across the carpet to show the baby how it moved. But just as she did, the child let out such an intense, bellowing moan that it seemed to blow Katya across the silk oriental carpet up into one of the couple's vintage Eames chairs.

"My gna gna," the baby screamed at Katya in despair.

"Sure, okay," Katya said, "your gna gna." Then I thought I heard her whisper the Russian invective *svoloch,* under her breath.

"Anyway," the baby's mother said, "he's a bit of a fussy eater, but when he likes something he eats *a lot* of it."

"That's for sure," the father said. "He *loves* fish sticks and peanut butter. Can you believe it?"

"Wow," I said.

As I made listless small talk with the couple, Katya's attention fell away from the baby and she started looking around the apartment. I could see her screw up her eyes into her comparing/appraising expression. She was impressed with the size of the place. Probably she estimated it at four times the size of the one-bedroom we'd just rented in Chelsea.

"Now, Katya," the mother said, "I hope you don't mind if I ask you this, but have you had all of your inoculations?"

"Which?" Katya looked up, puzzled.

"You know, typhoid, hepatitis, diphtheria."

"Oh, no," Katya said, "of course not. I've never had any of that."

"So she'll need inoculations then," the mother said, looking at her husband.

"No," I interrupted, "no, that's not what she means. In Russia they get inoculated for all that. She means she's never *had* those diseases."

"Oh. Oh, I . . ." the mother said. "So she . . . Okay, I see . . . Oh, she meant . . . Oh, I think we just had a little 'translation problem' just now."

The husband tilted back his head and shot out a projectile of laughter. He was only a few years older than I was and yet he seemed so naturally placed in his grown-up spread. There was something of the college frat boy in him, with his linebacker's body and his terrace of black gelled hair. I had a sudden flash of taking a filet knife to his scalp.

"Anyway, listen," he said when he'd stopped laughing, "Sally and I need to have a little tête-à-tête about all this but it seems perfectly cool to me. We'll let you know in a few days what we think. Personally, if it were up to me, Sally, I'd hire Katya right on the spot. I mean Sally, you're *fried*."

The couple showed us to the door and we went down into the subway to our next appointment.

Down in the subway Katya stepped over the orange warning line and went all the way to the edge of the platform. She looked into the tunnel in both directions. There was no evidence of trains. Only the sound of rats scuttling on the tracks and water dripping out of leaky water mains broke the silence.

"At least," I said, "they didn't ask if you had a green card."

"Yes, that's true," Katya said. "But I understand them. If it was legal it would be more expensive for them to pay me. Lena has the same situation with her baby-sitting. It's like in Russia: it's the black economy."

"Of course," I said. I turned away and moved my mouth around silently trying to think of a better way to explain it. No it wasn't exactly a black economy. More of a gray economy. It wasn't like Russia, where the mafia was bearing down on the population, squeezing every business affair until the limbs of the transaction turned black. This baby-sitting thing, it was just done. Everyone here started out a little bit in the black economy before passing into the white. I wanted

to tell her about all the humiliating jobs I'd had at dining halls and re-
tail stores and fast-food restaurants, but as I turned to her she walked
up, slid her arms underneath mine, kissed me, and laughed.

"Did you ever in your whole life see such a husband and wife?"

I tried to stay serious but a smile started to creep over my face.

"Or such an ugly baby?"

"Katya—"

"A head like a cosmonaut!" She chortled.

"C'mon."

"This is why you Americans got to the Moon. They breed you
for it."

And eventually it was all I could do to stop her from laughing and
get her into the train when it came.

We got off the subway and found the office of Seymour Brimmer, Esq., on the eighth floor of a nondescript 1950s skyscraper.
Brimmer's suite was at the end of a hallway on a floor that also
housed the consulate of the Dominican Republic. We shoved our
way through the line that had formed at the consulate door and into
Brimmer's office.

Inside, a secretary had us fill out some forms and, in a little while,
Brimmer himself appeared, a Greek paper coffee cup in his hand
and the ghost of a schmear on his lapel. He brought us into his office and put us in two swivel chairs in front of him. He took the
clipboard from me and looked at the forms I'd filled out.

"O-kay. What we got here? Nice young couple for a change. Let's
take a look. Yekaterina Romanovna Konstantinova, arrived eleven
twenty-seven ninety-one, on a tourist visa. What's the visa expiration date?"

"May," I said.

"Not much time," Seymour said. "Gotta move. Gotta move. On-
ward ho. Any relations here in the States, Ms. Konstantinova?"

"None," Katya said almost proudly.

"Nope-a-dope," he said and checked a "no" box with a flourish of his pen.

"Any political problems back home? Jewish, refusnik, Sakharov-booster, anything like that?"

"Of course not," she said.

"Too bad, there goes political asylum," and he checked another "no" box.

"Any skills, anything that would put you in a deficit professional category?" he asked brightly.

"I have a philosophy degree from best university in the Soviet Union."

"Insufficient," Seymour said. "Anything from the sciences—doctoring, nursing, computers?"

"Facial massage," she said.

Seymour lifted his head, startled, and took a good look at Katya for the first time. He seemed softened by her. "I'd be interested to find out all about that," he said. "That sounds interesting—and new. But that is also, unfortunately, insufficient."

"Oh," Katya said.

"Listen, dear, do you mind? I have to give you both a little speech."

"No, please. You must act according to your specialty."

"That I must. Okay, here we go. Ms. Konstantinova, living in America is a privilege, and like all privileges it requires certain adjustments. You'll both have to excuse me for putting this to you in the blunt manner that I am going to employ, but I must ask. I am obliged to ask, so here goes. Ready? Okay. Can you two tell me, are you, the two of you, *in love*?"

Seymour's question floated in the air above his desk and we all stared blankly into it.

"Let me put it another way," resumed Brimmer. "Is there any

possibility that whatever it is that now possesses you could be elevated to a higher level? Could this tender shoot of passion, could it be nurtured to grow into the enduring trunk of marriage? Now, I cannot counsel you to marry, nor will I, and I will have it duly noted that I have not done so. Evelyn!" Seymour shouted down the corridor, "Evelyn, can you come in here and witness this please, dear? Thank you, dear." A plump, middle-aged woman with soft eyes took up the stenographer's position behind us.

"Now then, as I was saying, *I cannot counsel you to marry.* Got that, Ev?" he winked at the stenographer. She nodded back. "It is outside of my jurisdiction and against the law for me to counsel you to marry. I am *not* a marriage counselor."

Here Seymour leaned forward and looked me square in the eye.

"But what I *am* telling you is that you two nice young people have quite a situation on your hands. I am describing your own reality to you. With no skills or legitimate American family relations, Ms. Konstantinova has absolutely nothing that the Immigration and Naturalization Service will consider meritorious of an American green card."

"Nothing?" I asked.

"No, nothing. Absolutely nothing."

"Vot kak okazyvaetsya," Katya whispered. So that's the way it is.

"However," Seymour began again in a fresh, new tone, "I repeat, however, if you did have the desire to make your attachment more permanent, merely to formalize what you already feel, then I believe you would find your circumstances *radically* altered. If you were to do so, then I could arrange all the associated paperwork for approximately one thousand eight hundred dollars."

"Why so much money?" Katya said.

"I said approximately," Seymour answered quickly.

"Approximately?" she asked.

"Primerno," I translated.

Katya mouthed the word "approximately" several times and then let her eyes wander around the office. She glanced over at me. I closed my mouth and my eyebrows arched up tensely all by themselves. Seymour focused on me for a moment. I blinked at him. He took out a fresh manila file folder from a box and started labeling the tab on it with my name. I felt as we do in dreams when we try to follow a story that involves us and yet doesn't involve us; where the conclusion, when it's reached, is already somehow known. Surprising but inevitable, a Hollywood producer would tag it, I suppose. And as I followed Seymour's logic in a spiral that led and could lead to one and only one point I felt my mouth getting dry and my throat muscles tightening up as if in defense of speaking or throwing up. All at once I found myself saying: "Katya, if it's the only way . . . I'd marry you."

She froze. She made a small sound. She seemed to be consulting some other person not in the room. Then suddenly she pulled on her fur coat and stood up.

"Oh, no," she said. "It's too disgusting. Married because some law tells you to do it? Oh, no, it's too disgusting."

Seymour looked up and then down and finished labeling the folder. He put our papers in his desk and locked the drawer.

"As I told you," he said, "I am not a marriage counselor but I am a lawyer and I've got the Dominican Republic outside my door waiting to get into this country and none of them think what I've mentioned is particularly disgusting. I've got you on file now, Ms. Konstantinova. This first visit was free, but the next one's gonna cost you. Good day."

We didn't speak of this conversation again. We tried to live in the brevity of our remaining time together and over the next few weeks she helped me put my apartment in Chelsea together. I sawed off the legs of the loft platform we'd taken from the place on Henry Street and made it into a ground-level bed. I took the wood scraps and banged them together into a kind of coffee table. To my amazement, it actually stood and only rocked slightly when a cup was removed or replaced.

My mother went through her storeroom in Connecticut and brought in some dusty old furniture—artifacts that I hadn't seen since my childhood. There was the latticed Indian screen that had once shielded Mom and Dad's bed back in the days of my earliest memories when there was still a danger of walking in on Mom-and-Dad. There was the French armoire that had stood in the foyer of the grand, three-story Tarrytown mansion Mom had been forced to sell to cover debts following the divorce.

Katya and Mom, it turned out, shared a talent for arranging large furniture in small spaces. They fed off each other's ideas and within a week there was both a coziness and a promise to the place. It was as if these old pieces of furniture from my parents' brief married life were the last seeds of an old extinct forest. Planted in fresh soil, they might grow again.

Mom helped us in other ways. She knew that you could link together a string of wire hangers, pass it through an old sheet and set up the whole thing as a curtain. She explained with a broad sweeping gesture, almost hitting me in the eye with a lit Virginia Slims, that you could transfer the debt from one credit card to another and put off paying the bill for two months instead of one. She showed us how any grain could be paired with any bean to form a complete protein.

And little by little things came together. A sale of dying plants on Twenty-sixth Street provided us with some additional decoration.

Katya trimmed them back harshly until there was almost nothing left of them but sticks. Then she fed them, sparingly at first, as if they were hostages. She whispered to them in Russian and upped their food and water. Day by day the leaves came, and soon a soft green glow filled the place on sunny days.

And in the evenings when we'd finally managed to get my mother to drift back to Connecticut in the Cordoba, we would put on one of Katya's strummy pirate tapes of Soviet protest songs and I would help her prepare traditional dishes from her mother's handwritten recipe book. Yeast-leavened blini with sour cream and chives; Ukrainian cabbage rolls stuffed with ground pork; salads of cucumbers and tomatoes cut into the smallest of cubes. Afterward she'd serve black tea, loose in a pot with a small dish of jam alongside. And over dessert we'd talk about traveling through Europe or Morocco or Australia. We even talked of touring Russia together. We planned a tour of the entire Golden Ring—the circle of stately medieval fortress cities that surrounds Moscow. And we dreamed of how at the end of our Russian excursion we'd settle in for August with her parents, napping the long days away on the wide porch of their peaceful summer house overlooking the shimmering Finnish Gulf.

During these times I even thought of reopening relations with my father and inviting him over. But then I remembered their huge East Side apartment and I thought about how they'd all come over and ask "where the rest was" and I'd have to explain in front of Katya that it was a good deal, that Chelsea was "an up-and-coming neighborhood," and that we'd been lucky to get in when we did.

But taken in broad strokes, the life we made during those short few weeks had the feeling of a hybrid—a hybrid that, given more time and nourishment, would have become viable. Even our sex life, which at first would have received a stamp of approval from the Soviet Central Committee, had started to change and adapt. We would twist and turn in the night and find ourselves joined sideways or backward, laughing at the absurdity of our position.

But then there were the mornings and work. Katya and I woke, bleary from the streetlights shining through the windows in our faces, our heads still ringing from the disturbances of the police precinct across the street and the unruly shouting coming from the crack dealers at the homeless shelter on the corner. We made coffee without a pot—just a plastic filter and generic brand coffee held over a cup. When one of us opened the front door to leave, the apartment filled up with the smell of Latin sauces stewed eternally on our neighbor's stove.

The couple we'd met in February hired Katya as their baby-sitter, and I temped, and Anne's friend continued to feed me the odd TV job. One production company even moved me up to "coordinator" status. A month before Katya's visa expired I got sent out to Passaic, New Jersey, for an A&P commercial where I was given a two-way headset that had a direct channel to the assistant director. This made me feel important.

The A.D.'s whiny voice started to irritate me, though, when it blasted in my ear. I got tired of hearing him say "let's lock it off, people" and annoyed at how we all had to tiptoe around the advertising client from A&P. Katya's blasé Soviet attitude toward work started to rub off on me and by the second day of the shoot I was dragging my feet. I muttered under my breath about how stupid A&P was. Finally I told the customers in the store that if they didn't like the shoot disturbing their shopping, then they should go to Grand Union up the road. When I said this I failed to notice that the channel to the A.D. was open.

"Uh, *pshhht,* Daniel, is that you there? Over, *pshhht,*" the A.D. said over the headset.

"Yeah, that's me . . . over," I said.

"Yeah, *pshhht,* come out to the production truck. *Pshhht.* Over."

The A.D. met me halfway to the truck in the parking lot, his headset hanging around his neck. He pointed his half-eaten Power Bar at me.

"Man," he said, "I'm sorry, but I have to fire you. But I'm gonna tell you why."

"You're gonna fire me?"

"Yeah, but I'm gonna tell you why."

"If you're gonna fire me," I said, "then I don't have to listen to why."

There was a New Jersey Transit stop nearby. The ticket back to New York was four dollars. If the production company paid me for a half-day, I'd still be up overall, at least enough to cover the minimum payment due on my Discover Card. It wasn't a major hit. Katya would be leaving in another month, anyway.

I thought about her, and tried to imagine how my life would be once she'd left. At least, I thought, there wouldn't be any more of this A&P crap. A&P, Grand Union, what's the difference? It's like Katya says—all one huge multinational mess controlling everything and everybody.

Once Katya left, I thought, maybe I would start working on independent films. I'd slowly work my way up. But as I thought about the path from production assistant to production coordinator to second assistant director to first assistant director, I saw such a shallow filling up of the days ahead that I groaned audibly out the train window.

A vague Ph.D. program in Russian literature started to take shape in my head. Once Katya was gone I might enroll at some isolated

New England university with deciduous trees and a crew team. I would take over a library carrel and study like I'd never studied before. I would examine Russia objectively, at a great distance. I'd learn Old Church Slavonic and read all the classics in the original. I'd read not just Pushkin but also the early monastic poets who came before Pushkin. I'd do my own translation of the *Song of Igor's Campaign*. I'd learn how to properly pronounce words that ended with that dodgy Russian character called the *soft sign*.

"And how does all this happen?" a voice in my head said as the train pulled into Penn Station. Who would pay for all this? Maybe I could get a grant? How do you write a grant? And who was supposed to give *me* a grant?

These things whirled around me as I walked back to Chelsea, just as the trash, uncollected because of another garbage strike, blew out of haphazard piles and whirled around my feet. Everything, every plan had a glum, Katya-less conclusion. I saw myself eating alone at Sam Chinita's, the aluminum Cuban-Chinese restaurant on Nineteenth Street. Yellow rice and black beans forever.

I was winded by the time I climbed up the six flights to our apartment. I went to unlock the door but it pushed open and I found Katya sitting at my makeshift coffee table staring blankly out the window into the police station.

"Home early?" I asked as I sat down across from her on a folding chair.

"I'm home for good," she said. "That nice husband is not so nice."

"What do you mean?"

"He told me he's very lonely and that I'm very beautiful. You see?"

"Jesus."

Katya winced a little at the curse. "And you?" she said. "Nice day at the supermarket?"

"Not so nice. I got fired."

"Very nice," she said. We went into the bedroom and lay down on the bed. She put her head on my chest. The apartment was unusually quiet—I'd never been in it at this time of day. It seemed almost peaceful.

"When I was small," Katya said, "we had a map of the world. My father made me look at it and he told me how much of it was no good. Nigeria, Mongolia, Mexico—I could have been born in any of those bad places. But I was born in the Union of Soviet Socialist Republics. I used to feel very lucky."

"Me too," I said.

"You know," Katya whispered, "this America will eat you whole, like a fish."

"Yes," I said.

"Especially when you're alone."

"Yes," I said.

"It's strange that we both lost our jobs today, at the same time."

"I know," I said.

"The same thing is against us."

"That's true," I heard myself saying.

"One person in this country will always lose."

"I guess."

"I wanted to tell you," Katya said sitting up. "I decided to accept your proposal. I decided that I want to be your wife."

"You did?"

"Yes."

The Russian phrase *shah mat* came to mind. Checkmate.

"When do we have to have a baby?" I asked.

"Not for a long, long time," she laughed gently. "We have at least a year."

The Ring

My mother gave us one of her old television sets just in time for Katya and me to catch up on the Los Angeles police beating Rodney King. I'd wanted to apologize to Katya and assure her that New York would always be safe from this. But when the cops who'd done it were acquitted and the riots started in South Central L.A., I felt like I was hiding something from her and that somehow we were going to get mixed up in it.

The riots spread east—from Omaha to Des Moines and then Chicago. The Friday after the violence first began, a crowd grew around the TV studio in midtown Manhattan where I'd been working for the last month. Around three o'clock, management closed the office. We were all sent home, as if a snowstorm had cut the schoolday short. I had some time, so I walked over to the jewelry district on Forty-seventh Street and took a look at the rings. It turned out they weren't expensive. One hundred fifty dollars would probably do it.

"What's her size?" the salesman asked me.

"I don't know, on the small side."

"Like this?" He held up a ring that would have fit my pinkie.

"Yeah, like that."

"You wan' it?"

"What if it doesn't fit?" I asked.

"Bring it back. What's the problem?"

"No problem."

"You want one for you, too? You get two, costs two-ninety. Save ten bucks."

"No, I don't need one."

"It's up to you, right? But if I was you I wouldn't want to buy a bicycle with one wheel. Know what I'm saying?"

"I don't like to wear jewelry."

"Most guys are like that. But you don't have to wear it. Just have it. You'll see. It's important," he wiggled his ring finger at me and winked.

I stared down at the rotating jewelry case.

"I'll just take one," I said.

I lay down the money and slipped out of the store. Katya had gone out to my mother's house in Connecticut for the weekend and I was going out to meet her. I had some time before the next train, so I put the ring in my pocket and walked down toward Radio City. The Rodney King beating was playing again on the screen in Times Square. People looked up. They were coalescing into groups and the groups were massing into mobs like some kind of chemical process. Blacks and whites were checking each other out as if to say, "So this is it. This is how it will go."

There was a whirring in my ears and every new block issued a threat. I found my brother Cam, still in the legal department at Radio City, clenching his fists and banging his head slowly but firmly against his monitor.

"Uh, uh, uh," he said. "Wang ate it all."

"What?"

"The Wang," he said again. "It ate the whole thing."

"They're letting me off early," I told him. "What about you?"

"*Were!* They *were* letting me off early and then this Wang just . . . just . . . *Wangs* me. Just *Wangs* my whole document." He cut his eyes at the computer monitor as if it were pure evil. I grabbed his arm. Cam is three inches taller and thirty pounds heavier than I am. That's the way it's been for the last ten years. But when we were kids, when he looked like he was about to take a swing at me, I used to grab both of his wrists with one hand until he backed off. I gripped his wrist now and he redirected the violence in his eyes from the computer to me.

"Just calm down, all right? It's just a stupid computer."

"Let go of my arm," he said.

I held on and stared him down. "C'mon, just forget it. Listen, why don't you come back to Mom's with me now?" Cam shook his arm from mine and logged off. We walked in silence over to Grand Central and barely made the 4:40.

Inside the train it was party time. The crowd was solidly Connecticut—not a single person of color had boarded. Leave the city to the jungle, they all seemed to be saying, rum-and-coke rattling in their plastic cups in the piss-coated bar car. I bought Cam and me a drink. We were pushed so close together in the train that I could have kissed him on the nose just by turning my head.

"You know," he said, speaking for the first time since we left his office, "you don't look so calm either. In fact, you look like a mess."

"Yeah, well . . . the thing is, Cam," I said, avoiding his eyes, "the thing is, I didn't tell Mom or anyone, but I'm gonna get married to-morrow."

He downed the rest of his drink, belched, and blew the burp in my face.

"Whoa," he said. "Well, what can I say? That's pretty fucking weird. Congrats, I guess. Is it like some kind of green-card thing?"

"Well, sort of, I don't know."

"Well, is it gonna be like a *wedding,* you know, like a big thing?"

"No, it's gonna be small."

"How small?"

"Small like if you came you could have a big part."

Cam and I and the other passengers drank and toasted each other and generally behaved like idiot diplomats being airlifted off the embassy roof in Saigon. But then we got off the train and the danger of the riots faded away. Housewives were waiting. Doors of German luxury cars opened, and I heard one woman say "Hi, honey," and it all seemed like nonsense.

We walked to Mom's from the station. I took us on a long, indirect route. We went past Michelangelo's Pizza where I had sat with a girl ten years before and asked her what records she liked. I took us by the high school auditorium where I'd slow danced to *Purple Rain,* holding a perfectly willing equestrian champion I was too afraid to kiss; then out into the town's periphery where the broadleaf maples held the moist heat close to the road even after the sun had set. All of it was so suffused with cicada-chirping, throbbing, teenage memory that Cam and I could barely look at each other. We turned in at the stone columns that marked my mother's driveway and came around to the back porch. Mom was in a deck chair in front of her rented cottage, a double scotch-on-the-rocks tinkling in her glass. Katya was there too, playing chess against herself in the twilight.

ᛒ

Two days later I sped a rental car up an incline and turned on a high, banked curve. I held the phone to my ear with my shoulder and glanced at the map on my lap. I straightened the wheel and looked up. All at once the branching, twisting California highway system laid itself out before me in the valley below. The producer's calm and modern voice was purring to me over the phone, giving careful directions and parameters. And I was so grateful for the miraculous invention I held against my ear—this *cell phone* as the thing had recently come to be called. I had never used one before, but within an hour of getting to Los Angeles the phone had become an indispensable device. It was helping me decode the mess of exits and overpasses ahead. The producer, twenty miles away in the TV studio office, had the same map as I did and he was telling me how a long green line on it would fork into an orange and a red one. But all at once the friendly lights on the phone blinked out and the device died.

I rattled and shook it and choked up. Other drivers crammed in the surrounding lanes looked at me as if I was some kind of mime-gone-mad, silently raging behind auto glass. I could hear a laugh track in my head, the bruise on my face throbbed, and all the absurd decisions I had made rushed out at me.

"Another decision! Another decision!" I chanted at the road. "There is a critical decision to be made now, right now! A Critical Decision." I turned it into a song:

Critical decision,
Critical decision,
Better go and make it,
It's a critical decision.

The five-lane highway would split in another mile. To the left would be South Central where the black kids mostly lived. To the right was the way to the Hispanic neighborhood where rioting had also broken out. What I was trying to figure out from the conversation I'd been having with the producer before the cell phone died was this: Did we need more Hispanic kids or did we need more black kids? It was critically important. The Producer of Special Programs had told me that I had to get a good color mix on the floor of the studio audience. "We have to bring these communities together," he had said. "These are the biggest riots in twenty years. The country's about to explode. It's historic."

Only a few hours after my wedding was over, the Producer of Special Programs had called me from the West Coast. He had flown out to L.A. and decided something had to be done about Rodney King. He said he needed a researcher and he asked me if I was interested and I could think of nothing else to say but "Sure, you bet," and I was on a plane before I could even consummate my marriage.

The idea was to bring together kids from all the different neighborhoods in Los Angeles and have them talk it through together with a high-profile television host. "Why was everybody fighting?" the host would ask them. We'd show them the latest footage of Rodney King in the middle of the riots. We'd show that moment when Rodney, tears on his scarred face, looked into the camera and asked all of us: "Can't we all just get along?"

The freeway banked up into the hedgework of hibiscus and bougainvillea and every gray space was soon filled in. I threw down the dead cell phone and in the end chose the South Central fork. It looked greener and more lush and I was thinking that things would just keep getting more luscious. But down off the exit ramp the green faded away. Little mounds of charred wreckage from the riots were spread here and there, sugared with sparkly, busted glass.

Lincoln High was easy to spot in all of this—a square brick prison-like structure minus the razor wire. The principal knew that the TV people were coming and she welcomed me in the parking lot with a weary smile. She paid only passing attention to the large black bruise on my cheek, figuring that it was all part of the recent unrest. I plugged in the cell phone in her office and she took me to a study hall where a class of tenth-graders waited. I told her I needed to get five good kids for audience-left, so we set about the business of seeing which of them stood out in a crowd.

"Class," said the principal, "this man is from a television company in New York. He's going to ask you some questions about the . . . the events of last week."

"Hello," I said, "does anyone want to tell me about why all these . . . um . . . events took place?"

Forty hands shot up and I called on a girl in pigtails at the back.

"Yeah, um, see, like, plate-glass window."

"Mmm hmmm," the crowd pulsed.

Then a fat boy broke in: "Yeah, like, and I mean, Korean grocery store!"

"Word! Mmm hmmm!" went the crowd.

"Yeah, and the brothers with the high-interest loans!"

"What are they talking about? What's the plate-glass window?" I whispered to the principal.

"That's the kind of window the African-American man was thrown through on the TV news just before the riots," she whispered back to me.

I spied one lone Mexican boy in the class. If he turned out to be good, if I could get him, then I wouldn't have to go to the Hispanic neighborhood after all. He didn't have his hand up, but I called on him anyway.

"What about you," I pointed to him, "what happened to you in the riots?"

The Hispanic boy ran his thumb and forefinger over the beginnings of a mustache and stared at me coldly.

"Fag," he said.

"I'm sorry?"

"Fag. How come the TV sent a fag to do this job?"

"I'm not gay."

"You're a New York fag."

"Look, I just got married," I said, my voice breaking.

"Ooo!" went the crowd.

"If you just got married," said the boy, "where's your ring?"

I looked at the principal. Where was the adult in this situation? C'mon, I thought, it's fifty against one. Who's going to hand out the demerits here? The principal looked down at the floor. She'd seen worse.

"C'mon, man, where's the ring?" The Hispanic boy felt his power, now the emperor at the coliseum.

"Where's the ring? Where's the ring?" chanted the crowd.

"A judge married us," I said. "I didn't need a ring."

"She pregnant!" laughed a girl from classroom-right. "That's why he di'n't go to no church!"

"Ahhhhh hahhhhhhh! She pregnant, she pregnant!" They all shouted now and looked at the Hispanic boy waiting for him to give the thumbs up or the thumbs down.

"So like, le' me get this straight," he said. "You're a fag, right, but you married her 'cause you made her pregnant, like, accidentally, 'cause it was dark!"

"Ahhhhh hahhhhhhhhhh!"

"And then, like, she beat him 'cause like he wun't do it after the wedding. That's how come he got that ugly bruise on his face!"

"Hey, hey, that's not what happened, that's not what happened at all," I said.

"Then what happened?" they asked.

And even as I felt these damn kids ruining the day and destroying my chances of ever working for the Producer of Special Programs again, I wanted to confess. I wanted to tell them how Cam and I had loaded up Mom's Chrysler Cordoba just twenty-four hours earlier; how Cam dug at me with the same line all the high school kids used when they saw that old car. "We have to be careful not to scratch the reech Corinthian leather," Cam said with his Ricardo Montalban voice.

Katya and her friend Lena got in the back. I started the car up and headed south.

"Hey, Katya," Cam said, "wanna Twizzler?"

"Yes, please," said Katya.

"Give me Twizzler too, please," Lena said from the backseat.

"Sure," said Cam. "Here ya go. Hey, is she from Russia, too?"

"Soviet Union," Lena said.

We drove out what was left of Connecticut, through the beginnings of New York and down the Henry Hudson Parkway. At Seventy-ninth Street we cut through the city to pick up the Queensboro Bridge. Summer had skipped over spring, and Manhattan was already tar-melting hot. There was no sign of rioting, but the streets were deserted and scalding little whirlwinds spun grocery bags and pages from yesterday's *New York Post* up into the air. I put down the window and the rot came in.

Cam turned to me and said something under his breath.

"What?" I said.

"On't-day oo-day is-thay," he repeated.

"I don't want to play a word game, Cam."

"It's not a word game," he whispered. "It's Pig Latin."

"Why are we speaking Pig Latin?"

He jerked his head in the direction of the back seat. "They can't decode it," he said.

"Oh, right," I nodded.

"On't-day oo-day is-thay," he repeated. Don't do this.

"Shut up, Cam."

He threw up his hands and was quiet for the rest of the drive.

Over the Queensboro and onto Long Island, things started looking up—little farms growing potatoes, for example. Pretty soon the gulls, which in Manhattan work a vulture beat, began to look like bona-fide seabirds. They dived and crashed and screeched and did all of those happy seagull things I remembered from the time when there used be something called summer vacation.

When I had last talked with Judge Corn he had told me that we should meet him on a stretch of beach in Quogue. It was supposed to have been empty this time of year. But what with the riots and the heat, the lot was nearly full and we had difficulty getting a spot on the beach for the ceremony. The judge didn't stand much chance of finding us. We didn't really look like a wedding party. I had a sport coat, tie, and chinos, and Katya's dress was beige, and Lena wore a pair of baggy silk Uzbek trousers. No way, the judge wasn't going to find us. He was already about twenty minutes late when I undid my tie. Cam had transformed into a super hero—windbreaker over his head in cape mode, his arms spread out as he flew after a flock of sandpipers along the tide line. Big, sumptuous green breakers rolled in while Lena trailed behind Cam with her shoes in her hand. The hell with it, I breathed, it was just another day at the beach after all.

But all of a sudden there was Judge Corn.

His big blue Ford crested over the space between the dunes, sparkling like a fresh-cut gem. Corn strode out in a wrinkled seersucker jacket that sputtered behind him in the wind.

We started walking down the beach. I tried to count how many paces it would take before we arrived at the spot we had picked out. But twenty yards short of our target, Corn stopped, opened a small book, and began the ceremony immediately, just as a pediatrician might shoot an inoculation into a child's arm before he catches sight of the needle. He took our hands in a strangely intimate way. He looked at us sadly and told us what a serious thing marriage was. His face was crinkly and kind. He asked us if there were rings and I told him I had only one and he said that was just fine. Then he tried to pronounce Katya's name:

"Do you Yek . . . Yekater . . . Yekaterine . . ." he said, pointing at Katya. Katya laughed and said her full-length, Russian-novel name for him. He winked at her and continued the sentence: ". . . take this man . . ." Katya did not know how to pronounce words like "thy" or "matrimony," so Corn returned the favor and said them for her. By the end there was so much mixing of lines that I thought maybe Katya had married Corn or Corn had married me, but he declared us man and wife.

The small crowd of weekend sunbathers lying around us stood up. Katya and I reached out toward each other and kissed. The sunbathers applauded. The waves and the wind had grown and I could barely hear anything over nature's ruckus.

Judge Corn pulled me aside right after the ceremony and whispered something in my ear.

"Thanks, Judge, I appreciate it, thanks," I said.

"No, no, don't *thank* me," he said. "I need . . . I'm sorry, I shouldn't . . . What's the name of your handsome best man there? Yeah, that fella. Yes, yes, thank you."

The judge took Cam with him down to the tide line and turned his back to me. In the wind I couldn't hear what they were saying, but there was some gesturing back and forth that looked a little like a Buster Keaton sketch. Each of them seemed to reach into each other's pockets and there was a lot of patting of lapels. Then the judge took a handkerchief out, sponged his forehead, and shook Cam's hand. He tipped his fingers to me in a half salute, got in his car, and rolled out between the dunes.

When the judge had gone we all walked back to the parking lot, each of us holding a glass. In the Russian tradition we were supposed to smash them for good luck. Katya hurled hers and it shattered completely. Lena threw hers underhand and only the stem broke away. I threw mine and it shattered. Cam wound up like a baseball player, let go of the glass, but sunk it into the dune where it stayed unbroken.

"What was the name of that nice judge?" Katya asked.

"It was Judge Corn," I said.

"No, it wasn't," said Cam. "It was Gorn. Judge Gorn."

"No, Cam, it was Corn, it says so on the wedding certificate."

"Yeah, well, who has the wedding certificate? I got it and I'm not gonna give it to you."

"C'mon, Cam, cut it out."

"What if I just tore it up?"

"Stop it. Just give it to me."

"Not until you pay for the stupid thing. But you can't pay for it 'cause you don't have any money. You're as broke as I am, aren't you?"

"What are you talking about?"

"I just had to pay the judge a hundred bucks for the ceremony. I'm not paying for it, damn it!"

"Cam, calm down, this is ridiculous."

"No, it's not. That's why you invited me, to pay for this stupid certificate."

"No, Cam, I invited you because you're my brother."

"Oh, yeah, right. As if this is what a brother's supposed to do! At least I'm supposed to give you the goddamned rings. But *you* didn't even have one."

"I didn't need a ring. That's what the judge said."

Cam looked at Katya. "In Russia, does the man get a ring, too?"

"Yes, that's the way it is in Russia," said Katya.

"You see! You *see*! Jesus, what the hell kind of wedding is this anyway? Why the hell am *I* here?"

And with this Cam caught my eye and saw that my hands were down. He pulled back his balled fist slowly and catapulted it forward. I don't know, Cam, I thought the moment before the painful thud on my cheekbone. Maybe this is why I invited you. Maybe for this.

Part Two

Evening in Brighton

A woman is . . ." Katya starts to say but then sees me prepare to lecture her on American rights and responsibilities. She seals her lips closed over Soviet dental work, which has recently started to go all wrong.

"What? A woman is what?" I insist.

"Beautiful. More beautiful than you. You shouldn't forget it."

The D train moves out over the Manhattan Bridge and the East River estuary opens up to my right. Halfway across, the engine gives up. The brakes hiss. A beggar who's already worked the car shuts up. Money is all about movement and you won't get a dime out of a stalled train.

"Ladies and gentlemen," a voice says over the loudspeaker, "may I have your attention. Due to a technical problem on the D line this train will be rerouted over the A line. I repeat, *This Brooklyn-bound D train is now a Manhattan-bound A train.*"

"What does it mean?" she asks.

And almost as if she is speaking directly with the conductor and not with me, the voice over the loudspeaker answers: "This means that those of you going to Brighton Beach will have to transfer to a shuttle bus at Broadway–Lafayette."

"Oh," says Katya.

"I guess we'll take the bus," I say.

"Maybe I can call my friend Misha," Katya says. "He has a car. He'll drive me anywhere."

"No, we don't need Misha," I say. "We have time."

We sit on the bridge for half an hour more and then the train moves eerily backward. In the tunnel it stops again and there is darkness and silence. It's okay, though. I've planned for this delay. Trains can never be expected to cross the border between Manhattan and Brooklyn easily. My grandmother will be waiting no matter what time we get there.

Back at Broadway–Lafayette, we board a bus headed for outer Brooklyn. We sit there in silence until we reach the other side of the Williamsburg Bridge.

"What bad thing are you thinking about?" Katya asks suddenly.

I feel transparent, in the way only a married man can.

"I was thinking about work."

"There's no work. Why think about it? What else were you thinking about?"

"I was thinking that everyone I know is leaving the City this summer."

"You know," Katya starts, "one day you could be alone and not married and all of your friends will be. Anne and Elizabeth—all of them. And if you keep behaving like this you will be by yourself.

You'll be in Yugoslavia or something, but by yourself. And you'll be unhappy."

After an hour of silence the bus lets us off at Sheepshead Bay and there is a long walk to Avenue Y and Twenty-fourth Street. It entails a jog of several avenue blocks inland—away from the immigrants' first foothold on America, north to the richer, but still fragile, low-income rentals of my grandmother's generation.

We walk, and the ritual goes like this: Katya goes ahead of me when the sidewalk is too narrow to accommodate us side by side. When there's room, she comes next to me but I hold the street side of the sidewalk to protect her. I've come to understand that Katya favors a nineteenth-century code of chivalry—as if those traditions that the rest of us have lost were frozen and preserved for the Russians in the amber of Soviet isolation. I gave in to the code once we moved in together. Now I open doors ahead of her whenever possible. I keep my eyes on alert for puddles—springing across them and holding out my hand to help her across.

"Are you telling your grandmother that we're married?" Katya asks.

"I haven't told her. No, I'm not telling her."

"You're so ashamed?"

"No. But my grandmother is—"

"What? Old? Fat? Stupid?"

"Traditional."

"So am I—traditional," she says.

We turn past the Golden Age restaurant, the place where we'll go later for a pale, geriatric lunch. Then another hundred yards farther we come to a flagstone path that's been cut through the sod. We walk up the path, and I ring the doorbell, and after a few preplanned seconds Grandma calls out: "Hey-lo-o."

"Oh, hey-lo," she says, crowding up to the screen door and fumbling with the latch. "Come on in. Come on in. I just spoke with your father and he told me that neither of you had a proper coat. So I says to myself, 'Why don't they tell me?' Anyway, fortunately I was just getting rid of some of your Grandpop's things—you know it's already two years since your Grandpop died? I can't believe it—anyway, I asked your father could you two gorgeous people use some coats? Because when I was cleaning out the closet I came across these beau-tee-ful coats. The collars are real leather. The rest is good Naug-a-whatchacallit."

By now she's all the way in the closet and pulling out garment bags and hatboxes. She's eighty-four but she's rooting around in there like a hungry raccoon.

"Oh, Katya dear, hold this bag, these are some feminine things that I'll show you when the man," she juts her thumb at me, "the man—oh, you're so gorgeous, I can't stand it—when he leaves us girls alone." Katya smiles flirtatiously and Grandma smiles back.

"She's pretty gorgeous, too," says Grandma, throwing Katya a smile.

Finally she's found the thing she's looking for. "Try it on," she says holding up a coat. I burrow an arm into one sleeve of the Naugahyde. It's tighter than upholstery and I can feel the stitching strain. "It fits!" Grandma cries. "Oh, it's gorgeous. Isn't he gorgeous?"

Katya raises her eyebrows and smiles, covering her teeth with her hand.

"Beau-tee-ful," she says and they both laugh.

Even if it's going to be lunch at the Golden Age restaurant, I'd like to eat something and move on. The odor in Grandma's low-ceilinged single-family-unit is sweet and stale and tinged by a toilet.

"So, you must be hungry," Grandma says as if reading my thoughts.

"Yeah, Grandma. Starved."

"Well," she says, "some of the girls helped me put a few things together."

She leads us past the out-of-tune piano into the dining nook. There are three kinds of sliced cheese, a bowl of potato salad and a breast of turkey. Two bottles of generic cola (one diet, one regular) and two bottles of seltzer. There's herring too and some other little things in bowls too small to contemplate.

"Weren't we going to the Golden Age?" I ask.

"Oh, ney-oh, ney-oh," Grandma says in her finest Baltimorian. "Jeez, I haven't made a normal lunch since your aunt Candice died. You know it's ten years almost since Candice died? I remember your grandpop, he just couldn't let it outta his head. He used to say, 'Why? Why did God have to take Candice? Why didn't he take me?' Well, God listened and he took Grandpop, too. You know, it's almost two years since your grandpop died. But your grandmom's still here!"

"You bet, Grandma."

Katya recognizes something of Russia in the salads on the table and she's decided to load up her plate. We take our food out to the back porch. I fill an old lawn chair that used to hold Cam and me at the same time. The sun and the sycamore trees mix like a cocktail and we sit in a green crème-de-menthe glow.

"So I was over visiting with your father and your stepmother the other day," Grandma starts, "you really should go see them by the way. Your stepmother looks gorgeous. I thought after she had Noah she'd never lose all that weight. Anyway, your little brother, Noah, he's such a darling, Noah he says to me, 'Grandma, how come you're so fat!' and I says, 'Noah, you should never call a woman fat,' and he says to me, 'Grandma, you're not a woman, you're my grandma!' What a character!"

Katya is pushing some herring around with a fork. It seems like she's bored, and this is always trouble. We've already run through the news of the last month. Soon we'll be into repeats. The repeats will run themselves down, too. If it goes on too long, Katya might say something.

"You know what else your little brother Noah told me?" Grandma bursts out quixotically, unexpectedly, almost youthfully. "He told me that the two of you got married."

The crème-de-menthe cocktail around us jiggles in the breeze. For the first time in many years, I actually look Grandma in the eye.

"Ub," I blub.

"Well, is it true?" she asks.

Katya squints at me.

"Grandma. It's true . . . I don't . . . Hmm."

"That's wonderful. She's gorgeous. You're gorgeous. What's the problem? What are your plans now? Where are you going to live? Are you going to move? Do you need some things? I have some china. It's funny, it's my wedding china—or maybe it was Candice's wedding china? I can't remember. But it's wedding china and I don't need it."

"No Grandma, that's okay, it's—"

"China is useful," Katya breaks in. "We have only three plates and two cups. The cups we have are too small. There are no of these things that go under the cups. What is it called?"

"Saucers!" says Grandma.

"There are no saucers. We have four forks but they are all differ-ent. We are using a sheet for a curtain. The blankets are old. We have no cool one for the summer, only hot ones for the winter. There is no small carpet to stand on after the shower. The apartment is next to the police station. There are criminals shouting all of the night. There is no alarm clock. We must wake with the sun. And this gets earlier every day as summer gets stronger and the days are longer. We could use this china."

The next twenty minutes are spent dismantling Grandma's china cabinet. No one has ever actually said yes to her when she has offered up her stuff, and she is a little taken aback. She and I are inside packing the chipped Wedgwood knock-offs into newspaper while Katya is trying on some "girl things" in the next room.

"You gotta watch her," Grandma starts in, "she'll eat you for breakfast. But she's adorable."

"Grandma, it's not exactly like it seems. It may be a mistake. You don't—"

"What's a mistake? Fifty years from now you won't even recognize yourselves. Just keep to the straight and narrow, if you know what I mean."

"But I'm not even sure I want to be married at all."

"Who wants to be married? It's just something we all do. You shouldn't be so tight-lipped about it—we all feel pretty shook up at first. I felt that way with Grandpop. You know how he used to carry on? God bless him, he drove me nuts."

Katya appears, flushed, angry, attractive. "If we are going to go to the market in Brighton," she says, "we must leave now."

"Already?" Grandma says. But she knows enough is enough. She can't help herself, though, and she throws in a few "you-just-got-heres" just to be sporting. Katya sidesteps to the door and we start to gather up all of the miscellany that's come our way today. With the dishes, the coats, and some leftover fruit—Katya and Grandma agree, you can't throw fruit away—all of it is quite a haul. We load it into a two-wheeled apparatus that Grandma has thrown into the wedding package. My grandmother's house is like one of those stores that's always going out of business—her prices have been slashed for the last ten years. It's a liquidation, going-out-of-existence kind of sale.

We backtrack across the mint-green wall-to-wall with my grandma inching behind in pursuit. We wave good-bye through the screen door and pull everything backward along the chippy flagstone, past the small businesses of Brooklyn with their signs that declare: "Russian Customers Welcome."

We make toward the water now. At the harbor we pick up Brighton Beach Avenue and watch the Latin alphabet surrender to Cyrillic. Katya grows excited when the smell of smoked fish comes into the air. She tastes the *tvorog* at the cheese counter in a Russian grocery store. She puts together the ingredients for a good cabbage soup. She pulls down four cans of Caucasian eggplant caviar—a cheap alternative in Russia, but expensive comfort food here. Katya does nice things with this food. I'm glad we're getting all of these cans.

We leave the last store, weighed down by the pickled and the smoked. Katya pulls out a candy from one of the bags I'm carrying and laughs as she reads the label. The candy is called Vecherny Brighton—Evening in Brighton.

"Vecherny Brighton. So funny. When I was a little girl, we had different candies—all of them from the Vecherny Factory. There was Vecherny Leningrad, Vecherny Moscow. I haven't seen those candies in so long. When the *perestroika* nonsense started, the Vecherny Factory stopped. And now I find Vecherny Brighton. I think here is the only place to find such things. It seems to me everything is upside down."

By now we've slipped through an alley that brings us up to the entrance to the boardwalk. We pull up our dolly one step at a time. At the top, an impossible ocean comes into full view. We roll along, the wheels wobbling over the splintery old wood. Katya's right—everything is upside down. When my grandparents first walked this boardwalk, they spoke English for the first time in their families' histories—Ukrainian Jews tanning out the last traces of their Slavic pallor in the Coney Island sunshine. Now I address my ivory-white wife in my halting Russian.

"*Nu?*" I ask.

"*Nu,* what?" she says.

"I'm sorry about my grandmother."

"I have no problems with your grandmother. We spoke. She told me about how you were when you were small. About your character. It's all very clear to me now."

"But what about that business with the china, and my little brother, and the coats?" I protest.

"It's true, it's embarrassing. But who will give you a coat if not your grandmother?"

Katya fishes out a candy for me. She unwraps it and hands it over. It fills my mouth with an intense sweetness that is un-American.

"Very sweet, yes?" she says.

"Yes," I say. "Very."

Outer Boroughs

M y name is Yekaterina Konstantinova," I wrote, "and I am a graduate of St. Petersburg University with over five years working experience in the health-care profession. I first heard of your dental practice from a friend who had received treatment from you. She told me about your expertise in the field and recommended that I contact you." The letter went on like this for two more paragraphs and then I ended it with a modest, supplicant closer: "If you should require a laboratory assistant or an additional staff person to assist with correspondence, I would be very much interested in discussing my candidacy with you further."

Of course Katya didn't have any health-care experience and I was pretty sure she didn't have any interest in dentistry. But her teeth had started rotting out of her head and I didn't have the money to handle it. It seemed like every other week she would damage a molar and excuse herself from the dinner table. I didn't know how she was managing to eat anymore. We'd been to two dentists, but both had reached the same conclusion: there was major work to be done. It could take months and the cost would be so great that many years would be required to amortize the bill.

And that's when I had the idea. It hit me one morning—a rare bolt of inspiration. Of course, if she worked for a dentist, the dentist would work on her teeth for free or at least at a large discount. All this *and* we'd have a second income.

I was in such a state after the brainstorm that I could barely stand the line at the copy shop. I printed out thirty letters, each one addressed to a different dentist. I had gone through the Yellow Pages and made a list of potential employers. I was careful to avoid all the ones with Slavic-sounding names. I also stayed away from the dentists who worked in the Outer Boroughs. I wanted uptown, stalwart, Yankee doctors with names like Barrow, Conway, and Keating. They should live in solid American neighborhoods, north of Fiftieth Street but south of Ninety-eighth. Those were the kind of dentists who could make use of a quiet, cautious assistant. Surely they'd see the way the Soviet doctors had ruined her teeth, drilling and redrilling them with blunt and filthy rotors until the crowns parted and crumbled to dust.

I bought a roll of stamps and organized myself a secret factory of correspondence on the kitchen counter. Katya was out with Lena and so I had time to carefully address each envelope. But as I started to seal the letters up, I thought I should really show one to Katya. What if one of the dentists called while I was out? Yes, showing her was better. Showing was honest. Showing was *real* marriage.

When Katya came home, I read her the draft. She stared at me with her lips wrapped over her teeth. I looked up when I'd finished reading. She asked me what a dental assistant did and when I told her, she looked at me as if I had just crushed a songbird with my heel. I let her know that there was plenty to do in a dentist's office, that in fact assisting a dentist was a whole profession—very well respected and well paid in the United States. Then I showed her the list of doctors and their impressive addresses to prove my point.

"But why aren't there any Russian dentists on this list?" she said when she'd scanned through the names. "There are many of *our* dentists in America."

"I wasn't looking for Russian dentists," I said.

"But I don't know the English words. I couldn't communicate with one of your dentists."

"You don't need to speak to the dentist! It's a physical job."

"What do you mean, *physical*?" she cried.

I tried to focus. I tried to think up some compelling, simple explanation. An explanation that could make its way through two languages. Nothing came. I stared down at the floor and walked away, whistling.

"Don't whistle in the house. You know what will happen," she said.

"It's already happened," I said.

"You'll see if you keep whistling," she said almost to herself, "we'll be even more poor. See what has happened already?"

She was right, actually. Something, some curse from the outside had come down on us and things were spiraling lower and lower. And who knew? Maybe it came from whistling too much. I had learned from Katya that there were a million things you had to avoid in the Russian home to keep bad luck away. One of those things was whistling. Russian superstition promises that if you whistle in your own home you're likely to go broke. Whistle in a friend's house— you'll wipe him out.

And I had been whistling in the house and all the work had dried up. The Producer of Special Programs stopped returning my calls. I had no benefits, no health insurance. I wasn't just writing job letters for Katya—I'd written dozens for myself, as well. I redesigned my résumé every week. One version cast me as a "television professional." Another claimed that I was a "Sovietologist." I sent one résumé off to a media company called GlobeNet. I sent another to an international mining concern prospecting for cadmium in the Russian Far East. Still others I sent to law firms cutting deals with former Communists. There was a gold rush starting in the ExSSR, *The New York Times* said, but it seemed like it would never trickle down to me.

I was turning in circles looking for work. Even if I'd been out of the house for only an hour I'd call in and check the answering machine thinking that someone might have left a message with a job. Sometimes when I'd call to talk with the answering machine Katya would pick up by accident. "Put it down, please!" I'd want to shout, "I want the answering machine, not you, not you! What can *you* tell me?" But instead I'd rein myself in and ask her delicately:

"Any calls? Any work?"

"No, no. Nothing, nothing," she'd say.

And I'd drop the phone, fuming at the bored way she'd said "nothing"—as if it was a matter that didn't concern her. "Nothing, nothing." Who cares, right? Who gives a damn that there's no money coming in, right? That the end of the month is fast approaching and soon we'll have to pay the rent and if we don't, if we don't, well, you'll see, you'll see how this country can screw you . . .

But I abided. I decided to try to stop whistling. I decided I'd do all of the other things required by her beliefs to keep the evil eye off our house. I'd stop shaking hands with people across thresholds, and when I stepped on someone's foot, I'd let him step on mine to prevent a fight. I'd even keep Katya from sitting on the bare ground in Central Park in order to "protect her fertility."

I'd do all of these things, but she had to stop too.

༄

Zhenya Gopmann was an old acquaintance of Katya's parents who had once lived near them on the other side of the Griboyedov Canal. In America, he lodged alone, in a far-eastern outpost of the Bronx. After I mailed the letters to the dentists I was hoping to avoid him. He was older and authoritative-sounding and like many of the Russians in the Outer Boroughs he held increasing sway over Katya's opinions. I was sure that if he learned about my plan he'd name some well-known fact that would make working for a dentist a black mark in the Russian god's book.

One morning while I sat at home waiting for the dentists to call, Zhenya telephoned to ask me for the Russian translation of the phrase "bird's-eye perspective." I told him and then he asked why we shouldn't all have dinner at his place that night. I suggested the next week would be better and he shouted, "Excuses! Delays!" and hung up. He called back a few minutes later and asked for the meaning of "trial by jury." I gave him my best answer and then he told me that dinner that night would be at seven o'clock and hung up again.

Zhenya had been a dissident in his youth. He had left the Soviet Union for Israel in the late 1970s and from there had leveraged his way into the United States. When he'd arrived he'd got his hands on a large piece of public housing and never let go. He worked as a clerk during the days and earned his CPA degree at night and eventually rose at his firm to become a senior accountant. By the time I met him, he was probably earning more than $60,000 a year. All the same, he continued to live in subsidized housing, far from Manhattan. His apartment was in a massive, ochre-colored project thrown up in hasty apology to the poor. Its hospital-huge bleakness poured down on me whenever we entered his courtyard; but it was the sheer size of the place that made Zhenya buoyant. He liked to show off his many rooms and spacious spaces at every opportunity.

"I don't understand why you live in that box down there in the Chelsea," he said when we entered his foyer that night. The little bald man rushed down his corridor, as if preparing for a Bolshoi-style leap. Then he turned and danced a pirouette in the grandness of his living room. "Do you know how much I pay for all this? Only four hundred seventy-five dollars. Four hundred seventy-five dollars, and I have ninety-seven square meters! How much do you pay for the apartment in the Chelsea?"

"Chelsea," I said.

"What?"

"We say just 'Chelsea,' not '*the* Chelsea.'"

"Yes, yes. How much in just Chelsea then?"

"I guess we pay probably eight hundred dollars."

"Eight hundred dollars! And how many meters do you have?"

"I don't know," I said, "we don't count in meters in America."

"We have thirty-four meters," said Katya.

"Thirty-four meters! Eight hundred dollars for thirty-four meters? But that doesn't make any sense at all! That is, let me see," he did the math quickly in his head, "that is more than twenty dollars for every meter! Katya, dear girl," he said switching to Russian, "I've made a remarkable discovery. As it happens, the new manager of this building is a very old, very dear friend of mine. He was my lieutenant back in the army. Fantastic, isn't it? We share cigarettes in the oil fields of Azerbaijan twenty-five years ago and we meet again in the Bronx! How many winters, how many summers we didn't see each other and now . . . Well, it's just fantastic.

"So, what I want to tell you is this: You can't imagine how many people are trying to get into this building. Usually it takes forever. Sometimes as much as ten years. But this old comrade of mine, this Kuznetsov, Sergey Maratovich, he said he'd be happy to have more of *us* in the building. He's capable of 'correcting the list' if you know what I mean. In your case, with the two of you, you could probably get a place bigger than this one and it wouldn't take more than a few months. You'd have room for a little one at last."

I avoided Katya's stare.

"That's nice of you, Zhenya," I said. "But I don't want to live in a housing project."

"It's not a housing project, it's *novostroika!*" Zhenya declared.

"It's not *novostroika,*" I said, "it's a housing project. It's for the poor."

"No, no, no!" Zhenya insisted, "you don't understand, it's *novostroika.*"

When Zhenya said *novostroika,* he had in mind the large, modernist towers that surround the hubs of Soviet cities. Many kinds of people live in Russia's housing projects—these *novostroikas.* Rich and poor, academic and mechanic. Zhenya and his people didn't care what a place looked like on the outside. As long as the interior was warm, clean, and full of homey bric-a-brac, they ignored the fact that they were encased in a husk of weeping concrete and exposed steel I-beams.

I suspected that Katya found the small apartment that I had picked out for us in Chelsea totally wrong. She wanted space and quiet. I had produced only thirty-four square meters, surrounded by bustling, disturbing commerce and a booming police station. I had put us in Manhattan where life was commercial, cramped, and unfair.

Zhenya looked at me with his eyebrows raised expectantly. I glared back at him. All at once he turned to the kitchen and broke off his talk of housing.

He seated us at his table, set with showy flatware, and we moved our way slowly through a three-course meal. Over carrot salad we spoke in Russian, with simple vocabulary for my benefit. We talked about politics and economics. There was much that I didn't agree with in the discussion, but I spoke rarely. I was stymied because whenever I tried to argue a complicated point in Russian I was in terror of bungling the grammar. I might start out correctly enough, but by the second or third subject/verb combination, my interlocutors would be squinting at me oddly. This would in turn make me more nervous and the sentences would speed up, almost of their own accord. And soon the conjugations would backfire and the nouns and adjectives would cease to agree in either case or number, and the subordinate clauses would lose their conjunctive tethers. By then the Russians would be staring at me sadly, shaking their heads as if they were looking down from a bridge into the scene of a senseless train wreck.

"The problem is," said Zhenya as we moved on to talk about George Bush and the recession, "there are no jobs for young people. The American economy has lost its ability to function."

I clenched my fingers around the stem of the heavy Czech crystal wineglass. If I squeezed hard enough, I thought, the top of it would pop off like a dandelion head.

"Yes, that's true," I said.

"It must be difficult for you," he ventured, "you have no real specialization. But you have Katya and she has a very strong character. That's very good."

We moved on to beef cutlets, followed by a cake with a thick, fatty frosting. Then tea with homemade preserves. I watched Katya closely, waiting for her to tell Zhenya that I had just sent off thirty job letters to dentists we'd never met. But Katya had promised not to say anything, and she always kept her word. No mention was made of dentists, even when Zhenya prodded her about work.

After a while neither of the Russians paid any attention to me at all. The conversation sped up and overtook me and I looked up only every once in a while to log its progress. They made their way past the usual milestones that Soviets ticked off when they came together in the New World: the poor education level of most Americans, the shock of seeing so many black people, the rising prices, the inhabitability of Russia after the fall, and news of the visiting Bolshoi Dramatic Theater of St. Petersburg's production of *The Three Sisters*. Eventually the talk trickled down into nostalgic sighs and musings finally ending with a murmuring, dreamy chant: "Ah, Russia, Russia."

The day after Zhenya's dinner party, a disturbance across the street in front of the police station woke us up early. It put Katya in a dismal mood. She asked me if there was anywhere we could go to get away for the day. I thought for a moment and then remembered how, long ago, I had helped my mother clear the grounds for the Wild Asia exhibit at the Bronx Zoo. And so I took us to the end of the line to the zoo's old North Gates and led her around the nineteenth-century grounds, past the oxidized-copper ape cages, the fluted gazebos, and the fountains with their friezes of leaping porpoises.

Whenever possible I tried to work out excursions like this—trips that brought us into contact with Old New York. If a rude hot dog vendor rebuffed her or if I caught her staring down a particularly wasted piece of the city, I would seek out a slice of preserved architecture and offer it up to her. "There was a time when Central Park was called 'the' Central Park," I'd say. "When you lived 'in' Twentieth Street and not 'on' it and there was no subway, only 'the elevated.'"

And even though these subtleties of English were lost on her, it didn't matter. I was more intent on incanting a spell than giving a philology lesson. New York had no center for Katya, no Admiralty spire around which the city could rotate. It had none of the fog Andrey Bely had painted over Petersburg, no Venetian-style embankments, no great, green Winter Palace. New York had to be talked into existence for her. Most of its past had been wooden and provincial and had rotted long ago underneath the pavement. So I sought out the older city's relics: James' Washington Square and Wharton's Grace Church, the Public Library and the Frick Collection.

I needed to do all this because Katya's hold on our life was weaker than I had anticipated. No, I would not *lose* her to Russia. That was clear now. But I saw that I could just as easily lose her to the Outer Boroughs. She could, at a moment's notice, just slip away a mile north or east into one of the Russian neighborhoods. Even at the Bronx Zoo there was this risk. There was an enclave only a few blocks away that would take her in, feed her cabbage soup and **pirozhki.** They'd whisper in her ears and reveal to her all the things that were out of joint in this place. More and more, I realized that life with Katya would be a struggle with these whispers, and that to keep her—to make an American out of her—I would have to physically pull her over to my side.

When we left the antique section of the zoo, Katya's dark mood returned and my Old New York illusion fell apart. We wound along the dull concrete path, past the makeshift Serengeti and through the American wilderness simulacrum with its sick timber wolves and fed-up bison. We floated above the park on the zoo sky tram, passing over a pack of sad tigers, moping away in five parched acres done up to look like the subcontinent.

The sky tram landed us near an exhibit called "The World of Darkness." The World's makers had permanently exchanged night for day and had added enough purple light for humans to see the subjects. Katya exchanged knowing stares with the bats and ocelots; in St. Petersburg it was nighttime, too. We stayed until the artificial sun rose in the World of Darkness and the last flock of bats scrambled back into their caves to sleep. Outside, the real sun disappeared into the Hudson and we headed on foot through the Bronx and then silently by subway back to Chelsea.

❧

The phone was ringing when we came in the door. Katya collapsed on the bed and I answered it.

"Hello, is dis the home of Yekaterina Konstantinova?" said a man at the other end of the line. It was a Russian, but I didn't recognize his voice.

"Yeah, yeah, hold on," I said and looked over at Katya. Here we go again, I thought. A new Russian now, another link in the immigrant chain. Just arrived from Leningrad, needs a place to stay, needs some information, needs, needs, needs.

"Can I tell her who's calling?" I asked.

"Yez. This is Doctor Konvay. I am answering the letter. Could I spik to Yekaterina Konstantinova?"

"This is who?" I asked.

"Doctor Konvay. Or maybe I must to say 'Doctor Con-oo-ay.'"

"Dr. Conway?"

"Yez."

"The dentist?"

"Yez. Doctor Gennadi Conway, D.D.S."

"Excuse me," I said, "but are you . . . Russian?"

"Yez."

"But—"

"Could I spik to Yekaterina Konstantinova?"

"Hold on." I called Katya over.

"Who is this?" I asked her before handing over the phone. "He's Russian! Did you tell Zhenya about the dentists?"

"Of course not. You told me not to."

"Here, take it then," I said.

She took the phone and leaned her ear into it. *"Da?"* she said. "Ah, Doktor Konvay." She tightened her mouth and waved me away. I left the room, but then came back and sat near her on the bed as she lilted back and forth. "Ah ha," she said. "Yes, Leningrad University, yes . . . No, not too long ago . . . Yes, it's very hard . . . And you? . . ."

She let out a cautious laugh. Then, in a feinting voice, she asked: "Is it true?" Pause with a smile and then, "Really?" I could hear Conway's answer come back through the tube in a gurgle of Russian, like water flowing from a forgotten tap, overfilling the bathtub and flooding the entire apartment. Before long Katya was drifting away from dentistry and her qualifications, which she had made light of from the very beginning of the conversation, and into other things. They were talking about the plays, about the upcoming production of Chekhov's *Three Sisters* at the Brooklyn Academy of Music. They talked about the poor education level of most Americans, and yes, there it was again, "Ah, Russia, Russia."

I scratched at my skull as if I was scratching to get at my brain. I paced the room and looked at the phone jack. Katya chortled on. There were some arrangements. *"Do zavtra"*—'til tomorrow—was said a dozen times and then, just when I thought the phone would be put down, a new thread of thought came unraveled and the interlocutors seized on it, teased it out of the fabric of their farewells, and worked it back into a new pattern of talking and talking. *Do zavtra, do zavtra,* again and again, until it was unnecessary to say "till tomorrow" because it already was tomorrow. Katya lay the phone carefully back into its cradle. All this had taken two hours.

"How can he be Russian?" I pleaded. "How? With a name like Conway?"

"There are many Russians with English names," she said. "Russia was a rich country once. Our problems now are just temporary. Before the Revolution we took from the whole world. Russia had maids from France and teachers from England. Some of those foreigners stayed and married Russians. Some of them liked Russia. Doctor Conway must be from one of these English families that stayed in Russia. You wouldn't believe it but Russia is a real melting pot."

<p>

Back when Katya had first come to America, we had made a silent agreement about money. No matter what I was earning, I would leave ten dollars for her every morning. I never asked her where this money went, indeed I never even mentioned it. It was always gone by the time I came home.

Starting a few months after Conway's call, more often than not I found the ten-dollar bill still lying on our coffee table. After a while I stopped leaving it and no mention was made of it. And one day when I checked my bank account I found that, instead of moving inexorably toward zero, my balance was actually going in the other direction: Katya had figured out how to make deposits. The weeks passed. The balance moved upward, higher and higher, approaching the $500 mark for the first time since our wedding.

And just as the fighting between warring nations tends to subside when their economies recover, so too did the anger and resentment between Katya and me start to die down after we each began to earn something. When she had first started working for Conway, her elaborate morning preparations had driven me crazy. She'd come out of the bathroom dressed more for a date than for a day of work at a dentist's office. She was over-rouged. Her blouse was too frilly and formal and her skirt not formal enough.

But when it became clear that she was maintaining herself financially and even to some extent maintaining me, her morning routine became increasingly endearing. Her eyes seemed to shine with a new light, and the fake green jewels she put on made them shine with double brilliance. A thought often grabbed me during those mornings. Maybe I should give this up, this attempt I was making to be independent and my silly forays into television and film. Maybe I should just throw myself at my father's feet and try to get him to loan me enough money for business school, for medical school—for anything professional and stable. Maybe what I needed was a *good* job and a house in New Jersey. We'd have a swimming pool and our kids would be beautiful. They'd have Katya's eyes and, with a little luck, they'd take their height from my family. They would be startlingly bilingual and they'd read and read. They'd read the Russian classics in Russian and the American classics in English. We'd be like the Nabokovs, damn it. Not ignorant, frightened immigrants, but real biculturals with one foot in America and another in the Old World.

But those thoughts were always too slippery to grab onto, and just as they were welling up into words Katya would disappear out the door with just a peck on my cheek and then up, up, up to Conway on the Upper East Side.

Something had definitely changed. The curse that had hung over us for so long seemed to be lifting. Even for me, a day or two of work started to show up each week. My temporary agency started calling again, and before long I too had saved a bit of something. Bush was voted out of office. The recession felt like it was breaking. It even seemed like we might be able to get away from New York for a few days. This Dr. Conway was kind enough, it appeared. I was sure he'd let Katya off for a little break.

I took Katya out for dinner to propose the idea of a vacation. I chose a restaurant that we hadn't gone to since the very beginning. It was a small, single-room French bistro in Greenwich Village. There was usually a long line out front. But this night we managed to get in after just a short wait. We got the difficult-to-get corner table and I ordered a bottle of Burgundy from the middle tier of the wine list. The restaurant was all glass on two sides and we could see lovers, gay and straight, amble past.

Katya was wearing a simple dress with a maroon-and-black pattern. It had a cut that made me realize shamefully that I had neglected for the last few months to tell her how beautiful she was. We joked about her Russian friends and my old roommates with light hearts and neither one of us felt any national indignation at the other's jabs. I quacked the way Zhenya had that night in his apartment and recalled the ridiculous idea he'd proposed that we live in a housing project way up in the east Bronx. She laughed and admitted that she was coming to like Manhattan and that it would be silly to move. We were Americans, adrift together, and our raft was a box in Chelsea. What difference did it make that I was fourth-generation American and she was first? Here, in this mad, vast city, any deal could be struck, any balance could be found.

The end of the meal came and we lingered over coffee. We ordered a dessert that was a kind of nut brittle topped with praline ice cream. Katya didn't touch it. "Go on," I said, "have some. Just a little won't ruin you." After some prodding she kissed me and took a forkful. She smiled at the first taste and then bit down. There was a sickening crunch. Her eyes filled with moisture. She excused herself from the table. In her haste, she left the napkin she'd used to cover up her mouth on the table. There, embedded in the dessert, were the crushed remains of one of her molars.

The talk of vacations ended. I hadn't thought about her teeth since she'd started her new job, but after that night, they came gnashing back at me. I called my brother Cam to see what he'd say, but he wasn't home and he had stopped returning my phone calls anyway. I even thought of calling my father to see if he could loan me some money, but I had let the silent treatment go on too long and now wasn't the time to introduce him to my new wife.

The figure those other dentists had estimated for fixing Katya's mouth pushed to the front of my mind again and it contorted all my other thoughts. I had assumed that with Dr. Conway it was all being taken care of somehow. The plan had seemed so good. Of course, if she worked for a dentist, the dentist would agree to work on her teeth for free. But he was a Russian dentist, after all, and maybe she didn't want him to work on her teeth, or maybe some bizarre, Byzantine arrangement had been reached between them. If that was the case, the deal started to look weird. What was she getting paid, anyway? I had never asked. These damn Russians, they had such abstract ideas about work and compensation.

One Friday, after she left for work, I decided I would go up to Dr. Conway's and speak to them both. The train let me out at East Ninety-sixth. I walked down two blocks to Ninety-fourth and found Conway's building on a very respectable block. Number sixteen was just off Fifth Avenue and in view of Central Park. It was a pleasant, shaded townhouse nestled between two auspicious-looking brownstones.

Inside the first set of doors was a panel of buzzers set in buffed brass. An elegantly embossed nameplate accompanied each button. I looked for Conway but there were no doctors listed. Only the low-ermost button had something close. "Helen Conway, MSW," it said. A paper arrow was taped to her nameplate and pointed down to a note below the intercom speaker. "Mail for Dr. Gennadi Con-way/Melnikov," the note said, "should be forwarded to P.O. Box 4120, Queens, NY."

I glared down the street to the mouth of Central Park. I turned a complete circle and then looked back at Helen Conway's buzzer. I took down the address and walked over to Madison, to the nearest pay phone. I called information. The operator gave me the same ad-dress, here, on Ninety-fourth Street. I asked for something in Queens but there was no Gennadi Conway—only a million G. Conways and none of them appeared to be dentists. I paced back and forth on Madison, thinking that maybe I should just go back home and wait for Katya. I turned back around, walked up the outer staircase to the landing, and rang Helen Conway's buzzer.

"Yes, I'm looking for Dr. Conway," I said when a female voice answered.

"Dr. Conway's in Queens."

"I'm sorry, I need to see him, and you've only given the post of-fice box down here."

There was a long pause.

"Hello?" I said.

"Are you from Russia?" said the voice finally.

"No."

"Then what do you want?"

"My wife's from Russia. She's working for him, I think."

"Wait there," she said.

A woman in her late thirties opened the door. She had dirty-blonde, frizzy hair with darkish roots. Sleeplessness had formed sexy indentations under her eyes. She shaded her face with her hand as she squinted down at me through the glass of the inner door. For a moment she looked as if she would turn around and go back up the stairs, but then she stepped out onto the outer landing wearing a pair of green wool socks.

"Here," she said and handed me a card. "Gena's there now. I don't know where the place is exactly. I don't go to Queens."

"Thanks. I'm sorry to get you out of the house this early."

"That's okay," she said, lighting a cigarette. She exhaled and lingered there as if once outside she no longer had the stomach for her apartment.

"Okay, well, I guess I'll go to Queens now," I said.

"Okay . . . Listen . . . if you see Gena, why don't you tell him Helen said hello, okay?"

"Yeah, yeah," I said hurrying down the landing, "okay."

"And, also, Gena's dropped the Conway. He's going by Melnikov again."

I rode the Lexington Avenue line downtown and muttered. Melnikov? *Melnikov?* Jesus. I transferred at Grand Central and asked the token-booth clerk which train I needed. It turned out to be one I'd never taken before. I was told to take it to the end of the line. The platform was on the bottom level, lower down below all the other lines. It took twenty minutes for the next train to come. I walked along the platform and counted the black gum blots. A panhandler too poor to afford a real instrument was plucking on a single string stretched between a stick and a washbasin singing:

This land is your land, this land is my land.

The incoming train scraped and screamed its way into the station. I got on and walked through all of the cars to the front. The train went forward in lurches and periodically peeked out from underground. Eventually it came into the light for good. The song kept playing in my head:

From California to the New York island . . .

When I came out of the station in Queens, it was as if I had entered another city altogether. There were no apartment buildings, no businesses. Just rows and rows of two- and three-family units, paneled over with aluminum siding. Oversized women with kerchiefs on their heads passed by, wheeling carts full of cans and used clothes. I looked at the business card again:

GENNADI N. MELNIKOV, DDS

Hygienics • Bridgework • Oral Surgery

I asked one of the kerchiefed ladies for directions to the street I needed, but she didn't understand. When I asked her in Russian, she threw her hand out in front of her—*"Tuda, molodoy chelovek, tuda"*— That way, young man, that way. I found a grayish-white house with the right address. The walkway was broken in places, and green mold was growing up the base of the siding all around the house. A row of Russian nesting dolls was perched inside one window.

I rang the bell and a heavyset Jamaican woman buzzed me in. She was sitting at a desk in an empty office with brown shag carpeting. She was dressed in a clean white lab coat.

"Yes, I'm here to see Doctor Melnikov."

"Y'avenappoin'mont?" she asked.

"No, no, I'm a . . . I'm related to . . . to . . . Yekaterina Konstantinova."

"Oh. Come in, then. Dr. Melnikov's just finishinafillin'. I'll go tell him."

I took a seat in the dark paneled room. Melnikov's walls were rich with information about new procedures. "Why not whiten your teeth?" asked one poster. In the corner a monitor showed a video loop of bad teeth morphing into good—spaces filled themselves in, gums turned from sick, white-flecked to healthy pink. And in among the different dental propaganda, little hints of another place—a smiling Russian clown on one wall; on another, a wistful, horizontal canvas of the south Neva embankment in St. Petersburg. Through the fog was the Admiralty spire and in the distance behind it, to the right, the dirty gold dome of St. Isaac's Cathedral.

And then, all of a sudden, there was Melnikov.

"Pliss," he said, "come into my office."

I followed him down a dark hallway. He was not an old man but there was something elderly in his gait. It's not that he was hunched, nor did he shuffle, but he lifted and planted his feet gently, like a man walking cautiously along a narrow beam. When he opened the door to his office he let out a small sigh and flipped on a light switch. It was a very clean, white room with all the modern equipment of American dentistry. He took a seat on his stool and offered me the only other chair. Then he pressed a button and raised and rotated me so that we could face each other on an equal plane.

"So," he said, "you are friends with the Yekaterina?"

"Yes, I really should have called you first but your card doesn't have your phone number. You've moved. I went to your other address. On Ninety-fourth Street."

He looked at the business card I showed him and shook his head.

"I was really not thinking when I make these cards. Somebody in Menhetten gave you this card?" he said.

"Yes."

"Who?"

"A woman named Helen."

"Ah," he said.

"She said to say hello."

"That's nice." He closed his mouth and stared at me.

"Listen, I'm sorry, I just wanted to find out from you how it's working out."

"Fine. There are no problems, generally. But exactly what do you mean?"

"I mean with Katya, is it working out?"

"With Katya?" he said, "I don't know. Have you seen her?"

"Yes, we live together," I said. "Actually, I meant her work with you."

"But the Yekaterina has not worked here for some weeks."

I could hear the fan ventilating the room and the ticking of the sterilization machine. I looked at the silver instruments lined up on a green-blue cloth waiting for the next patient.

"But she did work for you, didn't she?" I said. "I mean, where is she?"

"I no know where she is now. But yes, yes, she did work here."

"And? . . ."

"Well, you see, Yekaterina's leeter came at strange time. I just moved to the Queens from the Menhetten. Some things in the practice were not working. I needed some help and your—Yekaterina's leeter—it was so nice. Nobody in this country ever said I had such 'expertise' before. And her English in that leeter, it was so clever.

"When she first come, I am thinking maybe she can be some kind of assistant for me with the English for negotiations with these terrible HMOs. And also, you know—like receptionist and translator, she could be. We try this for some weeks, but her writing English is not so much better than what I have, I am sorry to say. I think maybe you write this leeter, no?"

"Yes," I said.

"Aha. Well, that explains it."

"I'm sorry." I looked at him and realized that actually he was not old at all. He might be taken for a man in his early forties were it not for the fact that his skin was washed out and dull, as if the luminance had been turned way down on his face.

"So," he said after a pause, "after it not work with the English, I think maybe she, the Yekaterina, can be as assistant in the practice. With the hygienics. And we try this also. But you must know Yekaterina is intellectual girl with the higher education. This work which I have for her—it is for the hands. She has much too beautiful hands for this. She is good girl. Beautiful girl. You should marry her," Melnikov saw that I wore no ring and he studied my face diagnostically.

"And what about her teeth?" I asked, "did you at least look at her teeth?"

"Ah," he said, "her teeth! It's such a tragedy. I am professional, and I love my homeland, but I cannot forgive them in Russia for what they do with the teeth. Fortunately, I have been retrained in this country, thanks to my former wife. She gave me so many things. Even her name. For a while. With that name, Conway, you can make a good life in America. But it is big shame for man to take a woman's name when she is no his woman no more."

"But you looked at Katya's teeth?"

"Yes, yes, I took a look, as you say. But I have not time for such big operation for no money. Maybe, we can find some arrangement with you?"

"I'm sorry, but I don't have that kind of money."

"I see." Melnikov started to ask me something, then stopped himself. Then he changed his mind again and asked me anyway.

"I'm sorry but you must tell me. You are good young American man. This is so rich country. Why do you not have the money? You have the beautiful, strong girl who is in love with you. You have the higher education—I can see. What can you not do with all of that?"

I couldn't answer Melnikov's question, and he wasn't going to press me. There was really nothing more to say between us. I wanted to get out of there, to call Katya, to get to the bottom of all this. But I had come far, come "as a guest" as the Russians say, and Melnikov's un-American manners prevented his letting me go too soon. We switched to Russian, and my lack of vocabulary made me more polite and pliable. I was cajoled into staying. He asked the receptionist to bring us tea and small cakes from a Polish bakery around the corner. We switched seats and Melnikov opened the window behind the dental chair and lit a French filterless cigarette. He asked where I came by my Russian and when I told him I had studied in St. Petersburg he brightened and told me he had grown up in Petersburg and taken his first degree there. He told me where he had lived, the funny aspect of his former neighborhood, and how it was, in fact, the same part of the city where Gogol's Major Kovalyov had lost his nose. We swapped jokes we'd picked up along the road—one about Gorbachev and Reagan exchanging secretaries that I remember being particularly funny—and then he walked over to a cabinet behind me that I knew contained a certain bottle reserved for special occasions.

It was just after quitting time when I left Melnikov's office. The Armenian cognac buzzed in my stomach. The houses around had lost what little color they'd had. I searched out a pay phone and punched in my home number as if I were accusing each digit with my finger.

I heard Katya pick up and laugh to someone out of earshot. Then she answered the phone in the Russian way: *"Slushayu vas"*—I'm listening to you.

"Katya?"

"Ah, there you are," she said. She too had been drinking. "We thought we'd lost you. Where are you, by the way?"

"I'm in Queens."

A pause.

"Ah ha," she said finally.

"Katya, what is all this? Why am I in Queens?"

"I don't know. Queens is not so bad."

"I just left Dr. Melnikov's office."

"So you're a secret agent now."

"He told me you hadn't been there in weeks."

"And I told you I didn't know the words of dentists."

Another pause, this time from my side. Over the phone I heard a man in the background, in our apartment, strumming a guitar and singing an Okudzhava ballad. Then I heard Katya's friend Lena say, "Stop singing. Let's drink to capitalism!" A glass clinked and the man's voice laughed back at her and started singing again.

"Katya," I said, trying to contain my anger. "It's not fair. You have to tell me. You have to tell me where you've been these last two months. You have to tell me where all that money came from."

"Have to tell you? *Have* to tell you? Why?"

I felt a thought boiling up inside me. Part of my brain scrambled to contain it, but the Russian ballad continued to plinky-plunk in my head. *"Po Smolenskoy doroge—lesa, lesa, lesa"*—Along the Smolensk road there are forests, forests, forests. I wasn't sure if I was hearing the song or imagining it. It droned out my reason. All at once my thought leaped out of its own accord, to drive away the song once and for all.

"You have to tell me, Katya," I said at last, "because you're my wife. Because we're married."

She cleared her throat, breathed in and breathed out.

"We are?"

"Yes," I said, "we're married."

"By the way you've been behaving," she said, a slight catch in her voice, "I wasn't sure."

The phone suddenly let out a blast of static. I realized that I was pacing so much that I had started to yank the cord out of its socket. I stepped gingerly back toward the booth and tried to keep still.

"You know," Katya said when the line had cleared, "we shouldn't be speaking like this now. This isn't a telephone conversation."

"Then what is it? Do you really think someone is listening to all this?"

"If someone is talking then someone is listening."

"And just what would they hear if they *were* listening?" I asked.

I heard Katya move into the bedroom and close the door and the guitar playing faded away. I heard her cup her hand over the receiver and whisper:

"They would hear a jealous husband with a weak character trying to pretend he has a strong one."

I listened to the crackling of the Queens–Manhattan trunk line. I took the phone from my ear and looked at it and tried to measure how hard I would have to throw it in order to destroy it. A faint voice came out of the handset and I pulled it back to my ear.

"What, what?" I said. "I didn't hear. What did you say?"

"I said that I'm going to the theater tonight. Zhenya got tickets for you and me. My friend Misha is driving me there."

"The theater?"

"Yes. Do you want to go to the theater tonight? Or probably you can't decide. Do you want me to decide for you? I can, you know."

"Which theater?" I asked.

"In Brooklyn. The B-A-M it's called. There will be a ticket waiting for you if you can ever make up your mind."

And she hung up.

๛

A jealous husband
with a weak character
pretending to have a strong one.

It was like a poem. A mean, marriage haiku that echoed in my brain as I walked through Queens. I headed west. The sun angled low and glared into my face. Dunkirk Street became Liberty, which in turn let out onto Jamaica Avenue.

Line one of the poem was definitely true: a thesis statement even. I was both a husband and I was jealous. We had established that and agreed on it.

Line two, "with a weak character," was more confounding. "A weak character," I said out loud, trying the phrase on for size. It was true that I had not exhibited great decision-making strength in the last few years. I hadn't really chosen a major in college or a career. Things had just sort of happened. But until now I'd never looked at my indecisions collectively. I'd taken each indecision one at a time and then moved on to the next indecision.

It hadn't occurred to me that there was a pattern in all this. Katya's phrase pointed not only to a pattern of what was, but also to a pattern of what would be. An endlessly replicating strand of weak-character DNA. Could it be true that there was an essential flaw in the machine of my character, like a broken tooth in a gear? That every time a decision came around, the bad tooth in the gear came round too, causing me to jam and break down?

"A weak character." There was nothing biting or cruel in the way Katya had said it. Actually, when I listened to her voice again in my head, she sounded sad and concerned—the way a doctor would sound, informing a favorite patient of his chronic condition.

But, really, a weak character? Surely someone's entire way of being couldn't be summed up in a blanket statement like that? Maybe in absolute Russia, but not here.

Then again, maybe we did do it here. Shrinks like my dad and his friends did all kinds of summing up. I'd overheard them at dozens of cocktail parties saying things like "He's manic," "She's totally borderline," and "They're chronically depressed." Those were certainly summations. Maybe even worse. Maybe they were equivocations. Maybe shrinks were avoiding the heart of the matter. Maybe in America weakness was coddled and obscured and given a fancy name for the benefit of the paying patient. Maybe those patients were just weak.

"A weak character," I said out loud again, this time a catch of panic in my voice. What could be done about it? Could I escape it? Maybe the only thing to do was to be honest and direct about it— to operate with a knowledge of my own weakness. Then maybe I could take strength from somewhere else or hide it away.

And this brought me to line three of Katya's haiku: "pretending to have a strong character." Was my lack of a strong character that visible? Was it like a physical disfigurement, like a hump on my back that I couldn't turn far enough around to see? And if it was that noticeable to a foreigner like Katya, was it even more noticeable to my countrymen—my friends, my family, my employers? Was it the thing that was standing between me and success? Was this why I was mired in temping and all sorts of other odd jobs while everyone else my age seemed to be slowly pulling themselves up above the tide line? If it was, then I was simply doomed. Doomed because I could only pretend to have a strong character when all the world knew I had a weak one.

And then I thought back to something Katya had said before we were married. "America will eat you whole, like a fish," she'd said, "especially when you're alone." If this was true, then me with my weak character—surely I was going to be swallowed like a minnow. Unless of course I could fortify myself—take something from Katya's character, which had been documented as "extremely strong" by everyone who'd met her. I saw in this a glimpse of the mysterious logic of marriage. Marriage was a merger. If properly carried out it allowed one to dilute one's weaknesses in the waters of another's strengths. And I started to realize that while it might be expensive and time-consuming at first, a merger with Katya might turn out to be to my benefit. If I could make a life with her, conceivably her very strong character could become *our* strong character and the two of us could become a couple that was stronger than average. And in the fertile ground of America a stronger-than-average-couple would certainly grow and prosper.

My march west had led me to the G subway line, the only direct connection between Queens and Brooklyn. An old, outdated train came into the station. I sat down in the car. The lights flickered on and off and the loser-smell of bad booze and homeless men hung in the air. I thought about Dr. Melnikov and how he had kissed me as if I were his son as I was leaving his office.

"With Helen and me it was different," he had said. "*She* was American and *I* was Russian. It could not work. But you and the Yekaterina—you are . . . opposite of us. You—the man—are American and *she,* the woman, is the Russian. A Russian woman gives everything of herself. When she loves you there can be nothing better, nothing more worthwhile. It is you—you who must be flexible. You must try."

The train stalled for five minutes. It started again but then aborted its trip several stations short of my stop. I got out and started walking fast. I sighted a white light in the distance and broke into a run. The Brooklyn Academy of Music loomed closer and closer until I could make out the marquee: "Tonight on the BAM stage," it said, "the Bolshoi Dramatic Theater of St. Petersburg presents Anton Chekhov's *Three Sisters.*"

I stepped inside the double glass doors. There was an intense odor of sweat and Russian rose perfume that was slightly nauseating. The lobby was filled with fussily dressed, older Russians. It was likely that the same crowd once gathered for the same play back in Leningrad twenty years ago.

I saw Katya's hair, uncoiled for a change, dangling over the banister of the mezzanine above. She and a gray-haired man stood next to each other in the bar facing Zhenya who appeared to be telling them a joke. Zhenya expanded and contracted his pudgy face and jiggled his shoulders up and down. Then he let his hands fly out in front of him. He twirled his fingers down in diminishing circles until they reached his knees. I heard him say "Boom!" and the three of them laughed until tears came into their eyes.

Zhenya caught sight of me below and waved me up. He handed me a flute of champagne and graciously brushed off the excuses I made about my appearance.

"This is my friend Mr. Kuznetsov," Zhenya said introducing the gray-haired man. "The one who manages the 'housing project' where I live."

"Sergey Maratovich," said the gray-haired man, offering me his hand, his name, and his patronymic all at once and smiling a mouthful of Siberian gold.

"A pleasure," I nodded.

"Also a pleasure," he replied. "I was just telling Yekaterina that we have put you on the waiting list in my building in the Bronx. I understand you have only thirty-four square meters now, in the Chelsea. Maybe soon we will have something bigger for you, ay?"

"Sergey Maratovich, Daniel," Zhenya called out to us, mirthfully changing the subject and flowing into Russian all at once. "Gentlemen, allow me to interrupt. I would like to propose a toast. And though this toast is usually reserved for the third round, I think it behooves us to move it up to number one, since we are in the company of such a beautiful woman. Gentlemen, let us drink to the ladies."

"To the ladies," we concurred solemnly.

"And their beautiful smiles." Zhenya winked at me. Katya and Sergey Maratovich struck up a conversation about apartment dimensions. Zhenya patted me on the shoulder and turned me away to the railing of the mezzanine. "Don't worry," he whispered when the other two were safely distracted. "Don't worry about her teeth. I've paid for the first bridge and Misha, that driver friend of Katya's, he's paying for the two worst bicuspids in exchange for her assistance on a small project. Her mouth was growing quite serious, you know—the infection was spreading."

"But . . . How . . ." I started to say. I wanted to ask him how this arrangement had been reached. I wanted to tell him that Katya had been lying to me, that she was supposed to be at a dentist's all along. I wanted to say that if he and this Misha guy, whoever he was, if they hadn't interfered maybe it would have worked out with Dr. Melnikov. But then I thought back to what I had said to Katya. That it was her responsibility to tell me. Because she was my wife. Because I was her husband. Because we were married. I turned back to Zhenya open-mouthed, my question trailing off into nothing.

"I know," he said. "I know you're worried about the money. Dentists in this country are very expensive and Katya says you worry about money constantly. Don't worry. You'll pay us back later. It's cheaper in the Bronx. You'll be able to save some money when you move there."

The house lights flashed. Zhenya placed his hand gently on my back and nudged me into the theater. I hung my head down and watched my feet move along the red-carpeted aisle. It was mesmerizing—the movement of my feet. One foot followed the other as if these feet of mine only took orders from each other. Of course the left had to move forward—if it didn't it would lose the right one entirely.

I looked up and I saw Katya walking briskly ahead. She too seemed transfixed by her feet. And why not? What would ever stop her stride? She had all the admirers and supporters that she would ever need. She had her green card and in a few more years she'd have her citizenship. How slow and weak and unnecessary I must seem to her. I watched her arms swing back and forth, carefree and happy. Her unfettered happiness bit at me. And the bitterness boiled up and began to condense itself into a dark and familiar shape. I felt like storming out of the theater. Making a scene. But just as the ball of my foot started to turn I saw Katya slow her gait and swing her right arm back. She opened and closed her hand twice and then stretched out her fingers.

"Dai ruku," I heard her whisper to me—Give me your hand.

I held my hand up and she not only took it, she clung to it. She pulled me toward her and circled my arm around her. She placed my hand so low on her waist that there was no doubt of our intimacy. We took our places in the theater and she nestled my hand in her lap. The seats were perfect. The richness of the velvet cushions and the tingling hush that came over the crowd silenced whatever protest I had left.

The curtain rose and I put on my translation headset. The actresses came on stage lilting and weaving in beautiful Russian. The English version came through the earphones as a dull, lifeless monotone. I knew I would quickly lose the story if I didn't use the headset so I took out one tube and listened to the Russian with my free ear.

The players were well trained and spoke clearly but the English translation was fuzzy and boring. As an experiment I took out the other earphone. My chest tightened and my eyes teared up. The Russian sentences held together. I suddenly had the impression that I was very cautiously standing upright on ice skates and gliding across a frozen lake for the first time. I was no longer translating in my head. I was simply listening and comprehending the original. I laughed when Katya laughed and choked up with the rest of the crowd. And all the voices of the Russians I had come to know over the last year returned to me with a clarity I had never heard before: I heard Melnikov's encouragements from his dentist's chair. I heard the heartfelt concern in Zhenya's voice as he tried to win us over to his housing project. And I heard the lost melancholy in all the confessions Katya had made that she'd proudly disguised as short, bitter rebukes.

Onstage a pretty actress whirled her arms around and around—free and dizzy. Yes, I remembered her. I knew who she was. I had read *The Three Sisters* in college. This girl was Irina, the darling of the family. She and her sisters were stranded far, far out—out in the outer provinces. They had lost almost everything. I knew this story. Goddamn, I knew it!

"Ah, v Moskvu!" the actress cried, and brought a lump to my throat as she did. "Oh, to go to Moscow! To sell the house, to finish with everything here, and off to Moscow!"

Beautiful Things

B ack in college, one of the lines I always got from my professors was that Russia never had a Renaissance and, as a result, the Russian mind has remained one-part medieval to this day.

As the weeks of our marriage turned into months, I came up against the medieval part of Katya's mind more and more. Night by night, Katya eliminated the baroque pieces of lovemaking we'd so adventurously composed during our courtship. Our positions were purified. Certain caresses were eliminated. And on the evening of our six-month anniversary, when my mouth drifted down over the soft rise below her navel toward the last gift of the night, her stomach stiffened and she sat up and said, "Stop. Please don't do that anymore."

She pared us down—all the way down to the bare crusader's thrust: the harder, deeper, and more severe, the better. Clothes were often left on, and many pairs of the strange Latin American underwear she'd taken to buying on Fourteenth Street were torn and discarded. I tried to ask her once if this was really what she liked, but she demurred: that sort of thing was not the subject for a conversation.

So I followed what I thought was her lead and carried on in the medieval way. As we progressed, she seemed to usher me back further and further to more primitive times. Even as her head banged up against the drywall behind us she would want to go further. Before long the rickety platform I'd knocked together from the remnants of our old loft started to buckle. And one night in November the hind legs of the bed caved in completely and I was suddenly slanted upward, literally climbing up into her. The destruction goaded her on. She rolled us over and used the new angle to throw herself down on me even harder than before, as if she were trying to get me to scratch an itch just barely out of reach.

Maybe it was the change in angle. Or maybe the frustration of conversing poorly in two languages all day long had finally sent us over an edge. Whatever it was, on this night as she slid and ground and crushed me I felt as if I were starting to get the point Katya was trying to make. I rolled us over again and went in further against her. I put my hands on her calves and pushed out. I expected her to resist, to push back and conceal herself as was her habit. But this time she seemed to come undone. Her legs parted to the horizontal. And with this change I moved strangely forward into a recess of her I had never occupied. I continued on and in that weird eyes-closed-sex-intoxicated way where length and depth can stretch and plumb beyond all reasonable dimension. I felt that I was making yard-long jousts, invading newer and newer territory each time. When I opened my eyes again I saw her round face illuminated by the streetlights, her eyes struggling toward something beneath their lids.

And all at once I felt what I can only describe as a small but significant opening in the barrier between us. In an instant I managed
to slip through. Her inner contours became a matched mold around
me. English words tumbled in my head with Slavic suffixes. And a
hundred memories of misunderstandings and half-steps sloughed off
of us—an unwanted, unnecessary rind.

I ripped further through the membrane that had separated us—
down, down, down into the center of her, down toward what the
chattering sex-voice at the back of my brain had decided to call
"her axis of power." Now the bed's remaining legs were wobbling
and the sheets were balled up at our feet and the cops outside our
open window were screaming and the air around us grew so hot and
thick that it felt like a new skin forming around us. And then all at
once this new skin seemed to gel and contract, forcing me down
into her in one vertiginous plunge.

And Katya suddenly paused. She didn't cry out. The corners of
her mouth only flattened. I could feel her try to control herself, but
still the inside of her legs trembled against my hands. She opened
her eyes and spoke.

"Da. Vot. Tochno."—Yes. There. Exactly. And then she "finished"
and I followed immediately afterward.

We fell asleep, grasping to each other and tilted uphill. We rolled
onto our sides but stayed joined, softening into one another.

Sometime in the middle of the night, I separated from her and
walked to the bathroom in the darkness. I flipped on the light and
looked at myself in the mirror. I looked strange, standing all by myself. What was this weird half-a-creature doing here—this Daniel-
recto without its Katya-verso? I could still feel the warmth and
closeness of her interior. I reached down to remove the condom.

There was nothing but an empty hoop of rubber.

I reached down again and pulled. Nope. Just me there. I scratched my head with both hands. I looked in the mirror again. The familiar, frightened, weak-charactered Daniel resurfaced and stared back. I opened the medicine cabinet. Katya's box of tampons mocked me. The box was utterly virginal. All forty wands were safely sealed away in their packaging.

"You must look at the Moon," Katya said when I returned to bed and told her about the ruptured condom. Her eyes were glistening and full of wonder as she said it. Her voice was calm and assured.

"The Moon?" I said.

"The Moon, Daniel, the Moon. Open the window and look at it. If the Moon is full, there will be a child."

I did as she said. I slid open the metal window casing and backed out onto the ledge as if ready to plunge Jacques Cousteau–style to the street below. I tilted my head back. The night glowed pink. A single cloud occupied the center of the sky, a ring of light surrounding it like a halo. Slowly the cloud slid to the right and behind it the Moon emerged—a sliver, a quarter, a half, gibbous and then completely, irrefutably full.

"Well?" she asked from the far side of the bed.

"Yes," I said, "it's full."

"I thought so," said Katya. "I felt it. Something very special."

"What do we do now?" I asked.

"We have no choice," she said. "Now we have to get a bigger apartment."

During the next weeks Katya was cautious in her movements. She took to wearing a plain, loose smock that her mother had packed for her when she'd left Russia. Indeed, there was a whole new protocol. A month after the conception when I started walking us toward the subway to go up to the housing project in the Bronx she looked at me as if I were insane.

"We can't take the metro. Not now," she said.

"Why not?" I asked.

"When a woman is pregnant," she said, "she must only see beautiful things." I must have looked exasperated, for she said to me sternly: "It's for our son, Daniel."

"You know it's a boy, already?"

"Yes, of course."

"How?"

"I just know."

Though it was only ten in the morning when we arrived, Zhenya greeted us with champagne and chocolate cake. We toasted to the yet-to-be-born "Danielovich." When Katya lifted the glass to her lips I pointed out that a pregnant woman shouldn't drink.

"You Americans and your superstitions," she laughed and drank the entire glass.

After the celebration, Zhenya took us to the housing project director's office. Sergey Maratovich greeted us kindly, offered his congratulations, and led us up to an apartment on the thirty-second floor.

Sergey Maratovich whittled away at the lock with a skeleton key and smiled his gold smile wryly at Katya. *"Poka afrikantsy zdes zhivut,"* he said—Africans are living here for the moment. "But," he said switching to English, "zay are in significant violation of zerr rental agrrreement." He poked his head in the door, made sure there was no one at home, and then held his hand out like an usher at a grand opera hall.

Inside was a vast, cavernous space. A hundred and fifty square meters, at least. The glossy lead-based paint was chipped and gray and marked with crayon. Dishes were piled up in the sink, and a beige carpet striated with coffee stains, rips, and frays stretched from wall to wall. I walked through the common room, past a few old lawn chairs, and slid open a glass door that stuck in its tracking. I slipped out onto the rusted balcony and took in the view.

It was absolutely and literally stunning. Identical yellow tower after tower stretched to the horizon, which was girded by the number 6 el and the tangled convergence of the Bruckner, I-95, the Cross Bronx Expressway, and the Hutch. Train and car noises blended together into a constant *shmmmm* that faded only slightly when I closed the sliding door again. Across the way on a balcony on the next tower a woman took laundry off a line and eyed me as I disappeared into the shadow of my future apartment.

"You are at the top of the list," Sergey Maratovich said, patting me on the back. "Now it is just a matter for the police to decide."

And yet the nightmare of our future home did not stay with me. We filled out an application and returned home and for the next few weeks we continued on as if in the sweetest of dreams. The closeness of the night when the bed and the condom had broken stayed with us. We spoke less and less. Words felt like ridiculous abstractions. "Yes. There. Exactly." We'd found that exact place together, and night after night we returned to it—two cosmonauts on an extended deep-space mission.

It was only after we had finished, in that gap between satisfaction and renewed desire, that the uncertainty grew again and started to gain the upper hand. I would detach myself from Katya, go to the bathroom and stare at the tampon box. Always it sat there: inviolate, pink and blue, feminine and prim. Sealed away forever in plastic.

If I hadn't felt similarly sealed away I might have asked some questions. I might have called Anne and grilled her on the details of the menstrual cycle. I knew Katya's suppositions were based on some kind of fact. I knew that the lunar and the menstrual cycle had a similar number of days. But was it so literal as Katya made it seem? Surely full Moon didn't mean full fertility? If it did, why had we American men not paid greater attention to it?

Maybe it was because we, unlike the Russians, were detached from nature. Less intuitive. Whatever. It didn't matter. Katya was definitely late; I was intuitive enough to track that. By my calculations she was already two weeks late. But that's where my knowledge ended. How many weeks late was too many? I didn't know. All I could do was look at the tampon box, close the medicine cabinet, stare at myself in the mirror, and make declarations to myself. "If this is going to happen we need to plan for it, not just go along with it," I said to myself. For Christ's sake, I thought, this is another human life we're making! It can't *all* be just a matter of fate.

Finally one evening after we had made love it was too hot to sleep. We got up and started boxing our things for the movers. As we sat there, naked and sweating on the floor, I steeled myself and asked Katya finally if she would consider taking a pregnancy test.

"A test?" she asked, laughing. "You mean with a rabbit?"

"No, no," I said. "It's simple. You can buy it in a store."

"But why test something you already know?"

I looked down darkly and shook my head.

She reached over and stroked my face softly, sweetly. "I know what you're thinking," she said. "You're thinking about what a stone around your neck this child will be. But it doesn't have to be that way. You and I are very different from other people. We're special— almost like one person. We can enjoy ourselves with this. He will be a part of *us* too. Very smart and very handsome, like you. He will be the best part of us. He will speak both languages beautifully. Like Nabokov. And some day we'll go back with him and visit Russia and stay at my parents' summer cottage. We'll pick berries with him in my mother's garden. It will be so peaceful and beautiful. Everyone will love him."

"But how will we manage?"

"You always find a way with such things," said Katya. "For my parents it was much more difficult than for us. My father was sent to the Arctic for two years after my sister was born. They managed. They were very strong about it. Anyway, what choice do we have?"

I didn't say anything. I quietly packed my college textbooks. I wondered to myself how much a visit to Planned Parenthood would cost. Would she get the meaning of *planned* parenthood or was everything just happenstance to her? I thought about Katya's father—was he *sent* to the Arctic on a business trip? Or was he exiled there? Did he feel lucky in a way when it happened? I looked up. Katya cut her eyes knowingly at me.

"Don't think such disgusting thoughts," she said.

We continued with our move but I was taking only half the necessary steps. I never told the landlord in Chelsea we were leaving and yet I'd called a moving company and arranged for a truck.

The morning in early December arrived. It was unnaturally warm outside and still the heat in the apartment was turned up full blast. I looked around the "box" in Chelsea for the last time. It wasn't so bad, actually. It had nice floors, high ceilings. There were a few hopeful signs that the neighborhood might improve. An American fresh out of college would be happy to have the place.

I shook my head. The signed contract for the Bronx apartment was in my back pocket. Katya had run downstairs to wait for the movers. I went into the bathroom to take one last look for anything that we might have forgotten to gather up. I opened the medicine cabinet. I shot an angry glance at those deceitful condoms. "Extra strength for the strongest gift of love" said the box. Yeah, right. I saw that Katya had forgotten her tampons. Maybe it was stupid to take them with us, but what the hell, maybe someday, a year from now, she'd need them again.

I reached out and grabbed the box. The plastic was loose. There was a tiny slit in the top. The seal on the cardboard had been broken and taped shut again. I picked up the box and stared at it. "Forty applications of freshness and comfort," it said. I carefully cracked open the lid. I counted the tips of the wands. Thirty-nine. I counted again. Forty. I counted a third time. Thirty-nine. I ripped open the box and took out the tampons and grouped them in rows of eight on the toilet seat cover. Four rows of eight plus seven is . . . thirty-nine. Or, three rows of ten . . . plus nine is . . . thirty-nine. I looked in the garbage can—there was a tampon wrapper! What a beautiful thing! I counted again. Thirty-nine. I giggled. I laughed maniacally. I pulled out the Bronx apartment contract. I threw up the toilet seat, scattering the tampons pell-mell. I tore up the contract and flushed it down the toilet. Thirty-nine! Thirty-nine! Thirty-nine! Yes! There! Exactly! I grabbed two tampons off the floor and started conducting a secret orchestra. "Thirty-nine!" I sang out loud. "Thirty-nine!"

"Thirty-nine what?" Katya said glaring at me from the bathroom door.

The Third Way

We entered the great silence then and retreated to our separate sides of the bed. I read American spy novels. Katya read the collected work of the Sri Vishnu Brahmaputra. When I would reach out to touch her she would look at me coldly and say, "What's the point? Why not use three condoms?"

And I would turn out my light and stare out at the police precinct and quietly obsess over that deeper part of her I had just lost. Yes, the time of her false pregnancy had been a time of fear, uncertainty, and anger, but it had also been a time of a different kind of intimacy. Now that it was gone, most of all what it felt like was an interrupted transformation. It was as if during those hot, close sessions together I had finally understood the logic of our isolation. I saw what Katya must have seen all along: that our marriage was peculiar but special and required a unique set of conditions to mature. Indeed, during that brief month, she had allowed me to see the pupate form of a real marriage.

But in my cowardly, weak-charactered way, I had destroyed it all. I'd flailed around with her tampons, celebrated the death of a life that had never come to be, and in so doing I had ripped open our chrysalis before our metamorphosis was complete. Now we lay awake night after night—separate, weak, and exposed.

Instead of a life filled with each other, there was now the special loneliness in our house that only two people can create together. Our phone seldom rang, and if it did, it was usually a new terrified-but-pretending-not-to-be-terrified arrival from Russia looking to grill Katya about shortcuts to life in the New World. The post was all outgoing: job letters, minimum payments on credit card bills, and entry forms for various sweepstakes contests.

It was therefore quite an event when two pieces of English-language mail arrived in our box one clear day in January. The first was a letter from a company called GlobeNet. I'd sent a job query to them months earlier, but unlike all those other companies out there, GlobeNet had reviewed my résumé with interest and responded. They were considering me for a position with their Russian Properties Acquisition Department. "Would you be willing," the letter asked, "to relocate to Russia?"

No, I couldn't relocate to Russia, not now, not with Katya's resident-alien status pending and the deep space between us still waiting to be regained. But the letter definitely had something positive to it. It felt like something I'd not experienced in almost two years. It felt like luck.

The second piece of mail, however, did not feel like luck at all. It was a postcard for Katya. It had three scenes of the Mormon Tabernacle and was postmarked Moab, Utah. The message on the back was written in large block capitals that caught the eye like a kidnapper's note:

BLESSED KATYA,

    MY TEACHINGS IN THE LAND OF THE SOVIET ATHEISTS ARE COMPLETE. I HAVE JOINED MY SAVIOR AGAIN IN OUR TEMPLE IN THE NATION OF *HIS* REVELATION. KATYA, DAUGHTER OF SALVATION, REMEMBER WE HAVE RESCUED YOUR IMMORTAL SOUL FROM THE LAKE OF FIRE, BUT YOUR SPIRIT WILL BE LOST AGAIN UNLESS YOU EMBARK ON AN ONGOING COVENANT WITH OUR *ETERNAL LORD JESUS CHRIST* AND HIS LATTER DAY SAINTS.

WITH ALL OUR HEARTS,

MARK

I put my GlobeNet letter away and forgot about it. I took Katya's postcard upstairs and threw it on the bed between us. She looked at it, smiled, and, to my amazement, explained.

It turned out that before she emigrated, before I ever knew her, Katya had come to know Christ. It had happened in a public bathhouse, far out in a bad district of St. Petersburg. A group of Mormon missionaries had set up a secret church there. It was a very basic arrangement—a table, some hard stools, a blackboard. The whole church fit in one of the unused shower rooms off the bathhouse's main atrium.

Katya rummaged through her suitcases as she was telling me this story until she found her Russian translation of the Book of Mormon. She showed me the inscription on the inside page. It was written in the same didactic, blocky hand as the postcard. This Mark from Moab had been the first to invite Katya to the bathhouse/church. There he had told her about Jesus and the state of Utah. He had warned her that the Russian Orthodox Church was imperfect and that the hand of God would destroy it by the end of the millennium.

I understood now why Katya had on occasion cited the Book of Mormon to me in order to make a point. With Mark as her teacher, she must have learned it thoroughly and debated its lessons in her clever way. I can imagine that it was probably frustrating for Mark. He must have had a quota of souls to meet in Russia and Katya probably stopped him up. They met regularly for four months and with each meeting Mark grew more committed to converting her. Finally during one of their study sessions together, he led her over to the cooling pool outside the steam room. Katya was pointing out a contradiction in Joseph Smith's writing when Mark turned abruptly to face her and pushed her backward into the water. She came up for air and it was at that point that Mark baptized her.

"So are you saying you're a Mormon?" I asked Katya when she'd finished her story.

"I'm not saying anything."

"And this Mark, he's back in America? What happens now? Does he become your priest?"

Katya held up her hand to me indicating a full stop.

I suppose I could have pressed her about all this further. I was her husband. She was my wife. We were married. But I felt that the answer for us was to get past all our words—back, back, back, past my insults to her femininity, past the aborted move to the Bronx, back to that territory of deep intimacy we had only begun to chart. The more verbal I made our relationship, the more remote that inner part of her seemed to get from me.

And I also didn't want to be part of the other badgering forces that were leading her to question her life in New York. On one front she had this friend Misha. Every week he'd pick her up and take her out to the dentist in Jackson Heights for hours of oral surgery. She'd come home in the evening and get right into bed. The anesthetic would wear off and she would clench her mouth closed over an ice cube and read far into the night. She read tirelessly, sometimes two books in a single evening.

It was during this period that she first came across the writings of the Sri Vishnu Brahmaputra. Someone had handed her a flier on the street and, soon after, she started checking his books out of the library. She kept his works stacked up on the milk crate on her side of the bed. She found out that Sri had a temple in Queens, not far from her dentist's office. After a while she started having Misha drop her off at the temple when the dental work was over. Eventually she changed the days of her surgery to coincide with Brahmaputra's weekly *puja*.

But just as with Mark, I left her alone on the Sri issue. I ignored the Sauna Mormons and the Queens Hindus, for there was still the most formidable foe of all to contend with: the Russians in the Outer Boroughs. The Russians exerted a tidal pull on Katya. When they telephoned, her eyes grew glassy and Soviet and she listened to them like the Manchurian Candidate. The spell would end as soon as she hung up the phone and I had reason to hope that she would come to understand that she was different from them. But they reached out for her constantly in clever ways and her bread-and-salt manners prevented her from keeping them out of our lives. So it was up to me to halt them and I spent a lot of time debunking their methodology.

Slowly I made progress. The Bronx apartment Zhenya had offered us had been a close call—for I found that the main weapon of the Russian was the gracious gesture. They used favors and vague gifts to get you within their circle. They flooded you with a generosity to which you could assign no precise value. Eventually their kindness lifted you off your feet and you would float around with them like victims of the same shipwreck—your goods, your time, and your currency all essentially common property, readily dispensable to any of them in the name of mutual survival.

I found out, however, that you could get out of their ocean by paying them back—tit for tat. If you did that, you humiliated them. You turned their broad waves of kindness into choppy, single strokes. Eventually, if you were rude enough, you'd pull the plug, drain the waters of favors and counterfavors, and finally be left high, dry, and alone.

Take Misha, for example. From the Russian perspective you could say we were associated—that he was doing us a series of favors. From the American perspective, though, he was offering a service. He provided a car to bring Katya out to the dentist. And so, every week I gave Katya a check to give to Misha for the gas and the use of his car. This little payoff kept Misha out of the house, which I knew was key. If I were ever to start speaking with Misha, have him over to tea, for example, I knew he would end up doing me another, more abstract favor because I was a friend of his friend Katya, and therefore *his* friend. Then I would be in favor-debt to Misha.

Already I had a favor-debt to Zhenya for the dental surgery bills. And Zhenya kept saying, "Move to the Bronx, save some money, then pay me back." Aha, I said to myself, another favor! Every few weeks he'd call us and give us an update. "That apartment is still available," or "No one's moved in yet. Sergey Maratovich, that beautiful ape, he's beating them away with a stick!" I didn't encourage him. Instead, to Katya's embarrassment, I made Zhenya take a signed IOU from me and forced him to accept interest payments, too.

When I had any spare money I sent him tiny checks for the dental work he'd paid for.

Yes, I was putting up a good frontal defense against the Outer Borough Russians. I really was. Even Katya finally agreed that their society possessed "a certain criminal element." She started to back off from them.

But then the Sri Brahmaputra outflanked me.

Katya told me one day that Sri's writings proposed "A Third Way" and she had decided to follow it, since, as she put it, I had offered her "no way at all." She became a vegetarian: not just a normal vegetarian, but a non-lacto-ovo vegan. She told me how Sri recommended drinking one's own urine in the event of a bad cold. She asked me, half laughing, which new name might suit her better: Rada or Sutyabhama.

Sri had his own publication, called *Ahimsa Explorations.* A subscription cost $119.98. Katya didn't ask me for the money, but the magazine started coming anyway. There were retreats advertised in *Ahimsa* that cost $600 for two days. The retreats were held "in laurel spas on the rich alluvial floodplain of south-central New Jersey." I noticed a weekend in early February circled on Katya's desktop calendar. "Retreat?" was written in parentheses underneath the date.

And before long she started meditating and chanting every morning. Acolytes from the temple began calling more often than the Russians, and the same glassy, Manchurian Candidate look would come into her eye when she spoke to them on the phone. She wandered listlessly about the apartment and grew animated only on *puja* days. We started making love again, but when we did, it seemed for another purpose. Her eyes turned dull and I could tell she was focusing on something outside of the two of us. When it was over she would climb off of me, return to the writings of Sri, and mutter to herself in a mixture of Sanskrit and Russian.

I could handle the Russians, but I didn't know what to do about Sri. I was galled that a woman who had digested all of Schopenhauer and Schiller could just accept this nonsense. If I had ever proposed anything as ridiculous as *Ahimsa Explorations* she would have called me "a typical uneducated American" and laughed so hard she'd have had to cover her mouth to conceal her dental work.

What was it that made her think Sri was so deep and new? Why had she thrown the heavy stone of her intellectual curiosity into *his* waters? I didn't know. But any American could see what Brahmaputra really was: the leader of a large and possibly dangerous cult.

I had no experience dealing with cults. I knew getting people out of them was a tricky business. I remembered reading somewhere that confronting people in cults only drove them deeper inside. With the wrong approach, someone as contrary as Katya could be driven right to the temple altar.

I needed information on the dynamics. I needed someone who dealt with family dysfunction—someone who had worked with sons and daughters who had got mixed up in this sort of thing. I didn't want a professional; I didn't want to bring a total outsider into our mess. I needed informal yet sound, fact-based advice. I needed some kind of therapist. As much as I tried to come up with a different alternative, I realized there was really only one choice. The only person who had enough skill and discretion to help us was my own father.

When we entered the restaurant, I saw that Dad had misunderstood me. He had brought Meredith, his fourth wife, and their child, Noah. Dad was restraining Noah's hands as he reached for Meredith across a corner table in the back of the dining room. Noah had just turned three and his golden hair had grown to shoulder length since I'd last seen him. Before he'd been just an infant, and I had assumed he'd always be an infant. But now he engaged his parents like a boy. His green-flecked brown eyes sparkled with the beginnings of human reason as he held up his index finger to argue a point with my father.

I had wanted to tell Dad to come alone to the restaurant. "Please don't bring Meredith and Noah. We can work that out later. There's something very important to deal with right now," I'd wanted to say. I had tried to imply it in my voice in the messages I'd left on his office machine. "I'm really sorry about what happened between *you* and me. I'd really like to see *you,* Dad. I would like *you* to meet Katya." Unfortunately, English only has the imprecise *you* at its disposal. There was no way for me to tactfully tell him that it was *tu* I needed to see and not *vous.*

My father stood when he saw me and beckoned me forward with a scoop of his hand in the air. He kept his white-haired head lowered as we approached the table. Katya looked around, as if wondering whether we might still be able to get a separate table in some other corner of the restaurant.

Strangely, I felt a rush of warmth as we approached them. If it was awkward it was also deeply relieving to see this tether to my former life. It suddenly seemed so utterly stupid. Had I really let almost two years go by without speaking to my own father? What had been my reasoning? It was as if another person had made that decision. I remembered it had started over a fight we'd had in his office before my going to Russia—something about trying to get away from labels, something he'd said about a Russia Phase. Whatever. I guess it also had something to do with Meredith and Noah, but now my problems with my own wife dwarfed whatever petty jealousies I'd concocted before.

Dad glanced at me briefly and then looked off in another direction. I could see him trying to gauge all this. I could see that he felt this moment might have cardinal meaning. He looked at Katya in her prim knee-length white dress, standing at attention with her arms at her sides, her round face and big eyes lowered. Yes, I could see Dad think to himself, I have to be careful with this greeting. And all at once he caught Katya up in a monstrous hug and kissed her moistly on the cheek. "Congratulations," he said, "welcome to the family." Noah pointed at the flower-shaped pin on Katya's dress and said, "Is it edible?" and we all laughed.

Throughout the evening, my father drew strongly on his professional training. I could see that Katya impressed him in her way— her beauty and her acuity had struck him as it had struck me on our first encounter. But Dad quickly recovered and removed himself from his attraction as much as he could. He sat back in his chair, kept his face clear and flat, and asked open-ended questions. He revealed only passing, surface-level information about himself. Katya did the same.

"You must miss your family," Dad said, filling Katya's glass with more wine.

"I miss my father very much," Katya said.

"You're very close with him?"

"I am very close. But it is not like it was with Electra." My father laughed. Katya didn't. "What is your opinion of the Freud?" she asked abruptly.

"The Freud?" my father looked at me for some explanation of this sudden change of direction. I shrugged. "Well, Freud . . ." He searched his mind carefully for a clear word. "Freud is a good base," he said.

"A good base for what?" Katya asked.

"For all of psychiatry."

"Daddy, no! No! Jung! Jung!" Noah shouted.

Meredith shushed Noah but he wouldn't stop crying until Dad turned his full attention to him.

"Yes, that's right, Noah," Dad said finally. "Jung was also a psychiatrist. Anyway, Katya—"

"Richard," my stepmother said, interrupting Dad, "don't patronize Noah. He wants to be *in* the conversation."

Dad composed himself and took a breath. He turned to Noah with a forced smile. "Okay, Noah," he asked, "what do *you* want to talk about?"

Noah pointed to the organic turkey sausage on Meredith's plate. "Is it edible?" he asked.

"Yes," Dad said, "yes, it is, Noah. The sausage is edible. And the salad and the potatoes are also edible."

"Nooooo!" Noah shook his head and kicked his feet against his chair.

Dad threw up his hands and turned away, back to Katya.

"I'm sorry, what were we talking about?"

"The Freud," Katya said.

"Oh yes. The Freud. Well, what I was saying is that Freud is a good base because he set out some fundamental directions to be explored—medically and therapeutically. You don't have to agree with his whole philosophy to see that."

"But do you agree with his analysis of dreams, of where they come from?" Katya asked. "Do you believe they have nothing to do with God?"

"God? Well, who's to say where God is in all this?" Dad said, confused, trying to keep up. "But, um, but as for dreams—well, it's been proven. Freud was right. Dreams are a strong phenomenal link between the conscious and the unconscious mind."

"I see."

"Why do you ask?" Dad said. "How do you Russians feel about God and dreams?"

"We Russians feel all sorts of things you couldn't begin to imagine," Katya said.

"I'm sure," Dad said, growing slightly vexed but still trying to keep the conversation light. "I meant, though, what do you do, personally, for religion?"

Katya opened her eyes wider than before, pursed her lips to a point and then tilted her head to the side. I clenched my teeth. Katya cleared her throat.

"Most of the time," she said, "I am studying with the Sri Vishnu Brahmaputra. Do you know him?"

Meredith and my father exchanged a glance.

"Yes," Dad said. "I know Sri. Sri is a scoundrel."

"Scoundrel?" Katya said. She didn't know that English word.

"You know, a crook."

"Crook?"

"He's got that cult out in Queens."

"Cult?"

Dad searched for a phrase that Katya would understand fully. "You know," he said finally, "like Stalin. A 'cult of personality.'"

"Stalin!" Katya answered, horrified. She cut her eyes at Dad and then at me. She put down her silverware and folded her napkin in her lap. She put both hands on the arms of her chair, ready, I could see, to push back and walk out of the restaurant.

"Dad," I said after a silence, "I think maybe you're oversimplifying. Maybe you shouldn't just dismiss it like that. Maybe you should just *listen* to Katya."

"Daniel, I wasn't dismiss—" I could almost see the hackles rise on the back of his neck. I held my breath as frustration filled up his eyes. But then he cut himself off and paused. He slipped back down into his chair, back into therapist mode. "No, of course not, Katya," he said. "Not like Stalin. How would you describe Sri?"

"He's like a teacher," Katya said. "Like that."

"Who's the teacher?" Noah cried.

"Noah, shush!" Dad barked.

"Is it edible?" Noah asked.

"Katya," Dad began again. His voice seemed to catch against something as it came out of his throat. "Everybody's entitled to their own beliefs, but I would feel irresponsible if I didn't tell you a little about Brahmaputra. You see, several of my patients were involved with Sri."

I exhaled with relief. Dad had zeroed in on the real problem. We weren't going to fight. He was going to give Katya some advice. He was going to cite some examples for her. The Russian mind loved examples. Dad really was good at this. He looked at Katya now with genuine concern in his eyes.

"Why are you telling me about your patients?" Katya asked.

"Well, I'm a psychiatrist, you see. I treat families, you know, parents and their kids, when they have problems. I had one patient and she was involved with Sri. She—"

"I know what a psychiatrist is. A psychiatrist is a medical doctor, no?"

"Yes—" my father answered her cautiously.

"Then," Katya said, "maybe you aren't allowed to tell me about your patients. Didn't you take the Oath of Hippocrates?"

"Hypocrite!" cried Noah, pointing at my father.

"Yes, Katya, yes, I did," Dad said with a forced calmness. "But clearly you don't really understand the way the Hippocratic Oath works. I know the medical profession is very primitive in Russia and there are many violations of privacy there. But you see, here, in

America, we respect those rights and just now I didn't tell you my patient's *name*—"

"You want to tell me her problems. It's the same thing."

"How do YOU *feel about that!"* Noah screamed, pointing at Dad.

"Noah, dear," my father turned sharply to his youngest son, "would you please wait until it is *your* turn to speak."

"You know, Dad," I said, using Noah's interruption to redirect the conversation back to Sri. "You know this really isn't about the medical profession. Maybe if you *listened* to her a little more about her situation with Sri—" I was trying to diffuse the argument and steer him away from defending psychiatry back to Katya's immediate dilemma. I hoped maybe he'd work some of his professional magic without referring to the profession itself. But now Dad turned back on me with his full wrath.

"You know, *Daniel,* I happen to know how to listen. In fact, I listen for a living. And when I hear you lecture me like that in that know-it-all way it's like I'm transported back in time and I'm listening to your mother all over again!"

"Edible! Edible! Edible!" Noah shouted.

"What are you bringing up Mom for, Dad? We were talking about Katya."

"Ed-i-ble!" Noah shouted out loud to the whole table, pointing at his forehead. *"Edible! Edible! Edible!"*

Dad whipped around to Noah. "What, Noah? What's edible?" he shouted. "Here, take my food, it's edible, all of it! Eat it all. It's all edible!"

"Richard, wait!" Meredith said. "Listen to Noah! Listen to him! He's not saying 'edible,' he's saying Oedipal. *Oedipal,* like Rex. That's amazing! Yes, Noah, yes. It *is* Oedipal, the way your father and Daniel are fighting!"

My father collected his thoughts. Meredith repressed a laugh. Noah said, "Ohhhhhhhh!" Katya excused herself. Dad watched her disappear into the ladies' room.

"Daniel. I'm sorry," he said, gathering himself up again. "But I haven't seen you in two years. And now you bring this woman . . . your . . . your wife . . . who's . . . who's . . . who's in a goddamned cult. For your information, Sri Vishnu Brahmaputra is worse than a scoundrel. He's a sex offender. He's a goddamned con artist. He's worse than Moti Lal, worse than Soba Roshi, and worse than Suleman goddamned Mufti."

"Then please, can you just *tell* her that?" I asked.

Dad looked at me and I could see the emotion recede and disappear from his face. "No, I can't," he said. "I can't help you with this. With these things, with cults, it has to come from somebody she trusts."

ॐ

Back at our apartment we undressed without a word and Katya got into bed. I kissed her neck. She stared up at the ceiling.

I had wanted to sleep on everything that had just passed. Nothing good could come from talking about it now. It was all a jumble of so many problems. But what Dad had told me in the parking lot after dinner was searing me from the inside. I had to say something.

I sat up in the bed. I tried to compose myself for what I was going to tell her. The street outside was oddly quiet.

"Katya," I began, "I'm sorry about my Dad. He gets worked up."

"Your father is a very intelligent person," she said. "He is a man to be respected. He has a strong character."

This remark made me feel both proud and jealous. But I had an agenda now and I took it all in the stride I would need to get through the next part.

"If you really think that, if you really respect him, will you listen then to what he told me?"

She looked directly at me. She seemed to be thinking past what I was about to say toward how she would react afterward. But she turned her attention to me again. She sat back on the bed, leaned her head against the drywall, and locked her hands behind her neck.

"Okay. I will listen. 'I'm all ears,' as you say."

"Okay, good."

I cleared my throat and began. Cautiously I started telling the tale I'd heard from my father. I tried to adhere to the rules of good storytelling. I tried to set it up well, making the main character speak directly to Katya. I told her about how once there had been a patient of my father's: an intelligent, sensitive young woman who, like Katya, had begun studying with the Sri Brahmaputra because of her deep intellectual curiosity. I told her about where she'd come from, how, like Katya, she'd gone to her country's finest university. I told her about the confusion that had enveloped her when she'd graduated from college and gone into the world. I told her how she had doubted Sri at first, how she was just playing around with his philosophy, how she even joked about it in therapy with my father.

But then somehow I got derailed and I found myself losing the train of the story and drifting back to other examples in history to other people who had been confused—to Siddhartha Gautama, Joan of Arc, Jesus of Nazareth, the Roman emperor Claudius. And I told little parables of their lives too. I weaved the patient's life back and forth with the lives of these great people, thinking I was giving it gravitas in the process.

By the time I reached the part about the patient's fall—the wrong turn she'd taken—I had become unhinged. I lectured her about how the patient had gone deeper into the cult, how she'd signed away not only her money but also her parents' country house. How she had been seduced by Sri's main acolyte, and that the man had passed on the AIDS virus to her.

And as I concluded the morality tale, ending with how the woman had succumbed fully to her temptations and died at the age of twenty-five, weighing only seventy pounds, starving in a halfway house in Hell's Kitchen, I happened to catch a sidelong glimpse of myself in our bedroom mirror. I watched my fists shake and listened to the rage in my own voice: I was the incarnation of a stultifying television evangelist.

I stopped talking. Katya was blinking her eyes slowly and had withdrawn to the far side of the bed. A minute passed.

"Finished?" she asked.

"Yes."

"Good. Now, may I ask you one question?"

"Okay."

"Do you enjoy destroying everything?"

She stared hard at me, utterly silencing me. Then she rolled away. "You don't know anything about me," she said to the wall.

She curled up in a fetal ball. I looked over at her five minutes later and saw that she had fallen asleep. On her milk crate were the few things that I had bought for her over the course of our two years together: long, tear-shaped earrings from a city on the shores of Lake Baikal; an opal pendant from a Forty-seventh Street jeweler—the stone had fallen out and I'd found out later she'd secretly replaced it to spare my feelings. The sight of these sad few things so carefully arranged on her milk crate broke my heart. I reached down for her hand. I took away the postcard of the Mormon Tabernacle she was holding and quietly clicked off the light.

Sleep came for me too, but it was a troubled, jittery slumber, syncopated by all the wine and espresso from dinner. I rolled over and felt Katya touch me. I reached under her nightgown and caressed her sides and woke: only a dream. She was as far away from me as she could get on the bed. I fell asleep again. Katya slid her hands in my underwear, I kissed her neck, and I awoke again far, far away from her: another dream.

As the blue light of the clock blinked three A.M., my eyes fluttered closed and the scene changed. I was walking on a sheet of cobalt-blue ice that had formed overnight on the Finnish Gulf. The ice stretched from what I imagined to be the wide portico of Katya's summer house all the way north to Helsinki. I stepped on the ice and walked until I found a labor crew that was laying rail across the frozen gulf. Someone was saying that it would be a direct Helsinki-Leningrad super luxury train. The slate sky parted and the sun glared down from above. I worried that the new heat would melt this perfect blue ice before they finished the rails.

As soon as I thought this, the ice did start to melt. It gave way behind me. I managed to pull myself back up on a round chunk. I put my arms around it and it pulled back at me. It was not quite ice now. Maybe it was a piece of machinery? No, it was soft and growing softer. Maybe it was a huge Caspian sturgeon that had blundered into the gulf? It grew warm and moist, and now slipped around on top of me, pushing me down under the water while I was pulling up on it. It smelled of honey. When I held it, I found I could grip it and squeeze it but then it would grow slippery and slide from my hands.

Somewhere in all this I slowly came awake to find Katya on top of me with her nightgown off, sleeping and not sleeping, rocking softly, crying in earnest for the first time since I'd known her. I felt around with my hand for a condom but I couldn't find one. It seemed that I was murmuring something to her, pouring it into her ear like poison. "Please, please," I was saying as her breath quickened and I drifted back toward the Finnish Gulf, "please. No Russian baby. No Russian baby, please."

༉

The next morning I woke early but Katya slept on past ten. I still had the blueness of the ice with me and it was rolling back and forth in my head like a marble. The color had the feel of a true vision. I paced back and forth trying to figure out what to do with the blueness in my head. I made some coffee. It came in a blue can—that got me too. After having a cup I realized I had to wake her. She opened her eyes. They struck me at that moment as fantastically beautiful eyes. I had always thought of them as green but now I saw the blue in them—concentric circles of blue and green finishing in onyx.

"Katya," I said, "last night . . . I had a dream—"

"Yes," she said, "about the Finnish Gulf. About the ice."

"Yes," I said, "there was ice. Blue ice."

She went over to her pile of suitcases. She opened one up and started rummaging through her immigrant debris. She pulled out a thick, handwritten document. It was a dream guide *samizdat*—an index of a thousand words with an explanation of their significance. Katya's sister, Liza, had copied it from someone and Katya had in turn copied it from Liza.

"The dream had ice, yes?" she asked. "Blue ice, you said, yes?" She screwed up her eyes. She held the dream guide away from me so I couldn't see it.

"Here it is," she said. "*Lyod, sini lyod*—blue ice. It means poverty. You will be poor. Maybe very poor. It's a very bad dream."

I dressed and went to my temp job at Morgan Stanley. I was on a two-week assignment entering reams of earnings numbers for a Sikh financial analyst. I felt extremely poor. Katya's interpretation of my dream felt like a death sentence. Blue was *blue*. I had the blues, literally.

❦

The letter from GlobeNet was still in my jacket pocket, and that afternoon I decided to call them. There was a desperate busyness in the background on the phone and they told me to come in as soon as possible, right after work if I wanted to. I arrived at their head-quarters at six-thirty. It was a sterile, new office in the Flatiron District. My interviewer, a nervous man with a clammy handshake, had culled my résumé out from all of the others and had liked me, he said, because I seemed like a risk taker. GlobeNet was a venture cap-ital firm, he told me, and they were looking for people willing to take risks. They were at this very moment, he said, buying television stations all over Russia and Eastern Europe. In time, he said, GlobeNet would create a seamless telecommunications network throughout the former Soviet bloc.

"You could help us, I think," my interviewer said. "You know about television. You know about Russia. That's a rare combina-tion. You could help us. Think about it. You could help spread de-mocracy."

"Could I bring my wife?" I asked.

"Bring your wife. Have some children. We have a lot of hope for Russia."

"But I have an apartment here," I said.

"We'll pay for the apartment. Money isn't the issue."

I walked home after the interview. All the way back I was think-ing how we might possibly move to Russia, how we might try to make a life there, this time on Katya's terms. Maybe if the equation were reversed, if I were the immigrant and she were the native guide, maybe that would suit our dispositions better. It made more and more sense as I turned it over in my mind. Yes, she's the one with the strong character, I thought. I'm the one with the weak character. I have no business calling the shots here. Yes, I thought, this could work. I was practically skipping by the time I reached our block.

But when I opened my door I found Katya sitting, staring dismally out the window. I couldn't bring myself to say anything. It was the day of her dentist's appointment and one of Sri Brahmaputra's holiest festivals. In spite of all that, she had decided to stay at home.

She got up, walked past me, and started making dinner. She was wearing a ribbed blue muslin shirt and a pair of chartreuse panties. She poured a cup and a half of flour into a glass bowl and mixed it up with some oil and water. She sent me out to the store for cherries, potatoes, and farmer cheese. When I came back, she was bent over the counter, rolling out a thin layer of dough. Her shirt was moist with perspiration and had climbed up her back, exposing the soft skin just above her underwear. I reached out to touch her there. She pushed my hand away and gave me a glass. She told me to use it to punch out little circles of dough. She stewed and pitted the cherries, mashed the potatoes, and mixed the farmer cheese together with some powdered sugar. She set a large pot of water to boil and began filling up the dough circles with different fillings. I copied her, but my dumplings were bulky and ugly and fell apart when they hit the water. Hers stayed together and they were nicely sculpted and uniform.

We ate them in silence, with sour cream. Afterward, Katya served tea in the Russian way—a small china pot with loose leaves on one side, and just-boiled water in a kettle on the other. A button in her blouse came undone as she poured. She sat back down, dumped her tea from her cup into her saucer, and dropped a lemon round in it. She slurped it up like a Tartar khan. The shift changed at the police precinct across the street. Off-duty cops lingered at the entrance and made a ruckus—much more noise than any crime I had every heard. I was about to tell her about the GlobeNet interview when she put down her saucer and spoke.

"Have you been to Utah?" she asked.

"Yes. I was there once."

"Was it okay?"

"It was okay. I was just passing through."

"Did you meet some Mormons there?"

"I don't know. I must have. I think everybody is a Mormon in Utah."

"And are the Mormons good people or are they a cult?"

"The Mormons? I guess they're all right. No, they're not a cult, exactly."

Katya gathered up our plates, cups, and saucers in her neat, efficient way. She rolled up the remaining dough from the countertop and put it in a bowl. She sprinkled a little water over the top and then covered it with a sheet of plastic wrap. She put it in the refrigerator. The cherry filling, the potatoes, and the farmer cheese she spooned into separate plastic containers. She stacked them one on top of another and then placed them in a shopping bag that had been neatly folded under the counter. Her legs disappeared into a pair of black jeans. She put on her green parka, picked up the shopping bag and a full knapsack I hadn't noticed before, and walked out the door.

A week later I received a postcard of the Great Salt Lake.

Part Three

Closed Cities

GlobeNet sent me to the closed cities: dark, isolated industrial
centers where once-secret factories fouled the parks and play-
grounds and the snow turned black before it hit the ground. People
watched a lot of television in towns like these. They came home
from their obsolete jobs, ate their simple dinners, and tuned their
sets for the rest of the night to the only local station on the dial.

I looked across the desk at the director of this final television station on my docket. In just a half hour more I would be done with
him, done with this whole tour of duty. I would climb aboard the afternoon flight and get back to Moscow by way of Novosibirsk. I'd
have a hot shower and arrange an international phone call. But this
damn director with sprays of dandruff on his shoulders seemed to
have lost track of time. He was talking without pause, like a man trying to fill in a deep hole with a tiny trowel. I smiled at him, pretended

to take notes, but really I was staring down at Katya's Great Salt Lake postcard—puzzling once again over its terse English message.

Is it possible I could belong to you?

The question on the postcard mocked me, mocked everything about my response to her leaving. There she had stood, wrapped up in her emerald ski parka, the magic Cloak of Confusion she put on whenever she made an important entrance or exit. And then she had opened the door and slipped out of our box in Chelsea as if she'd had as little connection to it as to a subway car.

I rationalized at first. I pretended it was just a pause, not a break. How could *she* leave, after all? How many times had she said to me, "Love is just the battle. Marriage is the war"? How many times had she reminded me of her parents' bond, holding steady from Khrushchev to Yeltsin while all we'd had to endure together was George Bush? Leaving just wasn't a possibility. She'd merely slipped away to the Outer Boroughs, up to Zhenya's house for a decent beef cutlet and some émigré consolation.

I'd called Zhenya the morning after she'd left and when he'd answered I didn't even think to ask for her. I just wanted her sent back. I told him I was sorry that I had forced Katya on him with no warning at all, that I'd hire a car to pick her up. But Zhenya only breathed heavily through my explanations and apologies, and when I'd finished he waited a full minute before speaking.

"You have completely ruined everything this time," he said. "At last you must be satisfied. She has left. She is so fragile and you are so clumsy. You really are a Neanderthal."

I drifted around the apartment for a week after that, completely Katya-less. On the chance that she might return or call, I rarely left home. I ordered in Cuban Chinese for every meal and sat by the phone and logged the full extent of the badgering she endured from the post-Soviet world. Three different men called from Petersburg asking if Katya had arranged their letters of invitation yet. A man who identified himself as the owner of "White Nights, the most famous club in Brighton Beach" telephoned to offer her a job. "I hear Katya is a good girl," the owner said. "A colleague gave me her photograph. She can choose: the bar or dancing." Katya's friend Lena phoned up three times a day to complain bitterly about baby-sitting. She talked on and on, about Russia, about the emigration of a splinter group of the Taganka Theater Company and their upcoming production of Trifonov's *Exchange* in a basement in Astoria. And while I wanted to cut Lena off, to demand if she'd had word from Katya, I stopped myself. I was Katya's husband. Katya was my wife. If there was an explanation for any of this it should come from Katya.

It did.

I grew more and more weary, sick of the feeble quaver of my own voice, sick of the nostalgic bleating of émigrés, sick of the lonely apartment and its ad hoc furniture. And then Katya's postcard came. "Is it possible *I* could belong to *you?*"—i.e., could I, a beautiful airy soul, be the personal chattel of a clumsy Neanderthal like you? Of course not. What had I been thinking? "Okay," I said to myself, "you want a strong character—watch this."

I called GlobeNet that same day and I told them I could leave for Russia by the weekend. I bought a very warm coat. My visa came express-mail and I placed our capsule in Chelsea in a state of suspended animation. I arranged her proto-religious library of Smith, Sri, and Dream Guide neatly on her milk crate. I pulled my mother's sheets closed across the windows. I cleaned out the fridge, throwing out the dumpling dough Katya had rolled out while standing at the counter in her underwear.

I was almost out the door to the airport and I might have even been able to leave cleanly if I hadn't remembered about the answering machine. I needed to change the outgoing message. I dropped my bags and ran back inside. I tried to think of an appropriate phrase equal to her postcard—some enigmatic place marker that would get under her skin if she happened to call. "Due to a professional commitment neither I nor my wife, Yekaterina, will be available for the next . . ." or "I'm out of the country at the moment. Katya, if that's you . . ." Every choice sounded either too cold or too plaintive. "Stupid, stupid, stupid," I recorded into the machine out of frustration. And just then the phone rang.

"Dai Katyu," a man's deep voice demanded when I answered the phone—Give me Katya.

"Kati nyetu," I said back—there's no Katya anymore.

"Where is she?"

"Utah."

"Yoo-teh?" the Russian pronounced accusingly, as if I were making up the name.

"No, really," I said. "It's a state."

"It's far?"

"All the way out west."

"Fucking shit," he said in English. "Such a long way to drive," and he hung up.

❧

The television station director had come over to my side of the desk and sidled up to me—closer than any American man ever would. He glanced at Katya's postcard before I was able to hide it in my GlobeNet binder. He touched my hand tenderly. "I have so much to show you," he whispered. He drew a map of Russia on a sheet of company stationery that was the same color and consistency as a grocery bag. He marked his city on the paper with an X. He drew radial arms out from the X, describing how the world would relate to X in the future. He asked me to imagine a time when this banished city would be an international business center with commodities exchanges and advanced telecommunications systems.

"So you see," he concluded, "if my company and your company complete our merger, you will have gained a strong, equal partner—not just a provincial television station, but the potential for an entire media production center! It's an exchange, you see. My television shows will be transmitted instantaneously over your satellite to every major city in the former socialist world. And to prove how valuable that will be to your company, I will now show you all of my programs."

"Programs?" I said. "I don't need to see your programs. I'm going out on the afternoon flight to Moscow, remember? I telegrammed you."

"Yes, yes, we tried to get you a ticket," the director said waving the suggestion away as if it were a bug in the air, "but there's no room on plane. The Chinese delegation is flying out today. And anyway you need time. We have so many programs—"

"But I . . . I have promises to keep. I have to make a phone call. I have to—"

"You have to see all the different varieties of our programs. Sports, music, news."

"Look," I said, "your programs have nothing to do with any of this. GlobeNet has its own programs. High-quality American programs. We don't need your programs. All we need is your antenna and your audience."

I had crossed a line, poked a hole in the director's fantasy, and now he glared at me, profoundly insulted. I paused. Flights to Moscow from towns like these were always inexplicably full and I realized that the director was the only local pull I had. He was the only man who would even consider securing my passage—today, tomorrow, or any other day.

"Okay, listen," I began again. "Give me a tape of your shows. I'll watch it, I swear. I'll send it express to New York. But if I stay here longer I won't be able to make my phone call. After all, this is a closed city—"

"Formerly closed!" the director insisted. "Formerly closed. The restrictions have been lifted. We are now as open as Nizhni Novgorod."

"Then can I call New York from here?"

"New York?" He paused and tapped his fingers together, counting, I think, the number of favors he would have to use to book my call. "Yes. New York. Why not? I'll look into it straight away," he said. "But in the meantime I have other programs to show you. I have comedy programs, talk shows, light entertainment—"

"Okay, but first things first. The telephone number I need to call is—"

"Now you just wait," he insisted. "I know what you *need*. I know who you are. We have other programs."

"I believe you. But—"

"We have explored other genres."

"Other genres?"

The director paused and swallowed.

"We have an erotic program."

I looked up at him and made a face that in America would have translated as "What the hell are you talking about?" But the director took my exaggerated expression to signify the most intense interest.

"Come, come," he said, "you'll take a look now. Our editor will show you everything." He pushed a button on a toy–red plastic intercom system and waved me down into my seat.

"Irina!" he called into the box. A dull buzz came back from it. "Ira!" he called again.

"Yes? What is it now, Timofey Arkadevich?" a long, slow voice said from the box.

"Ira, are those machines down there free?"

"Of course they're free."

"I've got a foreigner here," he said, winking at me. "I want you to show him our programs, all of them, if you know what I mean."

"Send him down," she said, a little laugh in her voice. "I've got nothing to hide."

The director led me out into the hallway and we fell into a bald groove in the communist-red carpet. Jets of smoke shot out from little recesses along the corridor, where men dressed in the same suits they'd worn every day of their working lives were getting down to the serious business of smoking. They were bunched around smoldering ash urns, talking about money. These conversation areas were "smoked out," as the Russians say. So smoky that they could only be used as smoking places for the remaining life of the building.

I nodded at a group of men smoking and thought about how this television station—this whole strange estate—would likely become American property soon. How weird—these worn-out carpets, these ash urns, this "Corner of Glory" ahead with photographs of veterans of the Great Patriotic War and honored members of the local collective farm—that it would all "belong" to GlobeNet. As it stood it didn't seem to belong to anyone, which was maybe why it looked so abandoned and so sad.

"Is it possible I could belong to you?" I had walked down dozens of similar corridors at television stations all across Siberia over the last two months, but this station with its deluded director seemed to ask this question more desperately than any before it. "Is it possible *I* could belong to *you*?" Was it really such a mean-spirited thing for anyone to ask, even Katya? I searched my mind and found that if I restrained my rashness and my anger just for a moment that there was quite a bit of room for another interpretation of her question.

I thought about "ownership" and "belonging." I thought about how awkwardly those notions move back and forth between English and Russian. Actually, the English word "belong" was a clunky, strange word for Katya to have chosen. And yet it was in her striving nature to use a word just out of reach of her competence. *"Vozmozhno li chtoby ya tebe prinadlezhala?"* That was what you got if you translated "Is it possible I could belong to you?" word for word back into Russian. There was something wrong in that. My feel for the language had been slowly improving over the course of my time in Siberia and as I said that clumsy sentence to myself I realized that no native would ever concoct such a phrasing.

Now as I rounded the corner of this poor, neglected television station, which nobody really owned or cared for, a softer, more figurative translation came into my mind for the first time: *"Vozmozhno li chtoby ya byla tvoey?"*—Is it possible that I could be yours? Could you keep me from becoming common property? Could you protect me as if I were a part of you? And, eventually, could we try to work it out?

If that had been what she'd meant in her postcard then I had done the very worst thing of all. I had left. I had abandoned her. I had relinquished my title and been placed at the bottom of a long list of those waiting to protect her. And though I'd tried to call her once from Moscow before leaving for the closed cities, all I'd got was my own voice chanting back at me on the answering machine, "Stupid, stupid, stupid."

Yes, by doing nothing to find her as she'd moved across the American West I had done the most stupid thing. My actions had answered her postcard much more succinctly than any letter I could have written. The realization came to me all at once and I blurted out, to no one in particular:

"Jesus Christ, I *really* have to call New York."

"Shas, shas," the director hissed. "I'll speak with the Ministry of Communications immediately." He muttered something else to himself and then suddenly stopped, looked at me, and smiled. "Ah, here we are at Irina's little house."

The director thrust his fingers into a hole where there should have been a knob and threw open a plywood door. At the end of a narrow room, a blonde smoked solemnly with her back to us. Smoke hung over her shoulders like a cloak. She faced a mass of ruined Soviet video machines, tangled together in a snarl of old cabling.

"Irina, here's our guest!" the director shouted. Her shoulders jumped.

"Timofey Arkadevich," she whispered, "I've asked you not to be so clumsy. You know I have a weak heart."

"Forgive me, Irochka." The director squeezed her neck and rotated her chair around to face me. She tucked in a platinum wisp of hair and raised her head. Her eyes met mine and then a slight, arrogant upturn came to the corners of her purple-painted lips. A strange quiver passed through my chest. Even though the colors were all wrong, every feature on this Irina's face seemed an echo of Katya's. She laughed Katya's little laugh and patted the seat next to her.

"Yes. There. Exactly," she said when I moved my chair closer to hers and pressed up against her shoulder. Her voice was soft and decidedly unprovincial, with the slightest trace of a Petersburg accent.

She pulled a dirty sheet from a bank of old Soviet televisions. Then she reached above me and took a videocassette from a shelf. Rose perfume and stale sweat came off her in coils. She bent down in front of me to find a switch under the table. She wore a beige, translucent blouse studded down the dorsal with a long row of tiny buttons and I could make out the word "Shazam!" embroidered across the back of her bra. Her hair was thick, with a Katya-like, 1940s wave blown in it. But unlike Katya, Irina pinned her plaits back neatly with a large plastic butterfly.

We both reached for the cassette at the same time and our hands touched. She smiled and thanked me and put the tape into the VCR. The gears in the machine groaned and we stared into the wobbly color bars at the head of the program.

"So," she said, "are you married?"

"Not really."

"What does that mean, 'not really'?"

I looked at her soft lips and at the vertical crack in one of her incisors. "No," I said, "I'm not married."

She made her mouth go flat and stared back into the monitor. An image popped up onto the screen and Irina gestured at it with her lit cigarette while keeping the rest of her body perfectly still.

"What kind of show is this?" I asked politely.

"I don't know. It stinks, whatever it is."

"Your director was telling me about another program."

"Oh, was he . . ."

"Ira!" the director broke in. "Show him the other programs first. Show him the news program. For God's sake, he's interested in information. Show him the news show. And then the music program. And then the talk show. Quick, quick, show it all to him!"

"Timofey Arkadevich, why are you so ashamed? It's a very professional program—"

"The news is *more* professional. And the music show will improve his mood. Enough of this insolence. Get going, Irina, stop dawdling."

Irina eyed him angrily over her shoulder. He shot her back an equally angry glance.

A different tape was inserted. The director slipped off to see about my phone call. But he knew the exact length of each one of his shows and he darted back in whenever a cassette was about to end. Irina would then, on his orders, turn toward the archive, arch her back, and pull down the next excruciating program. During these pauses I took a longer, sidelong look at her eyes. They really were the same half-moons as Katya's, and staring at them made my body ache. I tried to focus on their color, for that was the greatest difference. Irina's eyes were the powder blue shade of a high, hazy day. Her irises were edged by rings of azure, almost purple, and this feature was highlighted by the violet plastic butterfly in her hair.

It was three in the afternoon when a polar gloom descended on the town and the VCR finally gave up. Irina unscrewed a panel and stared blankly into the dirty jumble of wires. It was no use. The apparatus was frozen and the technicians were nowhere to be found. The erotic program would not be screened.

The director loaded me into his personal car and drove me out toward the only hotel in town. I sat hugging myself against the cold in his windy sedan. Seeing this Irina had somehow enhanced Katya's face in my mind and when I closed my eyes I could picture her fully, staring bleakly out across the Great Salt Lake.

I opened my eyes and glanced between the legs of a naked brunette spread-eagled across a calendar on the director's dashboard. Today was Wednesday, March 31. When I'd last called New York from Moscow I'd left a message on our machine, saying I would try again by the end of the month, after I returned from the closed cities. Now I was going to break that promise, too. I glared through the director's cracked windshield as we skidded around in the snow.

"I know what you're thinking," the director said to me contritely.

"You think I misled you. You think we don't really have an erotic program here. But we do. Believe me, we do."

"I'm sure you do," I said, thinking about my forgotten phone call and my missed flight. About the Chinese delegation on my airplane and the hot showers they would all get to take in Moscow tonight.

"Maybe we're different, we Russians," the director began again. "Of course we believe an erotic program should arouse you. I mean, imagine a beautiful girl in a field with her breasts bare. Imagine flowers all around. I don't think it has to be . . . well, you understand."

"I'm sorry, I'm not listening," I said.

"Well, I don't mean that I don't like to see a woman with a man's penis in her mouth. Who doesn't? But that's a private affair, you know? Not that it's unattractive to see a woman being penetrated forcefully from behind and to see her acknowledging that as a great pleasure. I mean all of that can be . . . well . . . stimulating, of course. But the problem was I just didn't have qualified people. Our cameraman didn't understand my concept for the film and then he and Irina worked up a conspiracy against me. They were both so busy with their own little ideas. They lack a certain vision. That's why I couldn't show you the film. The erotic project, as it stands now has no message. It is an artistic failure."

Once at the hotel, the director led me up fifteen flights of stairs to my room. He told me there would be a dinner party in my honor that night and he encouraged me to rest and not to go outside under any circumstances. Yes, yes, I was assured, my phone call would be arranged. It would take some time, but it would all be arranged eventually.

The walls of the hotel room were sewage-green. Above my head, a black water-stain bloomed across the ceiling like a storm cloud. The bed was narrow and cold. The sheets were pressed, starched, and filthy. There was a telephone by the bed. I picked it up. No dial tone—just a weak, pneumatic gasp that made it sound as if the phone were wired to the bottom of a well. I wondered who was First Secretary of the Soviet Union the last time the thing rang.

I undressed and shuffled into the bathroom. There was no real toilet or shower: just a single tap fixed to the ceiling and a hole in the floor with two foot-pads below. I stood on the foot-pads and turned the shower crank to the left. The water came out in a vigorous, rusty pour, so cold that it gave me an ice cream headache. There was a mirror about the size of a brick screwed into the wall. I could only see my face in it if I took two paces back, but at that distance I was pressed up against the slimy tiles, too far away from the tap to shave. I shut the water off and reached for the towel. The cloth went halfway around my waist. I waddled back into the bedroom and stared out through the window into this black-and-white movie of a town, still encased in snow even after the first day of spring. There was an annoying twittering noise coming from somewhere in the room. It sounded like a dying bird. I looked around for its source—a faulty circuit or a loose window pane. But then I found it.

The phone was ringing.

I picked up the receiver carefully and put it to my ear. *"Da?"* I whispered.

"Are you this Daniel from America everyone's been on my back about all day?" an operator demanded.

"Yes, that's me."

"You want to call America?"

"Yes."

"Why do you want to call America?"

"Business."

"Business," she said to herself in disgust. "Give me the number."

There was a snapping and twanging sound on the line, followed by a heavy gust of static. I remembered Katya's strange calls from

Russia back when we'd first met—how it had always sounded as if she were speaking from behind a closed door. Now I had a sense of what it was like to stand behind that door. The American ring came through as an aloof, insolent purr.

"It's ringing now," the operator said. "Be quick about your *business*. I'm not keeping the line open long." There was a shuffle and a click and the operator signed off.

The American ring rang on—as distant and as familiar as a childhood memory. Three times. Four times. Five times. How many rings was too many? I looked at my watch—it was four in the morning in New York. At least I wanted to hear my voice on the answering machine. I prepared myself for my own recorded rebuke: "Stupid, stupid, stupid."

There was a crunch and a ping. The two phone systems took measure of each other and synchronized. And then through the noise came the tremulous sound of Katya's voice in English:

"Two-four-three, eight-seven-eight-one," it said. "Leave a message for Yekaterina or the Gold Star Car Service. Beep!"

I stood there a moment trying to think of something to say. But as I opened my mouth, someone fumbled with the phone over in America. There was the whining of feedback and then the answering machine was shut off. Katya sighed sleepily in the background. A lazy, arrogant male voice shushed her and spoke.

"Da."

"Hello?" I said.

"Who's dat?" the voice demanded.

I hung up.

I knew the voice. It was the same one that had called the afternoon of my departure. The one that had asked where "Yoo-teh" was. The same one I'd heard singing Okudzhava's, "Along the Smolensk Road" while I'd argued with Katya over the phone from outside Dr. Melnikov's office in Queens. I had heard it so many times, but it had always been a background sound. The sound of some distant machine. Now I moaned to myself when I thought of it in the foreground—conveying great size and total ownership. "Who's dat?" the voice had demanded. What do you mean "who's dat"? I thought. Who the fuck is *dat*? Who's saying *dat* in my house? In my house we say *that*, not *dat*. And who should be asking whom "who's that?"

I fell back onto the bed and raked my face. I stared up at the black water-stain swirling above on the ceiling. It was all so far away and so completely out of my control. A twelve-hour time difference. The exact opposite side of the globe. Why didn't anyone ever tell me that if you dug a hole from home straight through the Earth you'd end up in Russia?

I felt something wringing me, from my feet to my knees up past my chest. My throat tightened. I thought I might throw up. There was no garbage can. I let out a sob instead. I smiled and sniffled and waited for the choking feeling to pass. I sobbed again. And that sob brought another sob. I opened my mouth and a moan came out. The water boiled up in my eyes and ran down my cheeks and wet the bed under my head. Shameful.

"Who's dat? Who's dat? Who's dat?" I cried out loud. I felt such a weariness. It came out of me in gasps and heaves. I cried until my voice gave out and my eyes burned and the black stain on the ceiling spread out into the blackness of approaching sleep. And when there was nothing else that could come out of me I felt myself sinking into the bed and my eyes closing. But the black cloud on the ceiling pursued me. It turned blacker and blacker, shiny-metallic, and finally came into the world as a black Lincoln sedan. It flashed its blinker and snaked through Brooklyn. It turned down Ocean Avenue and steamed past Avenues X, Y, and Z. It made one turn right and took a jog seaward where it picked up Brighton Beach Avenue. It straddled the road, squat and stout, as its driver searched for a parking spot near a store Katya likes.

"He will buy her some smoked fish," I heard my voice say. "She is still sleeping at this hour on a workday, and he will reward her laziness with some smoked fish."

Rows of long, fat American cars, the kind American-born Americans don't drive anymore, take up all the parking spots. But the driver can't be stopped. He plants his car in the Soviet way—vertically between two parallel parkers, almost pinning a passerby against a wall. He paces himself getting out of the car. He uses the automatic toggle to unlock his door when manual would have been quicker. He looks right, left, and even up and then swaggers into a store called *Zolotoy Kluchik*—The Little Golden Key.

Fish and cheese for her. Fish and cheese.

Misha lingers inside the store long enough for a laborer to paint one edge of a window frame a fresh shade of gold. The same color as the smoked herring he carries out of the shop. He gets back into the Lincoln and displays three golden still-lifes: kippers on a car seat; brassy sunglasses over tired eyes; a bulky Orthodox cross bouncing on a chest black and thick as a thunderhead.

Down to Knapp Street he motors, onto the Belt Parkway and over the Williamsburg Bridge into Manhattan. He avoids all tolls. He comes off the exit ramp onto Delancey and I can make out the decal on his door: "Gold Star Car Service: twenty-four hours a day, seven days a week." In the twenty-second hour of his shift, Misha heads up past Greenwich Village, along Eighth Avenue. He takes in for the tenth time that day the difference between proletarian Brooklyn and imperial Manhattan. At this I smile—at the size of the hurdle only three generations can build—but Misha shrugs the whole thing off as someone else's fantasy.

He parks in a loading zone and with the same slow, irrefutable pace he gathers up his keys and fish and scoffs at the useless police station before disappearing into the box in Chelsea. In the time it takes to devour a smoked herring, make love to Katya, and have a shower, he is back in the seat of his car. His hair is wet, gleaming, parted. It smells of my shampoo. He doesn't like the smell of the stuff, but he enjoys using it. The next customer who gets in his cab complains that the whole goddamn car smells like a fish store.

I woke to the director's shouting, "Vake up, sleepyhead!" He wagged his finger at me when I opened the door. "And you doubted me!" he laughed. "New York! New York! Everything is possible here, even such a phone call." He made me put on a suit and then we drove to a dark low building on the other side of town.

It appeared to be some kind of cabaret. It was hot and crowded inside and the air was bluish—almost more smoke than air. In the center of the dining room, just off the dance floor, an arc of lights had been set up around one of the tables. A cameraman was leaning on a chair, a cigarette dangling loosely in his lips and a coffin-sized Soviet camera balancing precariously on his shoulder. He snapped to attention when he saw us enter the room.

"Film our entrance!" the director shouted at him.

Someone took my arm. I looked over and saw Irina posing next to me in a purple-sequined evening gown. The three of us fell into a flying V with the director leading us slowly down the steps toward the lights. People at the other tables watched and the cameraman back-pedaled in front of us zooming in and out constantly.

"Try to smile," Irina said to me out of the corner of her mouth.

"What is this?"

"Shh. It's the news," the director whispered.

"What news?"

"You're the news. This is quite an event—the forging of a business partnership between your company and—"

The cameraman tripped over one of the power cords and fell back into the lights. Pop, pop, pop—all three bulbs broke and blew out the restaurant's circuit breaker. The smell of burnt hair wafted into the air.

"Damn you!" the director shouted in the darkness. A laugh flitted around the restaurant and in a few moments the auxiliary house lights came up dimly. The director pulled the cameraman up off the ground and hounded him over to another table. Irina glared at the scene, infuriated.

"Ruined again," she said to herself.

Irina and I took our seats while the director was forced to sit at the restaurant owner's table and make his apologies. Irina caught my eye briefly and then turned her face back to the dance floor. She had painted two stripes over each eye—one stripe was thick and blue. The other was narrow and violet and extended almost to her ears. It looked weird. I couldn't help staring.

As I stared, though, I saw again how the light entered her pupils along a familiar pathway. Her lids rose high in the center and then slanted off sharply at each corner belying the imposition of a Mongol gene sometime deep in her family's past. And I felt myself growing angry at her—at the way she took in the room with the haughty, cheated look of a deposed conqueror. It was so arrogant, so completely Katya-like, that her strange makeup job seemed more like a disguise at a masqued ball than a unique personal fashion statement.

"If you're going to keep staring at me," Irina said suddenly, "try not to look so miserable."

She drew a new cigarette from a pack and waited patiently until I realized she wanted me to light it for her. I fired the director's lighter, and a cloud of dirty gasoline tainted the air. She dipped down toward the flame.

"Never make a woman bend for a light," she said after she French-inhaled the first puff. "Never make a woman do anything that isn't graceful."

"I'm sorry. I wasn't thinking."

"Oh, you're thinking all right. You seem to be thinking about something very important. I wonder what it is you're thinking about."

"Your eyes probably."

"My eyes *probably* or my eyes for sure?"

"Probably, for sure."

"'Probably, for sure'?" she said with one dark eyebrow raised. "What exactly is your specialty?"

"Specialty?"

"Yes, your area of qualification."

"We don't really have that in America."

"You mean you have no higher education?"

"No, no. I do. But I have kind of a . . . kind of a general specialty."

"A general specialty. Interesting."

"Why? What's your . . . specialty?"

"Metallurgy," she said. She used all the curves of her mouth as she drew out the word. Then she made an O with her lips and blew out a smoke ring.

"Mostly I like to read though," she added. "I read all the time. I bet I've read more than you have."

"Probably," I said.

"I'm sure of it," she said. "I read all day long. You should read more. It's attractive for a man to be well read. You wouldn't think it, but the director of our television station—Timofey Arkadevich over there—he's read everything. And he writes poetry, too."

We were silent again for a minute. She smiled at me for the first time. I glanced at her breasts. They were exposed almost to the nipple by the deep V in her dress that started at her shoulders and stopped just short of her navel.

"Is it good?" I asked.

"Is *what* good?"

"The director's poetry."

"Oh, that. No. It's no good," she said.

There was a blare of music and the emcee came on stage to announce the beginning of the floor show. The first act was a People's Artist from the Great October Regional Ballet in Krasnoyarsk. She came out leading a small dog.

"You know, I have to tell you something," Irina said, her eyes fixed on the animal. "When I first saw you today, when I saw you walk into my room, I had a very strong feeling about you. I was thinking, I could make love to you. 'I could reveal myself to that man,' I said to myself right then and there. I had it all pictured in my mind. I saw you undressing me in your hotel room after dinner. I felt your hands on my softest parts. It was all very easy to see."

The ballerina balanced first on one foot, then on two hands, then on one hand. She whistled. The little dog leaped up on her chin. It stepped over to her chest and walked a jittery circle over the bottoms of her breasts. The dancer moved her body expertly, making sure it was not too sharply angled. This allowed the dog to continue its progress up her stomach and balance for a short rest on her pubic bone.

"So I thought," Irina continued, "Let's see where this can go.

And I asked you right away, do you remember? I asked you if you were married. Do you remember what you said?"

"Not really."

"That's right. You said 'not really.' You know, that's the worst thing you could have said."

The little dog caught his breath and started to walk up the ballerina's thighs until it got a pawhold on her kneecaps. It pulled itself up, took a breath, and then started up the last narrow passage. But on the way to her feet, the dog lost its nerve and looked out at the crowd.

"'Not really'?" Irina said in disgust. "What's that supposed to mean? If you had told me that you were married, I would have understood. 'Fine, I have other commitments too,' I'd have thought. 'Let's enjoy each other for this one night.' On the other hand, if you had said that you weren't married, well, then I would have wanted you even more. I might have even thought we could go further. But you said, 'not really.' My God, what a cowardly thing to say."

The dog on the dancer's calves craned his head toward me and whimpered. "Do something!" he seemed to be saying. But just then a woman in a glitter jacket and top hat strode out on stage. She held a biscuit above the ballerina's feet. The dog leaped for it. He chewed and swallowed and when he looked up he saw that in lunging for the biscuit he had put himself safely atop the ballerina's soles. The audience applauded. The dog whined. The ballerina punched him up in the air with her feet, flipped over, and caught him before he hit the ground. Then she bowed to the crowd and skipped into the wings.

"You see, Daniel, I've been thinking about you all afternoon," Irina continued. "I've been thinking about you in a physical sense and in a psychological sense. And I've decided that you have a problem. The problem with you is that you have—"

"I know. I know. I have a weak character."

"Yes. A weak character. It's nothing to be ashamed of. It's also a soft and gentle character. You just have to be careful who you marry. Who did you marry, by the way?"

"You've decided I'm married, after all."

"Of course," she said and stubbed out her spent filter. She flashed an amused, condescending smile at me.

"Okay," I said finally. "Her name is Katya. She's from St. Petersburg. She's Russian."

Irina's smile drifted into a frown. Then, all at once, she burst out laughing. "I knew it. I knew it by the words you use. By that terrified look on your face."

I blushed and this seemed to soften her.

"Where is she now, your wife?" she asked.

"In America, I guess."

"You guess?"

"I'm not sure."

"Would you stop saying things like that? 'I guess,' and 'I think,' and 'maybe,' and 'I'm not sure.' "

"It's just the way I learned Russian."

"You learned it wrong. It's unattractive. You should relearn it."

"Fine, I'll go get my textbook."

"*Nu,* Daniel. Don't be insulted. I'm only having some fun. Seriously, now, tell me all about her. Tell me about this mysterious Katya."

I looked up and stared right into Irina's face. Her lips curved up at the corners and her eyes laughed at me even as they sparkled. This was *not* Katya staring back at me. If it had been, I would have felt cut down by that arrogant look. I would have puzzled endlessly over the engine behind it. I would have worried about how, if I'd said what was in my heart, I would have accidentally stripped a vital gear.

"Are you so ashamed to tell me about her?" Irina chuckled.

Ashamed? No. But how to put Katya into words? Actually, I had never even tried. So much of being with Katya was about sensing her, not seeing her. Either we were crushed up against each other and she was too close to focus on or she was retreating, disappearing—a vanishing point. As for the intimacies of our marriage—they were like a kind of secret wartime code that we were unauthorized to reveal to those outside our two-person army. And one-by-one all the people with whom I might have once discussed Katya had dropped away—my friends, my father, my brother, my mother. Even Katya was gone now. And as I looked up at Irina—this weird Katya simulacrum who had made up her mind that she would never sleep with me because I had an irrevocably weak character—I realized that she was now the most intimate relation I had in the world.

"Well?" Irina asked smiling through the smoke.

I told her everything. I told her about our engagement and our wedding. I told her about Katya's nineteenth-century manners and her amalgamated religion and how she had beaten me at chess every single time but once. I told her about the night she first *finished*. I told her about her false pregnancy and her parents' many-gabled country house. I told her about the phone call I'd just made to New York and the man on the other end of the line who had demanded "Who's dat?"

"And what do I have now? This postcard, that's all," I said, showing the Great Salt Lake to Irina. "She asks me if she could *belong* to me. What does that mean? Is she asking me to come get her? I'm not really sure. I'm never sure. I'm not even really sure who she is. I've tried. I really have. I married her, for God's sake, but I still don't know."

Irina lit another cigarette, took a long inhale, and let the smoke come out her nose.

"You shouldn't try so hard. I can tell you who she is."

"You can?"

"Of course. She's a little Communist bitch."

Her pupils widened and her cigarette smoldered. She looked at her reflection in a spoon, fixed a smudge on her lipstick, and looked back up at me.

"Tell me," she began again, "have you ever heard the expression 'Party intelligentsia'?"

"I've heard it. I'm not sure exactly what it is."

"Well, I'll explain it to you. Let's look at this Katya a little more abstractly. My guess is she's a university girl, correct? History, philology, that sort of thing."

"Philosophy, actually."

"Philosophy fits right in. The thing is this: Your Katya has a problem with her pedigree. She's from peasant stock—that bit you told me about her drinking tea from a saucer betrays her. Her family owes its fancy city life to the Party. But since she's not stupid, Katya knows she has to do a little editing, especially in times like these. So she imagines herself part of an earlier century—a heroine from Tolstoy or, better yet, Pushkin. And like all those heroines, she's fond of our old Orthodox superstitions. She goes along with that mysterious nonsense about whistling in the house and stepping on each other's feet to prevent a fight. She keeps a dream guide in her drawer and has lists of lucky number combinations. Am I right so far?"

"She doesn't believe in lucky numbers."

"You get my point. Now, let's continue. As I said, she's from a good Communist family. She lives in a decent apartment in the center of Leningrad, which she imagines to be a kind of castle. She pays no mind to the fact that families like mine once owned entire buildings in Petersburg. That somehow doesn't fit into her equation of history. All her life Katya's felt ordained to follow her own reality— the path with the most connections. She can't help it. She feels a physical need to be close to money or power."

"But I don't have either one."

"Yes, but you could. Listen, with all this mess we've had, a woman doesn't know what to do. The only men with money or power these days are the kind that are fond of guns. And lately girls like Katya have been attaching themselves to characters like that chauffeur boy you told me about, the one who's using your shampoo."

"Go on," I said glumly.

"Danochka, Danochka, don't worry. Deep down, worthless little mobsters like this Misha disgust the Katyas of the world. Those boys are all wrong. Dirty. Crude. A different class entirely than you. And you, by the way, should take another look at yourself in the mirror. You're not unattractive. Not stupid. You could be a lot more, or at least you could fool someone into believing you could be more. And best of all you could do it without behaving like a hooligan. So you don't have money or power right now. Who cares? It's your potential that's interesting. If she helped unlock that potential then she would share in your journey and finally she'd be able to deserve what she has."

"Do you think I should go back to her then?"

"After everything I've told you, you still want her?"

"I'm not su—"

"Don't say it!" Irina said. "I don't want to hear 'I'm not sure' come out of your mouth one more time. And I know your Katya doesn't want to hear it again either."

"But it seems like from what you're saying that she . . . she used me in a way."

"We all use each other. It's how we survive. The question is, what are you using her for?"

"I'm not . . . I don't know."

Irina glared and shook her head slowly. I saw the last light of interest in me flicker out in her eyes.

"My God," she said. "She's really got something on you. Something very strong."

"Yes. She does."

"Then stay away from her. This is not the kind of girl to be unsure about."

The intermission of the floor show came and the director rejoined us. He was by then quite drunk. He was cursing to himself, complaining to Irina how he would have to sell something to pay for the restaurant's ruined circuit breaker. He begged me to buy his television station. He wanted to go to Paris. He wanted to study filmmaking at the Sorbonne.

A dessert was served, which left a petrochemical film on the inside of my mouth. The director sobered up a little. He ran his hands over his face and sighed. "You're right, you know, Daniel. This *is* a closed city. The restrictions have been lifted, but it's still closed. What can a person do here? There's nothing here but incompetence. The hell with all this. Let's go."

Irina and the director stood abruptly and I followed them out the door. The director put his arm around Irina's shoulders and she leaned slightly into him to keep him upright. His hand slid from her shoulder, down across the exposed skin on her back and over the roundness below. He hefted one of the cheeks of her bottom. Hefted, that was it—not a lascivious grope at all. He felt its weight and measured its tone and tautness. Irina, for her part, did not deflect his hand or even look at it. Instead, she took one step ahead of him so that it was visible to anyone who cared to notice that an important person was touching her in an intimate way. She knew she was being appraised and, knowing the qualities of her own gifts, she left the restaurant slowly, confidently, and with a clear knowledge of the night that lay ahead.

Homecoming

Valentina Stepanovna could see that I was tired, so she stood up from the kitchen table and led me to the bed where I had first made love to her daughter. I tried to resist—I had meant just to drop by—but my mother-in-law took my elbow like the tiller of a ship and steered me firmly to Katya's former room.

I had the weekend off. I'd finished with the eastern part of the former Soviet Union and now I was due to survey the west. In between I'd come back to Petersburg. I'd had in mind a kind of anonymous haunting of the city. I saw myself walking the same boulevards around Katya's house, dining alone at the Metropol Restaurant, and then slipping off on an overnight train to Belorussia by Sunday. But within an hour of arriving in St. Petersburg I found myself walking along the Griboyedov Canal. And before long I was in front of the

Konstantinovs' building. I punched in the code to the door just to see if I could remember it. And when the door clicked open I bounded up the stairs two at a time to their apartment.

"Valentina Stepanovna, come quickly," Katya's father said when he saw me. "Look, look! It's Katya's . . . It's our . . . It's Daniel." He moved to kiss me and shake my hand at the same time but the greeting got tangled up and finally resolved itself in an awkward, unmanly embrace.

Later, after I had drunk her tea and embarrassed her with praise for her homemade preserves, Valentina Stepanovna had me hold her hand while she climbed up a stepladder to the top of the wardrobe in Katya's old room. She came down with a duvet cover she'd embroidered herself and tucked a light summer blanket inside. Then, with her knees and shoulders, she did a surprisingly athletic clean-and-jerk move that converted the sofa back into the bed that I remembered. She stepped outside while I undressed, then she tucked me in and smoothed my forehead. She did all of this not in a loving way exactly, but in a manner that seemed above all professional.

"Daniel, dear," she said as she drew the lace curtains across the window, "you should think of this room as your room. Even if there is some unpleasantness for the moment with Katya. Feel yourself completely at home here. Dasha and I will leave soon and Roman Antonovich will take you up to our country house after you've rested."

"Is Roman Antonovich still here?" I asked, already nodding off.

"Papa has gone to the factory."

"What does he do now? Katya said he was involved in some kind of business."

"He's trading in butter, milks, and yogurts with several different fat contents. Quiet now. It's time to rest."

Homecoming

✌

I slept a stop-and-go sleep. Each time I woke, I struggled to get out of bed. What was I doing napping here? I needed to make my excuses and leave. But when I started to rise, the cool cotton and the gentle summer dusk lapped over me and I slept on. I heard the pleasant, ordered sounds the family made as they prepared to go to their dacha. At one point I had the impression that Valentina Stepanovna was standing over me, staring, and I thought I heard my niece Dasha run in and kick my slippers.

"Get him out of *my* room!" Dasha cried.

"Shhhhh, easy now," Valentina Stepanovna said soothingly and I dropped off again.

The hours passed and Valentina Stepanovna and Dasha left. The apartment grew quiet. I didn't know whether I was supposed to get up or sleep on until morning. Actually, for all I knew, morning had already come. It was the time of white nights in Petersburg and the light from the window was the same as it had been when I'd first lay down—almost the same, in fact, as it had been on that white night with Katya nearly three years ago. All of her things had been left exactly where they'd always been—her weird American books, her archery bow, her plastic Finnish tanker advertisement in the curio cabinet. It seemed almost logical that Katya would sneak in the door now, slip into bed, and pull the blankets around us. The only thing that broke the spell was her giant Bob Dylan poster. The poster was still there, of course, but now Dylan looked a good three years younger than I did.

I sat up and thought about getting dressed, but considering even that made me confused and dreamy. If I stayed in this house, what was I supposed to wear? Was I expected to lounge around in my boxers, flip on the gargantuan Soviet boob tube, and joke around with my father-in-law like one of the family? Or was I supposed to sit at attention, wear my best, most Western suit, and discuss politics like a proper foreign guest? I crossed the room and found that Valentina Stepanovna had already addressed this problem. A yellow-and-red polyester jogging outfit was laid out neatly on an armchair. Pinned to it was a note written in easy-to-read block Cyrillic letters: DANIEL, HERE IS A PRESENT—FOR YOU!

I put on the suit and looked around for my slippers. My niece had kicked them under the wardrobe, all the way to the wall, and I had to lay on my stomach to reach them. One had gone to the left, the other to the right of a wooden box. I pulled out the slippers and the box as well. There was more Katya memorabilia inside: a photo of her in a red neckerchief, her arm angled across her flat, twelve-year-old chest in an earnest Pioneer salute. Another from the same series showed her taking an archery lesson from her father. Roman Antonovich's big arms smothered her and the bow while she looked sternly ahead at the target.

There was more underneath the layer of photos. Certificates of excellence in political philosophy, riflery, and "big tennis," whatever that meant.

There was also a stack of about a hundred letters from America.

I blinked at the letters for a moment. I placed them carefully on the bed. An almost sexual flutter passed through me, staring at that neat, bound-up pile. Of course there was no way I could read them. I'd be no better than a petty KGB investigator if I did. Yes, there would undoubtedly be something important in this correspondence, for it was all addressed to her sister Liza, Katya's most intimate relation. There would be details of her life, probably even something about the nature of her feelings for me. And her reflections might lead me toward all sorts of conclusions.

But the evidence would all be tainted. And when I imagined an impossible future where Katya had come back to me, I could see this betrayal multiplying itself out. The secrets I would have learned from the letters would fester for years until some horrible moment when I would get drunk and confess everything and she would order me out into the street and I would have to go live with one of our children.

I plucked the cord that bound the envelopes. It was cinched as tight as a guitar string on all four sides and the letters themselves could not be examined without untying the knot. Only the postmarks and the return addresses were accessible. The addresses were written in English but followed the Soviet format—backward, with the name of the city first, then the street, then the sender.

I flicked through the corners and saw the dates and the cities change. February 14, 1993, the day before she left me, was the last one from New York. After a month they picked up again in Utah. There were unfamiliar small American towns called Moab, Ephraim, and Nephi; then came Provo and finally Salt Lake City. She must have lingered in Salt Lake, for there was no correspondence from her for several weeks. What had happened to her there that had caused her to stop writing? Something significant, it seemed, for when the correspondence resumed again, it did so in a flurry. She wrote a letter every two days between mid-April and the beginning of May as her postmarks drifted back eastward: Omaha, Chicago, Fort Wayne, Akron, the Bronx, and finally Manhattan once again.

I flicked back further in time to see if she had marked the same moments that had stayed with me. It seemed she had. There was a letter written the morning after she had *finished*—the date of the November full moon. There was a thick one on the day of our wedding and another thick one following the evening of our engagement. There was no denying it. This pile could very well contain the key to it all—a kind of Katya Rosetta Stone.

I pulled at the end of the string to see if it would loosen. It would not. How unfair. Why did it have to be tied up so tightly? Wasn't I being honest? Wasn't I just trying to learn the nature of our process and then find out why she abandoned it? I didn't deserve this obstacle. Some Russians I knew would even call it fate that I had found these letters. No doubt they recorded scores of hollow impasses that a simpler marriage would have effortlessly plowed through. But I hadn't had a simple marriage. I'd had a mess. And now here was a kind of legend to that mess. How easy it would be—to go through every letter and note each mistaken impression. And once I had this overview I could plot the route I had traveled that stretched from that first white night with her all the way forward to my present exile. And then I could put an arrow on the map that said "You are here."

I fingered the bundle. I picked at the knot tying it together. It was a complicated one, with multiple crossovers and smaller barrel-shaped micro knots inside, designed, it seemed, so that only its creator would be able to replicate it if it were untied. I found a pen and paper and drew a schematic of the knot and then carefully annotated my diagram as I undid each loop. It took about half an hour. Finally I reached the last crossover and pulled. The string fell away. I opened the first envelope and unfolded the letter inside.

Page one began with a diagram of a knot.

"Dear Liza," Katya wrote to her sister. "This is a special knot I learned from my book *More Knots by Houdini.* You are to keep all of my letters from America tied with this knot since our correspondence is intended for your eyes alone. If you don't follow my directions I will be forced to stop writing you. Also, from now on, when we correspond, we will use the special alphabet." The handwriting then switched to an elegant calligraphy that was as beautiful as it was unintelligible. I could only make out one English word scattered throughout the text: the word "Daniel."

૭

Katya's father woke me a few hours later. He handed me a fifty-pound gunnysack of butter as soon as I met him in the hallway. He led me silently out into the street to the bus stop. We rode the bus without a word for an hour to the end of the line and then humped our butter half a mile more to a field of tent-sized metal boxes.

"You always have to pay, don't you agree, Daniel?" Katya's father said as he threw down his own load and started unlocking one of the boxes. "Always you have to pay. Back in 'fifty-four, when I was your age, they . . . invited me to the coal mines up in the Arctic. I learned that lesson then, I'll tell you. There was one fellow—he gave the commandant a lot of trouble. Well, they took away his boots and they gave him twice as much to carry! He got so tired that he couldn't even—"

A tall man in a suede coat appeared from behind a row of boxes and stared at Roman Antonovich. My father-in-law muttered a greeting to him and fell silent.

"But that's all in the past," he said when the man had disappeared from sight again. "Of course I've made some mistakes, believe me. I was strong-headed when I was younger. Not like you. You're lucky to have your particular kind of character. Not me. I didn't listen to anyone. And the funny thing is that the Party understood my character better than I did. They could see I was strong but that I lacked discipline. My internal forces were working against each other. I was a divided man. So they made me do a little work up north. So what! Some whiners like that Solzhenitsyn you see on TV all the time these days call it a 'labor camp.' But I'll bet you Solzhenitsyn was the type to make another man carry his load. Not me. I did my share. It built me up. Made me stronger. And after I paid, well, you see, I was rewarded."

My father-in-law pulled open the last of five padlocks and with a flourish swung open the door of his metal box. Inside was a tiny yellow car. Roman Antonovich took out a chamois cloth and carefully buffed it, all the while whispering to it, calling it "little sparrow," or "my sweet one," or "my little paw." The car was of Ukrainian manufacture—"Zaporozhets" was its trademark. Nowadays young people were calling that line of cars "Academics" since only school-teachers or moldy college professors were thought to drive them.

We jammed the butter in the trunk and then squeezed into the little cockpit. The car ignited with a single twist of the key and we putted out past columns and columns of concrete apartment complexes. Cranes hung still in the air like the hands of a stopped watch. Then all of a sudden the city ended and the Academic was buzzing like a high-speed lawnmower through a dense forest of birch and fir. Twenty miles up the road we veered off into the woods and found a concrete box that capped a deep hole in the ground.

"Water, Daniel, water," Roman Antonovich chuckled. "You need water, don't you agree? What can you do without water? A person can die of thirst, you know. Believe me, I've seen it happen, even in the snow."

He lowered a bucket into the chipped cement well casing and slopped water over his shirt when he pulled the bucket up again. A tornado of mosquitoes swirled around his head.

"Ho, ho, look at the mosquitoes, Daniel, look at 'em all, they're everywhere. That's summer for you, ha-ha! Of course this is nothing compared to the way it was in the Arctic." SLAP! "Ahhhh! Got you, you miserable bastard!" The mosquitoes had bitten up nearly every free blood vessel on his face and he was red and raging. He huffed and puffed and fired the little car back to life. "That's right. You got to have water. Water, water everywhere but not a drop to drink . . . But I want to say a word or two on this matter with Katya.

I just want you to know that she has a harsh and demanding character: very tough, very difficult—I wouldn't have had it any other way. There's a chance she might be too much for you. If she is, just send her back. I know how to handle her."

We rounded a glade and then started toward the Finnish Gulf. We came over a bluff and the gray-blue sea opened up before us. Below I could see a few of the rambling old wooden summer houses, built before World War II when Finnish barons still controlled this territory. The houses were many-gabled, with wide porticos and large porches. They were lovely, I had to admit. I wondered which one of them nestled in the firs along the shoreline belonged to the Konstantinovs. But just when I thought I had picked out the house that matched Katya's descriptions, Roman Antonovich swerved sharply to the right and headed inland along a muddy river. Fifteen minutes later we pulled into a village and stopped.

"And here's Katya's little gemstone," my father-in-law exclaimed.

Country house, summer cottage, country cabin—none of those names fit the structure ahead of us. The Konstantinovs' was a foundling dwelling, assembled from pieces of plywood scrap and nails of different lengths. A corrugated tin roof brought to mind a Bombay shanty. Out back a railway car salvaged by my industrious father-in-law was due to be gutted and connected to the main building of the complex via a Habitrail-like plastic tube.

The family plot was abutted on four sides by other huts, which in turn were besieged by even more. In fact, in the space of a few acres, hundreds of tiny summer shacks were pinned up against one another like graves. They would have multiplied out further had their advance not been checked by a fetid little pond at the perimeter of the colony.

The ground in front of the Konstantinov house was clearly under the supervision of my mother-in-law. The land teemed. Every meter

was planted with some necessary crop. Even the flagstones that led
to the front door were interlaced with white-flowered potato plants.
Looping around the house were concentric rings of berry bushes:
first raspberry, then black currant, then red currant.

We got out of the car and I caught a whiff of raw sewage in the
air. A man with a ruddy face appeared from an adjoining dacha
when he saw us. "Roman Antonovich," he boomed, "I just wanna
say that I just wanna say . . ." He charged in front of our path with
a half bottle in his hand. My father-in-law tried to push him out of
the way.

"Not now, Mitya."

"*Nu,* come on, just one little glass, I've got some herring for a
chaser—"

"No, no, not now."

"Hey, who's this . . . guy?" he said, thumbing me.

"That's my . . . It's Katya's . . . This is our Daniel."

"Ah, the American spy! Well, how do you, do you, do?"

Roman Antonovich whispered something to the man and the
two bumped chests a few times until my father-in-law silenced him
with a block of butter. The man stumbled back to his hut holding
the butter over his shoulder like an American football.

Inside the house Roman Antonovich expanded and exclaimed:
"Well, this is our little month in the country." He made relaxation
motions and sighs, but in time he grew agitated and left to cover up
his car. His activity grew more and more frantic and soon he was
moving wood around, pulling potatoes, and hefting and replacing
the flagstones.

"Oh, the water!" Roman Antonovich shouted. "Valentina Stepanovna's making soup. I must bring in the water!" He picked up the
two canisters of spring water and lugged them over to a tank he'd
fashioned from an abandoned septic system.

Homecoming

It was warm and moist in the kitchen. Valentina Stepanovna bent over a cutting board loaded with things she'd grown. My sister-in-law, Liza, strummed a guitar somewhere in the distance while Dasha played a hopscotch-like game and shrieked her way around the living room. I was forced into my jogging suit and slippers, "for relaxation purposes." I stood by my mother-in-law while she cooked. It seemed the quietest place in the house.

"So," Valentina Stepanovna sighed, "this is how we take our vacations. What are your impressions?"

"It's somewhat different than Katya described it."

"Yes, well, Katya always has her specific way of looking at things."

She began loading up the now-boiling cauldron with potatoes, beets, carrots, and dill. The Plexiglas window over the stove steamed over, and outside Roman Antonovich, racing through his different chores, blurred from sight.

"Valentina Stepanovna," I said, "I think you live very nicely."

My mother-in-law pursed her lips in a way that in Katya always signified grave doubt. She poured some water sparingly from a jug, rinsed her hands in a rusty basin, and then poured the water from the basin into a second jug reserved for dirty water. She wiped her fingers on her apron and spoke with her head lowered.

"It's sweet of you to say these compliments, Daniel, but they're untrue and you know it. Katya's written Liza. We hear from her a little about your problems with our Russian life. I understand you, really. She'll never admit it to *you*, but Katya has the same problems. She has very specific ideas about how her life should look and how people should behave."

I paused for a moment before my next question.

"And what about me?" I asked softly. "Did I behave properly?"

"You behaved according to your character."

"But did she love my character? Did she actually love me?"

Valentina Stepanovna lifted her head and looked diagonally across my face, missing my eyes. "Of course, Daniel," she said. "Katya loves you the way I love Roman Antonovich out there. All you need is patience. You'll make your peace with each other. I know you will. Soon you'll understand that love is just another obstacle." And here she tested the boiling soup's texture and finding it to her satisfaction she smiled to herself, as if to say, "Well done."

૭

The family came together at last over the afternoon meal. I started to say something with my mouth full, but I was hushed by Dasha with an admonition Katya often used on me: *"Kogda ya yem ya gluh i nyem"*—When I eat, I am deaf and dumb.

"Duckling!" cried Roman Antonovich, massaging Dasha's head too roughly. "*Nu,* stop it!" Dasha howled back.

When we'd finished the soup I brought out a bottle of French Armagnac I'd found in a specialty store on Nevsky Prospect. Roman Antonovich poured himself a tumblerful and drank it down as if it were cream soda. Then he reached behind my chair and pulled out an old guitar with a snapped sixth string.

"Liza, play something, sing something!" He shouted at my sister-in-law, thrusting the guitar in her face.

"Later, Pop. I'm still eating."

"But that's your specialty, isn't it? Folk songs, right? Women, women everywhere and not a one to sing. I'm surrounded by them and they don't even do womanly things! Go on, Liza, I insist. A song for your . . . for this . . . for our Daniel!"

Liza took up the guitar and started finger-picking. She sang a folk song in a way that indicated years of lessons. Her voice was strong, well trained, and hopelessly off-pitch. When she'd finished, Roman Antonovich snatched the instrument from her hands.

"That-a-girl. Now I'll show you how it's really done." My father-in-law wrapped his body around the instrument and pulled at the peeling strings with his fingers while he sang:

Dasha, Dasha, Dasha, who's that duckling Dasha?
Daniel, Daniel, Daniel, catch that duckling Dasha!

Dasha giggled weirdly and began beating the rhythm on the back of my chair: *"Dasha! Dasha! Dasha! I'm that duckling Dasha!"*

She screamed and started flying circles around the table until she tripped and banged her mouth on the stove and began to cry.

"Pop, enough," Liza hissed. "*Mamulya,* Pop's had too much to drink."

"Who are you to say?" Roman Antonovich shouted.

"Roman Antonovich," Valentina Stepanovna said firmly, "it's enough now."

Roman Antonovich stopped cold like a man pulled over for speeding.

"Maybe you're right, maybe you're right," he looked down at the salvaged linoleum floor tiles and his mouth moved silently as if he were communing with someone not in the room. Then he turned to me with watery eyes. "You know, Daniel," he said, "what you're seeing here is not what it really is. This is no kind of family. Katya has a difficult character, but it's a strong character. A strong character, damn it. She knows how to keep a target in her sights. She should. I taught her how to shoot! I learned my lesson with Liza. Look at her there with her useless singing and her spoiled little Dasha holding on to Katya's room for dear life. And look at me, a man, a strong man getting weaker by the day, surrounded by these girls, with no help to be found on this entire continent!"

The holes in the sky's gray slate had been mended and the sunshine, which had somehow managed to leak through all day, was finally blocked out. Thunder rumbled, followed by a trickle, then a downpour.

"Water," whispered Roman Antonovich. He stood up suddenly, pulled a punctured slicker over his head, and threw the door open. He flew out into the rain, which was now falling in great gobs and quickly turning the grounds into a muddy floodplain. He rounded the back of the house hauling from this place and that every hollow object he could find. Water coursed through the garden, inundating the flagstone and rising upward, dangerously close to the lip of the doorframe. Bit by bit Roman Antonovich assembled an army of plastic buckets, paint trays, bottles, and jars. Through the Plexiglas, the women and I watched him, a mute conjurer raging at his containers. All his hard work paid off though, for the rain persisted and the containers filled up and overflowed.

The Overcoats

Russia and her satellites spiraled below all expectations. Yeltsin blew up parliament, war rolled over the Caucasus, and the infrastructure of the ExSSR, already so bent and broken, was whipped like a donkey to carry its load one more mile down the road.

I continued my survey. Through Western, "European" Russia, GlobeNet sent me, to the ruined medieval fortress cities of the Golden Ring. Then west to Ukraine, over the Pripet Swamp, birthplace of the Russian nation. And finally back eastward toward Belorussia, skirting along the southern edge of the Chernobyl nuclear cloud.

At a certain point I found myself on a bus, stopped in front of a cafeteria near the Ukrainian-Belorussian border. The driver announced an hour for a meal but most of the passengers decided to smoke instead. They filed out of the bus and I saw them gather in a loose circle in the snow outside my window. Each of them wore a different kind of fur hat. From above they looked like an impossible gathering of forest animals: a raccoon, a fox, a rabbit, an ermine, and a timber wolf with a long tail. When I walked past them I saw that they were showing each other their new passports: Ukrainian, Belorussian, Lithuanian, Moldovan, and so on.

"This passport's even more worthless than the last," one of them said.

"There's nothing we can do about it," said another.

"It'll be like this for a thousand years," said a third.

"Hey, brother," one of them called out to me, "what kind of passport did they give you?"

"Foreign," I said and slipped into the cafeteria.

Even though there was nothing wrong with my coat, nothing dirtier about it than the rest of the filthy canteen, the old woman at the door made me check it. By the time I got in the chow line, it was clear that I needed it, for it was as cold inside as it was out on the road. Wind blew through cracks in the windowpanes and when customers entered, the door slammed behind them, bouncing and rattling a half dozen times before settling ajar on its crooked frame.

The server spooned me a puffed egg square that she said was an omelet. It had a wrinkled, waterlogged skin and small bits of fish inside. For an appetizer I had a choice of either beef suspended in gritty gelatin, or chicken soup. I chose the soup, which was tepid and came with gray stew bones rolling around on the bottom. To drink there was a glass of icy fruit compote with an apricot pit submerged in it like a depth charge. My chair was metal and cold and I pulled the sleeve of my sweater up to cover my fingers. Only the spoon protruded when I ate.

I finally gave up on the meal when I realized I wanted my Eddie

Bauer Permafrost coat more than anything on my plate. I shoved my tray away and went over to the coat-check lady. I demanded my coat. I shook my fist. She bristled. She reached back and felt for the sleeve. She could tell from my accent and from the texture of my coat's shell that I was a foreigner, maybe the only foreigner that had ever come here. This seemed to make her angrier and she pulled on my coat carelessly without noticing that one of the other hooks on the rack had caught the back flap. She yanked sharply and the hook wedged itself deep into the Gore-Tex. She yanked again. There was a ripping sound. Feathers puffed out into the air.

Both of us paled. The woman's voice caught in her throat and her filmy eyes came alive.

"Young man . . . Please . . . Forgive me."

I walked out into the snow, my nose tingling with the beginnings of tears. I put on the coat. One of the men in the circle of smokers— the ermine—saw the long rip down the back. "Oh dear God!" he said. "Young man! Your coat!" The other men turned to look. Soon they were all shouting: "Young man, your coat! Your coat!"

"I know, I know," I said. There was nothing to do. No one in the whole new country of Belorussia had the technology to repair Gore-Tex. I took my seat in the bus and tried to lean back into the tear. The engine started and we continued on, eastward toward Minsk.

It was such a long and important road—the only road, in fact, be-tween two republic capitals. Why hadn't they built it properly? It made no sense. This choppy two-lane catastrophe was all ruts and pointless switchbacks—worse than the worst American country lane. The bus bounced furiously and my head banged against the window every time I dozed off. I was trying to keep my back pressed up against the seat, but the bus jerked and tipped on the curves and rattled over the potholes and I kept needing to readjust myself. Each time I turned, a puff of down squirted out into the air and I wanted to cry out: "This is so unfair."

But was it? How weak I was. Really and truly weak. What was my coat problem compared to the suffering of the Soviet Union? Sixty million tortured and killed. Millions more exiled. Poverty for the rest. In front of me a pair of men turned the lapels of their thin wool coats up and fell fast asleep. What did they earn each month? Forty dollars? Fifty maybe? Certainly not enough to buy even a damaged Eddie Bauer Permafrost. And what kind of coat had they given my father-in-law when he'd been sent to the Arctic, to the labor camp that he claimed wasn't really a labor camp?

I tried to imagine the thoughts that went through my father-in-law's head during his exile. How had he preserved himself? How had he reached that strong-charactered moment where physical suffering became an irrelevant detail? I cleared my mind. I imagined Cold as something abstract—something completely separate from me. Once separate, I started to shrink it down: from an iceberg to a snowball to an ice cube.

Just when I thought I had reduced it to a harmless blue marble, a tune appeared at the very bottom of my thoughts. It was something from long, long ago. From the very beginning of the whole Russia thing. It came clearer. Yes, the song was from a college musical I'd seen freshman year—an adaptation of Gogol's short story *The Overcoat*. It concerned a poor clerk who spends his life's savings on a new coat only to die of exposure when his coat is stolen. The lyrics of the title song of the musical came back to me now:

An overcoat! To keep one warm.
An overcoat! A friend in the storm.

I found that I was suddenly able to remember the whole song, and the cold rushed back into my body as I sang it. My back went numb. My teeth chattered. And the tune kept playing in my head—all the way on the bus to Minsk and then on the overnight train from Minsk to Moscow. I sang it to myself the following morning on the streets of Moscow as I went from department store to department store:

When your life is tearing at the seams,
An overcoat gives life to your dreams!

By the time I had walked the length of the Arbat and made a full circle of the Moscow Garden Ring, the feathers in the upper bulkhead of my coat had all blown away. It was three in the afternoon and the sun was gone. Cold air filled in where the down had been and the back flap sputtered in the wind that swept over the Patriarch Ponds and down the alley of spindly linden trees known as "The Boulevard." In Moscow's new stores I'd found Braun coffee machines, Toblerone chocolates, and light Hugo Boss suits for spring. I'd found hundreds of pounds of Norwegian smoked salmon and vinyl covers that fit the latest model of BMW exactly, but there were no coats. There were Russian nesting dolls with the faces of the last ten American presidents painted on them, there were fake Orthodox icons inlaid with fool's gold, there were wing-tipped leather shoes from Italy, but there were no coats.

I saw a travel agency with a poster of Egypt in the window. It looked very warm. I went inside. They had camel treks from Luxor to the Red Sea. They had gambling tours of Monte Carlo and the Gold Coast of Spain. And they had airplane tickets to America.

I bought one and flew to New York the next morning.

༄

The best, most miraculously American thing of all was that I
didn't even need to buy a new coat. I had the airport limousine drop
me off at an Eddie Bauer retailer on lower Broadway. I lay the
wounded Permafrost on the counter and the salesman said he would
replace it free of charge.

"I'm sorry, guy," he said, his fingers wiggling in the hole. "This
really shouldn't happen to a Permafrost." He went into the stock-
room and came back with a new coat.

"Here," he said, "try this."

In the time I'd been away, a successor to the Permafrost had been
invented—the Eddie Bauer Arctic Explorer. Whereas the Permafrost had been a dull forest green, this one was electric blue. It was
more elegant than the former coat—tucked and plaited attractively
at the waist and tapered at the sleeves. And it was warmer. Much,
much warmer. Warm enough to protect me from a hundred Russian
winters. The stitching was twice as sturdy. It was good—extremely
good. It was so good that I wanted to show it off. I called my father
and told him to bring my brother Cam and meet me at a restaurant
in Chinatown.

༄

"What kind of coat is that?" Cam said blinking at me. "It's like an
Everest coat or something. Is it reversible?"

My brother was looking more fit than I'd seen him since high
school. I knew from a few brusque phone calls that he'd had some
success while I'd been away. But seeing him now drove home how
much life had turned around for him. Cam had always had a thing
for superheroes who could change their form. When he'd lucked
into a temp assignment at an animation company he'd finally made

use of this obscure passion. *Shapeshifter,* a rare comic book from the 1960s he'd shown to his boss, got optioned for a television deal, and now Cam was helping to produce the movie. Money literally fell out of my brother's pockets in crumpled balls when he took his hand out to shake mine.

"Yeah, well, it's called an Arctic Explorer," I said to him. "It's not reversible, but the hood detaches."

Delicious appetizers appeared. I counted the total on the plate, divided it by three in my head and quickly ate my share. When I had finished, Cam noticed me drinking the dipping sauce with a teaspoon and pushed one of his dumplings toward me. I ate it. I looked up. They were both staring at me.

"So," my father said, "when is the Russia Phase going to end?"

I poured the dumpling sauce out of my teaspoon back into the common bowl. "I don't know," I muttered, "soon as the job's over, I guess."

My father adjusted his belly so that it hung symmetrically in front of him. "Daniel," he said, "your brother asked me not to say anything, and I realize you may not want to hear this, but I think Russia is a losing proposition. It's not panning out like everyone thought it would. An investment-banker patient of mine just fired all his Russian analysts."

"What'd he do?" I asked. "Send them back to Russia?"

"Back on the boat," Dad said and popped the last dumpling in his mouth.

"How 'bout you?" Cam asked. "When are you getting back on the boat?"

"They're expecting me in Moscow on Friday."

"What're you doing until then?"

"I . . . uh . . . I guess I'll check out what's going on at my old apartment."

My father cleared his throat. Cam smiled and started doing calligraphy on a napkin. Then he looked at me dead on.

"Is Mrs. Zhivago still there?" he asked.

"Katya? Yeah, she's still there."

A waiter wheeled over a cart with a whole Peking duck on it. The neck was broken, allowing the head to touch the golden-brown back. The waiter sliced pieces of the crisped skin off and placed them one by one on rice pancakes. He dribbled hoisin sauce and sliced scallions on top and folded each of them up with two spoons. When everyone had a portion, Cam rubbed his hands together and stretched his arms out.

"Well, why don't you stay with me until you go back?" he said. "I bought a place. It's like all the way the hell out on Avenue B, but it was cheap."

"A straight shot to me on the bus, if you take the Second Avenue line," Dad said.

I had shoved half the duck pancake in my mouth. The Sweetness of the hoisin sauce, one of the Five Chinese Jewels of the Taste Sense, mixed with two of the other jewels in my mouth: the Bitterness of the scallion and the Saltiness of the duck. I chewed and swallowed and crammed the rest of it in my mouth and nodded yes, not to Cam, not to my father, but to the duck, sitting there with still more golden skin on its carcass.

The windows in Cam's apartment went from floor to ceiling and he didn't have any curtains. As I was falling asleep on his futon couch, I thought that I should tell him about Mom's trick of hanging sheets from coat hangers.

But when I woke the next morning I looked out my brother's living-room window and realized that he might not want curtains

after all. His building bordered Tompkins Square Park—once one of
the most forlorn lots in Manhattan. It had always seemed to me that
when you really bottomed out, when you unequivocally punted on
life, you ended up in Tompkins Square. There had been a village of
tent dwellers down there just a few years ago, and bleary, broken
men used to wander its walkways as often as patrol cars and baby
strollers passed below me now. Here again Cam's eye for spotting
shapeshifters had paid off. When I stopped thinking about the tents
of the past and just looked at the park for what it was—what it was
rapidly becoming—I saw that Cam's view was nothing short of
spectacular.

There was a quaint dusting of snow over the resodded greenways,
and a few brown leaves clung to the old oaks near the Temperance
Fountain. Across the way a work crew dismantled the last of the
scaffolding on a townhouse they'd just finished refacing. I was suddenly furious.

"Who the hell do they think they are, fixing up that building?"

But where had that voice come from? It was a weird Soviet
voice—sad, jealous, resentful. Jesus, what did I care what they did
with that building?

I jumped out of bed and tried to shake the voice out of my head.
I draped my new coat over my shoulders and paced back and forth
across the big open living room. But the voice still muttered on. It
muttered about the unfairness of it all, about America's unearned
opulence, about the excessive amount of space in this one-person
apartment. Out of the corner of my eye I thought I saw where
the voice was coming from. Someone was tracking me. Crossing the
room as I crossed. I looked to my right and saw him—a strange,
hunched man scuttling in the shadows along the back wall. I turned
to face him. He did the same.

It was then that I remembered that for some stupid reason, probably inspired by a comic book, Cam had decided to mirror the entire rear wall of his apartment. I walked toward the mirror and looked at myself walking. I seemed to trudge, barely lifting my feet. My coat hung over my naked body like a big blue pelt.

I stopped a foot away from my reflection. Two new furrows marked the sides of my mouth. A kind of middle-aged muzzle was emerging. I turned away from the front view and glanced sidelong at my profile. What early hominid was this? It was as if with each month I'd been in Russia I'd been going backward along that picture of human evolution: from proud, progressive *Cro Magnon* to dimwitted but tool-using *Australopithecus.* My lower jaw jutted out and my cranium appeared smaller and sloped at an angle unworthy of *Sapien sapiens.*

I stuck my lips out and puckered. I went "ooh, ooh," like an ape. I scratched my underarms like a monkey. I blew the air from my cheeks.

Out came a whistle.

I stopped immediately. Bad luck—an invitation to the evil eye itself. Everyone knew that whistling indoors brought poverty. And Cam with this new place and all this great new money, well, you know . . . I tried to remember what it was the Russians did to reverse an unlucky thing like whistling indoors. Did you spit over your shoulder? Did you throw salt?

The alarm clock went off in the next room. I heard Cam yawn on the other side of the wall. The bedroom door flew open and he walked out wearing a red silk robe with twin F-16 jet fighters embroidered on its lapels. "Hey buddy," he said. He stepped into the bathroom and started to whistle.

It was a very catchy tune. Something from the 1930s. Something that must be a joy to whistle.

I felt my mouth puckering again. I felt my cheeks fill with air and I whistled. I couldn't stop myself. I found that I was not only whistling but also listening to myself whistling. I was making that warbling kind of whistling sound, the sort of sound they made in old musicals. I never knew I could make that sound. With the Russian prohibition on whistling, I hadn't whistled in years and in the interim something seemed to have changed in the shape of my lips. I had become a fantastic whistler. I sounded like a canary—a canary on a short furlough from the mineshaft of the Russia Phase.

"When is the Russia Phase going to end?" What a strange question for Dad to have asked. As if after all these years Russia could still be a phase! Oh, please, Russia wasn't a phase. It wasn't even just a physical place anymore. Russia was my life. The lens through which I had chosen to look at life. I couldn't just slip out of it like Houdini cheating his way out of a knot. Russia was all knots: once you escaped from one all you did was get yourself tied up in another. I just had to accept it. I could escape Russia about as easily as I could escape my own character.

Besides, what was I supposed to do without Russia? At least with GlobeNet I was respected. Russians often called me "Mr. Daniel" and Americans in Russia referred to me by my title: "Director of Former-Soviet Acquisitions." No small accomplishment for a man with a weak character.

There were hundreds of television stations in Russia and I had promised to acquire them all for GlobeNet. It would be incalculably weak to quit now, to leave GlobeNet in the lurch. Especially when I could feel the wisps of strength starting to build in my temperament. I had a new coat now. With that coat who knew how powerful I could grow and what obstacles I could overcome? Maybe someday, everyone, Russian and American alike, would see me coming, smile, shake my hand and say: "It's always a pleasure to see you, Daniel. You have such a strong character."

Cam sauntered out of the bathroom, a towel around his head like a Sikh.

"Cam," I asked, "do you think I have a weak character?"

He cocked his head at me and screwed up his eyes. "A weak character?" he said. "What the hell does that mean?"

Cam went to work, leaving me alone with my ruminations and his back issues of *Shapeshifter*. Over the course of the morning I developed a little routine. I would read an installment of *Shapeshifter* and then I'd pick up the phone and dial the first six digits of my home number. My thumb would float above the seventh digit for as long as a minute. Then I would put the phone back in its cradle and return to *Shapeshifter*.

"Abandon all form!" the Shapeshifter would cry out and begin his transformation. First he would turn into a swirling blue cloud. Then he would shout "Take shape!" and the cloud would reconfigure— sometimes as an animal, sometimes as an electromagnetic field, sometimes as a larger, more powerful version of a man. You could always tell the new form was the Shapeshifter by the pulsing edge of blue surrounding his character.

In episode two I found the Shapeshifter's signature superhero weakness: he had no permanent form. He could hold each shape for only three hours. After that he'd have to retreat into shapelessness again and reemerge as something else. Like all superhero powers, shapeshifting was as much a curse as it was a gift. "She would love me," the Shapeshifter exclaims tragically at the end of episode five, "if I could only hold my form!"

The poor Shapeshifter. I knew how he felt. I read the bubble over his head again and again. I dialed my home number for the fifteenth time. But this time, for some reason, my thumb hit the final digit. I heard Katya's voice on the answering machine:

"Two-four-three, eight-seven-eight-one," she said. "Leave a message for Yekaterina or the Gold Star Car Service. Beep!"

I hung up immediately. I read more comic books. I dialed again. The answering machine once more. I hung up. I read another three episodes. I dialed my number. Katya and the Gold Star Car Service. I hung up. "Take shape!" the Shapeshifter cried out, again and again. I pulled on my clothes, threw on my coat and set out from Tompkins Square Park, west, into Chelsea.

Cam's was not the only neighborhood in Manhattan in transition. When I rounded the corner of my old block I saw that Eighth Avenue had brightened. Instead of a dark, dirty furrow, it now seemed more like a narrow isthmus of prosperity connecting my building to the mainland of the good life. The clean-up that had started to the south in the early eighties had resumed and was now making its way up past Twenty-third Street. It was possible to imagine that a stretch of exclusivity beginning below Houston would one day spread north along the West Side, past Hell's Kitchen, all the way to Harlem. Every store on my block sold muffins. The police station across the street had grown quiet and peaceful and appeared to be more in the business of handing out traffic tickets than dealing with violent offenders.

I looked at the buzzer panel and saw Katya's name, written in both Latin and Cyrillic characters. A Gold Star Car Service sticker had been stuck to the outside of her buzzer—marking territory but not yet an integral part of the nameplates beneath the glass.

I pushed her button and waited. No response. I pushed again. Still nothing. Finally I took out my key and let myself in. I climbed up the six floors and opened my own door for the first time in nearly a year.

The air inside the flat was warm and stifling. I took off my coat and sat down at the coffee table. I had noticed in the ExSSR that Russians liked a room to be about five degrees warmer than was comfortable—a little bit of extra heat, just in case. Katya had achieved this effect in our apartment by sealing all the windows twice with plastic. Two space heaters, switched off but still warm, were set up on either side of the living room.

And the living room—it had become a kind of poor mock-up of the Konstantinovs' living room in St. Petersburg. Polyester lace curtains hung over the windows in place of my mother's sheets. All the assorted bric-a-brac from Katya's suitcases—small Orthodox icons, birch chips with peasant village scenes burned in them, a biography of Bob Dylan in Serbo-Croatian—all this stuff had been exhumed and spread out over the walls and floors. A few pieces of cheap antique furniture gave a fussy grandma's-house feel to it all.

But there was also a sad disorder. Drawers were open. Piles of clothes were scattered about. A hundred different books—Russian and English—lay bent back, furiously bookmarked or open-faced on the floor, as if she had been trying to research some impossible term paper.

I did not know if there was a place for me in all this. I picked up a pile of her underwear, folded it, and put it back in a drawer. I gathered a stack of books and put them in alphabetical order on a shelf. It broke my heart, the chaos that had come upon such a neat and arranged person. But just as I was about to start in on the bedroom I saw the coat.

It was a huge leather sheath, smothering one of my mother's chairs. The man who wore it was a two-hundred-pounder with big hulking shoulders and an inscrutable stare. Misha, in other words. I went over and touched it. It was soft and strong. A thousand-dollar coat, at least. I dropped the pile of clothes in my hand and reached for a piece of paper.

"Katya, I'm back," I wrote. "Call me at Cam's if you want to see me." I left the number and backed out of the apartment. I walked briskly, almost sprinting out of the neighborhood. I was all the way to Avenue A when I realized I'd forgotten my Arctic Explorer.

I hid out at Cam's for the rest of the week. The day of my return to Russia loomed closer and closer and I found myself dwelling on the miserable bus ride to Minsk, the windy cafeteria, the bony gray soup, and the fishy eggs. When I closed my eyes I saw beef suspended in gelatin.

I needed things and I wasn't doing anything about it. I needed a birth certificate. I needed a medical check-up and I had two cavities to fill. I needed a huge number of consumer goods but I couldn't seem to list what they might be. There were by now many Western products available in Russia, but the inventory in the post-Soviet stores seemed as if it had been collected during the haphazard spree of a desperate shopper. There were staplers but no staples, jeans but no socks. If you weren't careful you could end up carrying a redundant suitcase halfway around the world.

Most of all, I needed my Arctic Explorer. I brooded over it and over Katya. Both of them seemed held hostage by that huge leather coat. I lay like a sick man on Cam's futon couch and waited for her call.

On the evening before my departure Cam came home and we ordered in. Cam tipped back with his beef chow fun in his big red adjustable armchair and studied his Shapeshifter storyboards. For some reason the sight of him pissed me off. Here I was, barely holding it together, having to go back to Russia, a place that Cam couldn't even imagine, and there he sat all snug and cozy in that ridiculous Barcalounger.

"You're really into this stupid Shapeshifter thing," I said to him finally.

"Yeah, so? You're really into this Russian gulag thing."

I put down my egg roll.

"But Cam," I resumed, "I mean, Russia's a country. The Shapeshifter's a comic book. I'm living through a political phenomenon. The end of the Soviet Union—it's the most important event of our generation."

"Shapeshifter's cooler," Cam said and turned a page without looking at me.

"You're so ignorant. Why don't you read a real book for a change?"

"Real books are boring."

"You're the epitome of the ignorant American."

Cam folded up his storyboards and took off his glasses. He massaged his eyeballs. I clenched my fists, expecting him to shout at me, or worse, take a swing. But Cam slid his hands from his face and lay them flat on his thighs like the Buddha. He spoke to me calmly, the master of his temper.

"You know, Daniel," he said finally, "you could learn a thing or two from the Shapeshifter."

"Oh, really? Like what?"

"The Shapeshifter doesn't get bogged down. He gets himself in a mess—he changes."

"Some things you can't change."

"Like what?"

"Like . . . like, I don't know, your character, for example. If you have a weak character you have a weak character. That's just your lot in life. You can't get out of it, like, I dunno, like Houdini getting out of a knot."

"The Shapeshifter would disagree with you on that one, buddy boy."

"Oh, really? Well, I don't think the Shapeshifter is such a great authority on character. He has no permanent form!"

"Who, Daniel, has any permanent form? Houdini was a Hungarian Jew. He came here and became an Italian escape artist—just another shapeshifter. There's no shame in it. Americans can get out of anything. That's what we're good at."

I stared down and kicked a nail that was sticking up from one of the floorboards.

"I don't know why we're talking about all this," I said. "The Shapeshifter is a stupid superhero."

"The Shapeshifter is an American, Daniel. And you know what? The Shapeshifter wouldn't go to Russia without his stupid coat."

Cam's taunt bit at me as I started out coatless toward the west, my hands thrust in my pockets, the wind picking up and blowing trash in my face. "Abandon all form!" echoed in my ears and I felt like a swirling blue cloud floating across Broadway, across University, Fifth, Sixth, and Seventh. I shuddered as I approached my own building almost in the way I shuddered when I thought of beef suspended in gelatin. I walked up the stoop and stepped into the inner lobby. I turned to the panel of buzzers, ready to punch out its little black eyes. Ibarra in 6B, Gurkin in 6C, and then, there, finally, Konstantinova/Константинова in 6D. My finger hovered above the buzzer and I paused. The Gold Star Car Service sticker had been hastily ripped off. All that remained was a fragment of the decal: the final letters "I-C-E."

I thrust my key into my lock and bounded up the stairs. I threw open my door.

All the iconography had been removed from the walls. The clothes had been packed up and stowed neatly. The polyester lace curtains had been taken down and replaced by my mother's sheets. And in the center of the room, draped over a chair like a fur on a throne for a restored monarch, was my royal-blue coat. I sat down and wrapped its sleeves around me. My rival's leather coat was gone—banished from the kingdom, it would seem. I was lord over all I surveyed. All I had to do was plug myself back into the Daniel slot. I had a brief moment of comfort.

It was all there in front of me—the very shape of my once and future life—the counter where we would roll out dumpling dough again. The bed where we would have our strange, deep sex. And I could see before me a series of future scenes that were as clear as memories: a weird walk down Brighton Beach Avenue, adhering strictly to nineteenth-century protocol; an admonition against whistling during a dinner party; an eerie silence imposed in an argument at its most crucial point; a viewing of a Russian feature film followed by a sad session of mourning for the loss of a country I never really had.

Whose slot was this really? In a way it was neither mine nor Katya's. It was a space created by an odd moment in time, when everything seemed deeply unsure of itself—a strange world of incomplete metamorphosis for creatures who could bear neither Russia's cocoon nor America's free flight.

"Take shape," I whispered to myself. I put on my coat and walked out the door.

℘

The rain that had begun as a drizzle had frozen and turned into wet snow. The wind had shifted over to the northeast and the precipitation was driven parallel to the ground straight into my eyes.

The gust caught the edges of my coat and blew it wide open. I tried
to hail a taxi. They were all off-duty or full. I thought I sighted one
free cab but a man in a tank top charged past screaming, "Mine,
mine," and grabbed it. I started eastward. In this weather it would
take me forty-five minutes to get home. I could handle it though. I
had my new coat.

When I left the protection of the buildings along Twenty-second
Street I caught a full gale coming down Seventh Avenue. Parked cars
had become whitish mounds, skyscrapers—obscure, glowing phan-
toms. Blown-out umbrellas cartwheeled down the streets and all the
storekeepers had pulled down their metal grates. I stepped off a curb
into a deep, icy puddle. Slush washed over the tops of my boots and
accumulated at my toes. I could barely make out whether the traffic
lights were red, green, or yellow.

I still had my hand up in the air in that pointless-but-hopeful New
York gesture, as if I could conjure a taxi out of thin air. And really
the snow was so thick by now that it was completely possible a cab
might see me in my electric-blue coat before I saw it. Which is what
happened. An off-duty limousine—a black Lincoln—pulled around
the corner and stopped. The automatic window came down.

"You're for the east?" a voice said from the darkness.

"Yes," I said.

The driver muttered something to himself and then hit the automatic lock release. I got in. The driver was barely visible from the
back seat. Different stickers for rock bands, nightclubs, and cigarettes
were plastered over the partition and I could only make him out between the decals.

"It's okay if I smoke?" he said to me.

"Sure."

"Good."

He didn't seem to want to get going right away. He opened the door to keep the light on and counted a handful of cash. When it was all straight, he put the wad of bills in his pocket and started up the car.

"This weather is shit," he said as he pulled down Seventh Avenue. "I hate driving in this shit."

"Yeah, I know."

"No, really, do you know? It's shit, really shit."

I couldn't make out his eyes in the rearview mirror—the brim of his chauffeur's cap concealed them. I could see his hands on the wheel. They were large but somehow delicate. His shoulders were half a foot broader than my own and they filled out the full frame of an expensive leather coat.

"I know the weather's shit," I said finally, "but it beats Russia, I guess."

"Ah, so you know our Russian winter?"

"Yes."

The driver powered his window open and looked up in the rearview mirror again. "I tell you something, Mister. You feel this coming in the window now? This weather is shit. *Real* shit. It's not better than Russia, I tell you. In Russia they have a dry snow. In Russia they let you use the chains. Here, no chains."

"Well," I said, "they don't let you use the chains because they destroy the roads."

"And then they fix the roads. No problem. Everybody has a job. Mister, you mind if I stop one second? The engine making noise I don't like."

"Sure, okay."

He grabbed an oily rag, popped the hood, and slid out of the car with the engine still running. I tried to get a glance at his face but the open hood was in the way. I could see his arms working on some piece of machinery inside the engine. When he tugged at it, the car revved and roared. He pulled it again and again and the car roared louder. Then there was a sucking noise and the sound of something clearing a valve. The idle of the car came down several notches. He jumped back in.

"That's better," he said, this time in Russian with an accent from the deep provinces.

"Seems like you really know cars," I answered back in Russian.

We turned east on Fourteenth. The driver took no notice that we now spoke in his native language. He powered down the other front window and shouted back at me. "You know, brother, you're wrong. I'm not particularly interested in cars. I am interested in machines. That's mostly because I'm interested in how things work."

"You're a mechanic?"

"Once. Once I worked with machinery. Very complicated machines I worked on. Are you familiar with the city of Murmansk?"

"In the north, right?" I said.

"That's right. Above the Arctic Circle. I fixed machines up there when I was in the navy."

"Oh, yeah?"

"Yeah."

I was hoping not to continue this conversation. I didn't say anything, but he didn't either. It was as if he was trying to out-silence my silence. Finally I spoke.

"What kind of machines did you fix up there in Murmansk?"

"Atomic submarines."

"Hmm."

"Yes. Now *that's* a machine. So subtle."

"I'm sure it is."

"Yes, I'm sure you're sure. You're sure of everything, aren't you? You're a smart guy. But you know what's an even more interesting machine?"

"What?"

"This country. These United States. This country is something unbelievable. It's a composite machine. An interconnected crushing web of machines and micro-machines all working in concert toward a common objective. There are devices here: hardware as well as software. There is one machine here that measures your profits. It looks in your wallet and in the pockets of your pants when you're sleeping. It figures out the minimum that can support you. It looks at the woman next to you and calculates the algorithm. It looks for the answers to two questions: How much does he have? How much can he afford to lose?"

I nodded along with him. It was only another ten blocks to Cam's house. At best he would get another few anecdotes in. He lit a third cigarette and offered the pack to me, backhand, over his shoulder. I took one—in Russia I had learned to smoke out of politeness. I leaned into him and let him light me up with the orange-hot cylinder waving unsteadily near my face. The traffic signal ahead turned red. He grabbed the wheel quickly and slammed on the breaks. My face hit the back of the seat, breaking the cigarette in two.

"Sorry," he said, "you okay?"

"Yeah."

"Okay. Good. So I'll tell you about the next machine. There's a second machine that is in charge of obsessions and catastrophes," he continued blowing smoke out the window through the corner of his mouth. "It's more sophisticated than the first machine. It analyzes the raw data that the first machine gathers. It channels everything you can lose in a single direction. Usually in the direction of a woman.

"This isn't too complicated for you, is it? You're an educated man. You know what I'm talking about."

"Actually," I said, "I have no idea what you're talking about."

"Of course you do. Of course you do. You, of all people, should know." He paused and shook his head and was silent.

"Say you meet this obsession," he began again after a minute. "The perfect woman, let's say. She's intelligent. She understands you. When you play chess with her, she beats you, but she loses sometimes when you play. Just enough so that you don't get frustrated. She's with you. You're in this together. I mean, you can't make it in this country alone. When you're alone, this country will eat you whole, like a fish."

"Yeah?"

"Yeah. Definitely."

"Oh."

"Now, as I was saying, you have this perfect girl. But then the machine, it goes to work on her teeth."

"Her teeth?"

"Yeah, her teeth. Her teeth are a mess. Bad government. Bad genes. The machine can use any excuse."

"So?"

"So her teeth break. And you decide to fix them. Maybe you drive to Queens to fix them. Maybe you hear about another dentist over in Jersey. You drive and drive. And then the principle of driving is established. You keep driving. In time, another thing breaks. One time you drive all the way to Utah to fix it. Mister, you know how many hours it takes to drive to Utah?"

"How many?"

"Depends," said the driver, "depends on the car. Driving to Utah can break your car, believe me."

We had reached Tompkins Square Park. We'd driven by Cam's house once and now we were circling back toward it again. The new bars and clubs around the park glittered through the sleet.

Someone outside the Odessa Restaurant waved at the driver as the car passed by.

"Anyway," he continued, "the important thing is, you understand that to keep this girl you have to keep driving your whole life. But that's okay. She's a perfect girl, right? And you're with her. Sure, you have your problems. People come and go. But you can work it out.

"Maybe one day you're shopping. Things are looking up for a change. And she sees this coat. She says, 'You'd look beautiful in that coat.' So you buy it. I mean, you don't want it, but it will make her happy, right? So you spend a thousand dollars on it, but it's not enough.

"One day, maybe even today, maybe she does something or maybe sees something you don't want her to see. So you start to argue. It gets pretty bad. Very bad, actually. And then all of a sudden you realize—the machine and her—they're working together against you! The knot pulls tight. Together, they are so powerful. And it's all you can do to remember to pull your fancy coat out of the closet.

"But the machine won't even let *that* go. The coat catches on something in the closet. You pull. It rips. You rip your fucking coat. See? See this bullshit on this thousand-dollar coat?" The driver slid the partition all the way open. He ran his hand to his collar and showed me a long vertical tear in the leather of his coat, just next to the stitching.

"This sort of thing, this malfunction is caused by the third machine," he continued. "Did I tell you about the third machine yet?"

"Not yet," I said.

"Well, this third one is tailored to your character. It's the one that takes the legs out from under you. The one that says, 'You are nothing.' This machine looks at what's left. It looks at your age and your health. It uses the most powerful of Zeno's Eleatic paradoxes—the one where the arrow goes halfway to a wall and then goes halfway of the halfway remaining, and so on. The machine measures how much is left and tries to balance exactly how much it can push each American. Jewish-American, Italian-American—it doesn't matter. It just tries to push you as far as possible within your programming. Do you know this paradox, by the way, Mister?"

"Yes," I said, "I know it."

"Well, if you know it then you know that if the arrow goes more than halfway to the wall in any one shot, then the equation is ruined and it will eventually hit the wall. Have you ever hit a wall at full speed?"

"No," I said.

"Me neither."

He jammed his foot on the accelerator and threw his cigarette butt over his shoulder into the back seat. He used his knees to guide the steering wheel.

"Now this machine has problems. It needs work. The other two machines are perfect, but this machine, well, I've figured it out. It doesn't work for us Russians. It's not adjusted right. And the reason is this: a Russian person is absolutely committed to his direction. He has to be. How else would he survive the idiocy of the Soviet state? He doesn't care about circumstances. He doesn't care if he's gone more than halfway. He doesn't care about the wall. If he hits it, he hits it. Big deal. That's the natural fate for his character." He had his hands back on the wheel and everything was in place again. "Oh, I'm sorry, we've passed your house three times. I should stop. But you know, I can't stop. My foot is on the pedal on the floor. There is no gear shift. Your American cars have me in automatic—that's a bad thing to put in the hands of a Russian. I can just keep my foot here forever."

"You can just stop here."

"Why here? Why not uptown? Why not Brooklyn?"

"Because I live here."

"No, you don't. *You* live in Russia. That's why you speak Russian. You're just visiting. You're experimenting with a different machine."

"My experiment's over," I said.

"Yes? Yes? And what did you learn? What's your analysis? What did you learn?"

Misha turned onto Delancey Street and was speeding east, faster and faster, flying toward the Williamsburg Bridge and the Outer Boroughs. The speedometer waggled back and forth between 80 and 120 mph.

"I learned," I screamed over the roar of air, "I learned that I can abandon all form."

"All form? *All* form? What form?"

"My Russian form!" I yelled.

"And what about your wife? Can you abandon her too?"

The light ahead turned red. Misha swerved into the other lane and a fleet of Chinese delivery trucks blew their horns.

"Yes!" I screamed out. "Yes. I can."

Misha hit the breaks. The wheels locked on a patch of black ice and the car skidded diagonally before stopping just before the Williamsburg's first strut.

"I don't believe you. You can't just escape! She's perfect."

I looked at him now head-on.

"She's not perfect for me."

I unlocked the door and pulled on the handle. Misha hit the auto lock and resealed the door.

"Wait. Do you mean to tell me that you think you can just walk away? That you can end everything? Just that simply? What about the consequences?"

"They're your consequences."

Misha breathed heavily for a full minute. Finally, I heard the automatic lock pop open. I paused. For some reason I felt I should pay him for his services. I reached in my pocket. In addition to a ten-dollar bill I had an envelope from my Moscow travel agent. It would of course take some doing—changing of names on the flight manifest, typing over the old information—there might be some suspicion. But plenty of people knew how to forge documents in Brighton.

"No, no," Misha said when he saw me starting to pay him, "really, you don't have to."

"I insist," I said. I gave him the ten dollars and my return plane ticket to Moscow. "Take this," I said. "I don't want this ticket. Maybe you can use it."

Constructive Abandonment

My procedure had no motion. I had no grounds. No index number had been issued and I could not be referenced by the court. I did not exist as far as Uncontested Divorces was concerned. This annoyed the clerk who heard me. He was a slight man with a long, red braid. He was called Ruby.

"Who is initiating the motion?" Ruby asked and then took a giant bite out of a turkey sandwich.

"I don't know."

"Then how do you expect to have any motion at all? Come on, who's initiating it?" He swallowed.

"But that's what I'm asking *you*," I said.

"*I* can't tell *you* who's initiating the motion."

"Okay. But I'm here. Doesn't it mean that I'm initiating the motion?"

"Not necessarily."

"What should I do, then, to initiate the motion?"

"I can't tell you that, sir."

"Why?"

"Because the law prohibits me from providing legal counsel."

"But I'm not asking for legal counsel. I just want to end this thing."

The clerk put down his sandwich, wiped his hands and then looked at me directly for the first time.

"What are the grounds for the motion, sir?"

"I don't know."

"You need to establish some grounds. Somebody has to have done something wrong. It has to be somebody's fault. Whose fault is it?"

"I don't know."

"Who left whom?"

"It's not exactly clear—"

"Somebody left somebody. *Who* left *whom*?"

"But—"

"*Who* left *whom*?"

۵

Who left whom? I found this unfair and difficult to answer. In Russia, no clerk would be so bold. In Russia a person gets married at a ministry and divorced at a post office. What business was it of this Ruby?

What *were* my grounds and who *was* initiating the motion? Ruby offered me only one clue. He had me purchase a divorce kit that contained twenty blank forms in quadruplicate. These forms implied all kinds of culpability. There were medical certificates to document physical abuse. There were worksheets to calculate the cost of rearing an abandoned child. There were annulment forms that required the intercession of a religious official. There were all these opportunities for confession but no instructions.

So what to do about my scenario? Which form did I use to express the fact that Katya was painfully unclear? How would the court come to understand that the mysterious force that ruined our marriage was my own character—as strong perhaps as any character but hopelessly divided against itself when it came to Katya? And how would Ruby process the despair of beef suspended in gelatin?

As it started to sink in that I was actually beginning a divorce process, the shameful phrases from my parents' divorce bubbled up in my head: "It will be a protracted custody battle," and "I feel no desire to contest that issue," and "She's asking for alimony *in perpetuity.*" I had been the smallest of children when I'd heard that kind of talk and it had sounded like aliens speaking. Surely these words weren't meant for me. They were for men like my father—men who marry four times and wake with the dawn to pay down their debts.

And when I asked my father if he could help me with the forms, he only shook his head and backed away, terrified. "Get a lawyer," he said. "Get a good lawyer. An extremely good lawyer."

I knew only one lawyer: Seymour K. Brimmer, Esq., the man who had first counseled Katya and me to marry. And I thought as I headed back to his office that in a way it was all his fault and that it was only fitting that he should fix what he himself had put in motion.

The same line still waited outside the Consulate of the Dominican Republic near his door, but the consulate had expanded and now occupied half of what had been Seymour's suite. He no longer had a secretary, nor a corridor, nor a proper desk. He had just a single room with a computer credenza. We sat very close, in very small chairs.

"I am *not* a divorce lawyer," Seymour began. "My business is immigration and naturalization. My knowledge of divorce is coincidental. It arises from the anecdotal, seeing how one common consequence of marriages between Americans and foreign nationals is divorce. I can represent you, if you like, but I repeat, I am *not* a divorce lawyer."

"I don't want to be represented. I just want some information."

"Information is not *cheap!*" he said, and as he said it, he ascended a musical scale with "cheap" marking the high note. Then, once up there in the higher registers, he descended the scale for emphasis: "Information is not cheap." He made a break and began in a new key.

"This is your, let's see," he rifled through a filing cabinet. "Let's see . . . this is not your first visit, I see. Client appeared three-eleven-ninety-two with one Yekaterina Romanovna Konstantinova. After inquiring, client implied he was *in love* with Ms. Konstantinova, expressed interest in *intent to marry,* reviewed process for completing forms pursuant to statute so-on-and-so-forth of U.S. immigration and naturalization laws.

"It's a pretty lengthy record already. Clearly, this is not your first consultation. I will, regrettably, have to charge you for my time."

"How much?"

"One-fifty."

I gave him the money. Seymour quickly pocketed it and his demeanor changed from a pre-meal anxiety to that of a full man.

"So what is it you want to know?" he said, lighting a cigarette, inhaling deeply.

"I want to know the grounds. I want to know who is at fault. I want to know who initiates the motion."

"Excellent questions!" he said. "Important questions!"

༄

When Seymour had finished his explanation, I left him and went to the coffee shop below his office. I sat in a booth and sorted the contents of the divorce kit. On the first form, in a space marked "Grounds" I wrote what Seymour had told me to write. I wrote "Constructive Abandonment." Below the grounds was a short essay section.

"Describe the grounds," asked the form.

I wrote what Seymour told me to write: "On or about February 1, 1993, the defendant, Yekaterina Romanovna Konstantinova, began refusing to have sexual relations with the plaintiff." This seemed more than enough, but Seymour had insisted I go on. "There was no good reason for the refusal of sexual relations," I wrote. "There was no mental or physical reason why the defendant refused sexual relations."

There was more to write. "In spite of the fact that the plaintiff on many occasions pleaded with the defendant to have sexual relations with him, the defendant refused." Then a beautiful coda: "The parties have not had sexual relations since February 1, 1993."

Seymour had concluded that constructive abandonment was the only kind of grounds that worked for me. It was actually too complicated. I didn't understand.

"You see, it has to be *her* fault," Seymour had explained, "because you want to be in control. It's very important that *you* control the divorce process. For you to control the divorce process, it has to be her fault. That's the way the law works. She errs, you complain. What did she do? She left you. What do you do? *You* divorce *her.* Q.E.D."

"But she didn't leave me exactly, Seymour," I said.

"Right. Exactly. That's the problem. She came back from wherever she was—Utah, you said, right?—and came right back to *your* house. But you, see, *you* screwed up. You left. Now *she's* the one oc-cupying the marital residence. She's in the house and you're not, so it's really *you* who left *her* as far as the law is concerned."

"But I didn't really leave—"

"Yes, you did. You left. You left her all alone. It's your fault."

"Is it really my fault?" I asked.

"It is," Seymour said. "It is in the eyes of the law. That's why we have to figure out a way to make it *her* fault."

"And how do we do that?" I asked.

"Well, that depends. What do you think she's going to do? Do you think she's going to contest?"

"I don't know. She might. But I don't think she would even know what that means. Why?"

"Well, you could try infidelity, but infidelity's tough to prove. If you think there's a chance she'll contest, it's better not to open that can of worms."

"So what do I do?" I asked.

"Well, there's something obscure, but it might work. For you to make a legal complaint against her, she has to have left you in some other way. She has to have left without physically leaving. See what I mean?"

"No, not at all."

Seymour cleared his throat. "What makes a marriage a marriage, my friend? S-E-X. If there had been no sex, then you would have been just two people sharing an apartment, not husband and wife. So, you see, if you can show that she refused sex then the court will see that *she's* the one who left the marriage. That way she doesn't have to have left your residence, just your bed."

"But she didn't leave my bed!" I'd wanted to say to Seymour. That wasn't the problem. We were making real progress there. It was the *marriage* that was the problem. If there had been no marriage maybe we'd be necking on the G train or making love on a peasant stove in Perm or in a sunken honeymoon suite in Jersey.

But I didn't protest. Instead, I described the circumstances of her constructive abandonment again and again. I wrote them on a form called "The Complaint." I copied them out on "The Judgment," on "The Decision," and confirmed them on something called "The Affirmation of Regularity." I bundled all of it up and took it down to the county clerk's office. From the end of the Uncontested Divorces line I spied the same clerk on desk duty again. I was sure to draw him. Ruby stood leaning on his knuckles with his red braid over one shoulder and his pen tucked behind his ear. He slashed through his opponents one by one. "This is inadequate. File this upstairs with Records. Go to the fourteenth floor to Judgments. *Get this damn thing notarized.*" I arrived with my neat stack and placed it before him. He looked up and I thought I caught a half smile of recognition.

"What's this?" he asked.

"It's my divorce. I've got my grounds."

"That's very nice for you. Congratulations. What do you want me to do with it?"

"I want you to take it. File it away, please."

"*File it away?* Where would I 'file it away,' sir?"

"I mean, don't I just give this to you? Haven't I finished the procedure? Off the record, I mean."

Ruby pressed his lips together and took my papers. "Off the record, let me see. Here's the Complaint, Judgment, Affirmation, Notary Statement, uh huh, yes . . . Regularity . . ." He grew silent. He took in a long breath, held it, and leafed through the rest of the stack. At the last page, he exhaled. "Sir, off the record, I feel obliged to inform you that these documents suck."

He glared down from the counter and blinked.

"The law is not a boat," he continued. "You can't sail it whichever way the wind blows. To get a divorce you must commit to a series of discrete actions and then record those actions in an exact and pre-specified order."

"But my lawyer said I just needed some grounds."

"Sir, and again, I offer this to you totally and completely off the record, if you were to tell me that your lawyer is a five-hundred-pound hairy ape, I would not be in a position to dispute your claim."

"So you're saying it's not over."

"It has not even begun."

"But how does it begin?"

"You must serve a summons and she must answer that summons."

"You mean I have to see her again?"

"You must see her but you must not be seen by her," said Ruby, grown oracular. "The summons must be served, but you cannot serve it. You must find an objective party to serve it. How's her English?"

"Not perfect."

"Then you should be there when it is served, to ensure that it is served correctly and that she understands it. I would advise that you, an intelligent and English-speaking fellow like yourself, I would advise, off the record, that you guarantee the serving."

"Then what?"

"Once the summons is served, you must find a way to get her to sign this waiver," he handed me a new form. "This waiver is her declaration that she agrees to all terms. If she signs this waiver then you are exempt from any moral or financial obligations. If she signs, then your divorce is truly uncontested."

"But what happens if she doesn't sign the waiver?"

"Then, sadly, you and I will never see each other again, because *I* work in *Uncontested* Divorces. Next!"

Before this last discussion with Ruby I'd never wanted to officially engage Seymour K. Brimmer, Esq., as my lawyer. I thought that there would be broad repercussions that could not be anticipated. Again, those divorce phrases from early childhood came to me. "The legal fees were enormous," "I should have settled out of court," or "My lawyer asked for a retainer of *twenty-five-thousand dollars*." But someone had to serve the summons. A blood relative like Cam seemed less than objective and I had no one else I could really trust. All of my friends were shocked or abroad or at graduate school somewhere. So I thought of Seymour. He knew me. He knew my case. He had met Katya. At least he knew the tricks an immigrant could pull in this kind of a mess. These were the kind of things, anyway, that Seymour impressed on me when we met again in the coffee shop underneath his office.

"An immigrant woman," said Seymour, pocketing another $150 payment, "a Russian immigrant woman in this kind of situation is like a cornered animal. Imagine, you are taking the golden key away from her. You are going to take this animal out of her very nice habitat. You're gonna put her on an Aeroflot plane and send her back to godless Russia. What would you do? You'd do anything, I think."

"But Seymour," I said, "that may be true, but why didn't you tell me more about the divorce process? I can't help but think that this whole thing could have been accelerated if you had told me how the entire process is supposed to work."

"I'm sorry. Forgive me. I made the assumption that you were familiar with the basics of the law. I've been practicing for a long time and I don't even think about the summons, the waivers, et cetera. And, well, truthfully, all of us are looking for some kind of commitment. You didn't want to retain me. It was a disincentive for me. If you had retained me to do the whole thing, you'd be done. But you didn't, so you aren't. Don't blame me. I'm not responsible. I can't control your decisions, your emotions. I am *not* a psychiatrist. So what's it gonna be? Are we in this together or what?"

"I don't know, Seymour. Why don't you serve the summons and I'll deal with the rest?"

"But what about the waiver, huh? Who's gonna do that? You gotta get her to sign that waiver." Seymour's eye suddenly gleamed golden, and something passed through my mind. I saw a not-too-distant future in a courtroom, me with a different lawyer, maybe even my father's lawyer, and over in the plaintiff's booth, Katya with Seymour next to her, suing me for alimony in perpetuity.

"No, Seymour," I said. "Just the summons, please."

We met in the early evening in Chelsea on the stoop of my building. I felt weak-kneed as I rounded Seventh Avenue past the former SRO housing unit. The fat cops across the street eyed Seymour. I rang the bell. Katya was there. She buzzed us up.

She was waiting for me on the landing of the sixth floor. "*Nu, Daniel*," she said. "How many winters, how many summers has it been?" She moved toward me. But then the smile on her face faded and she stopped short. Seymour huffed up the last set of stairs. "Good day," he said.

"Why is *he* here?" Katya asked.

"I'll explain later," I said. "I have to stay outside for this first part. Leave the door open, in case you don't understand something."

She looked from Seymour to me and from me to Seymour. Her lips trembled. And then, all at once, the anxiety in her face vanished behind some instinctual flat Soviet expression reserved for interrogations.

Seymour sauntered in and I could hear him unclick his plastic briefcase. "Are you Yekaterina Romanovna Konstantinova?" he asked.

"Yes," she said.

"Is this you?" said Seymour. If he was following our plan, he was by now showing Katya the photograph of herself at our six-month anniversary dinner.

"Can it be me?" she said. "No. I look too ugly. No, it can't be me."

"I would urge you to cooperate, Ms. Konstantinova."

"Yes, yes, that's me."

"Okay, so that's you, right?" asked Seymour.

"Yes, unfortunately."

"And now, Ms. Konstantinova, I must ask you, are you in the military?"

"Yes," she said.

"Really?" Seymour asked.

"Actually . . . No."

"Well, which one is it? Yes or no?"

"No, I am not in the military. Unfortunately," she said.

"I'm asking you because if you are serving in the military you are exempt from all responsibilities in this matter."

"Maybe I should join the military? Is it true they let you keep the gun?"

"It's too late to join now."

"If I had only known . . ."

"Okay, okay," said Seymour, his voice growing shrill. "So that's you in this picture, right? And you are not in the military, right?

Right. Okay. Now, this is your summons. Your husband is suing you for divorce. You must answer this summons within thirty days, or default. Do you understand?"

"Yes."

"Completely?"

"Yes. I understand everything, except for 'summons' and 'default.'"

"Come on!" Seymour cried. "Summons and default! That's the whole point!"

"A summons is a *sudebnaya povestka*," I said from the corridor, "and a default counts as a *neyavka*."

"Ah, now I understand. That's okay. I'll ask you to leave now."

"It would be my pleasure." I heard a briefcase click shut. Seymour walked out of the apartment and handed me the waiver. "She's all yours. And, by the way, off the record, she's still quite a dish, your wife." He scuttled down the stairs and disappeared.

I came around from the stairwell. She held open the door and I went inside and sat at the makeshift coffee table I had nailed together when we had shared this place and I had thought myself a carpenter.

"Katya," I said, "there's this waiver."

"Now what's that? All of these papers. It's so complicated, really. In Russia we do all of this at the post office."

"It's a waiver. It puts an end to all of this. You need to sign it and we have to get it notarized."

She read it through, turned it over, and then read it through again. "Nice waiver," she said.

She reviewed it a little longer and got out her dictionary. She asked me a few questions. I helped her with the words "affidavit," "counsel," and "pursuant." She laughed when she read what I had written for the grounds. Then she smiled open-mouthed for the first time since I'd known her. Her teeth were now white and flawless. She put up some water for tea. I took off my coat. She took off her shoes, her earrings, and her necklace. She wiped some moisture and an eyelash off my cheek. I helped her off with her shirt and her cotton trousers, and she took me inside to our marriage bed where we destroyed the grounds altogether.

୧୨

Only then did I realize how many voices had gathered.

There was Irina, the platinum blonde in Siberia who'd pegged Katya as "a little Communist bitch." There was Katya's father, who'd described her character as "harsh and demanding" and who had advised me to send her back to Russia when I couldn't take her anymore. There was the driver Misha and his insidious machines. There was Seymour K. Brimmer, Esq., who thought of her as just another immigrant gold digger. And there were Cam and my father, standing up in the bleachers and booing her team from the sidelines of the Russia Phase. It was as if an entire Politburo had assembled in my head in the last year and conducted a show trial—not just against Katya but against the entire philosophy of Katyaism.

But now as I moved against her I understood that there was no philosophy. I looked into her eyes—which were open and looking into mine for the first time ever during sex—and I saw that there was only Katya. The blankness of the Soviet interrogation stare was gone from her as were all the labels put upon her by others. We seemed to come untethered from everything people had said, indeed from everything that we'd said to each other. Our experience of each other faded and all resistance left our bodies. The medieval rituals disappeared too, and we turned and rolled and realigned as fluidly as the Shapeshifter—passing from form to swirling cloud to form again.

And as we both reached the end of things, her legs relaxed, came undone, and opened to the horizontal. And I found that I was able to enter that recess in her again as easily as I might have opened a book to a bookmarked page. How I had fantasized about this moment of return!

But even now, as I was both fantasizing and actually experiencing finishing with her, I could sense that it was not some psychospiritual territory that I was regaining. The more the labels faded away the more I saw that getting to this place was as much a question of rhythm and angle and properly applied force as it was a matter of pain and suffering. Once the physical things had been aligned, the reaction came regardless of the rest. And the reaction was intense but typical, surprising but inevitable. She froze and stayed perfectly still. "Yes. There. Exactly," I heard her voice say in my head. And then the two of us softened into each other and fell asleep.

"Chto by sluchilos?" Katya asked me a little before dawn—What would happen?

A police car left the station below and hooted its siren once. Common sparrows were doing away with the night, chirp by chirp, and a flat, dull light started to come through the tops of the windows.

"What would happen if what?" I answered back in Russian.

"If I didn't accept your summons. If I didn't sign your waiver. What would happen then?"

I looked over at her. She had put her nightgown on. She looked as if she hadn't slept. She was facing me, her head propped on one hand.

"It depends on the circumstances," I said.

"Which circumstances?" she rolled over to me and dug her chin into my sternum. "By the way," she said, "your Russian improved while you were away. Before, you spoke like a monkey. Now you sound like a Yugoslav."

"I appreciate that."

"I know you do," her smile faded. "Tell me, though," she said, "what will happen if I don't sign your waiver?"

"Well," I began cautiously, "you could challenge my summons in court, and then we would let a judge decide."

"I see," she kneaded my thigh with her hands for a minute, "and if we went to a judge," she said, "would I get to have some sort of . . . alimony?"

My heart skipped a beat and I fought back a gasp. I shut my eyes tight, hoping that this dawn conversation might not be happening— that it was all just a dream, a late-night/early-morning phantom that would disappear when exposed to light. Maybe I had in fact walked out the door after Seymour had served her the summons and I was now safely back in Cam's apartment, sleeping with a whole width of Manhattan between my lawfully wedded wife and me. I opened my eyes cautiously. Katya was staring at me. She seemed to note every change in my expression.

"Are you frightened of the waiver?" she asked.

"I'm frightened of its implications."

"Do you really want me to sign it?"

"If you signed it, then there would be nothing forcing us to be together. We could be together just because we wanted it. Not because some document or our families or our governments said we were together. No labels. We wouldn't pretend we were making a family. We would just be together. There wouldn't be anything at stake."

"What you mean," she said, "is that if I signed the waiver, you'd have nothing to lose."

I tried to think of a better way to explain it to her so that she would understand. Some simple and sophisticated thing. I searched for the words in Russian and in English, but then I looked at her and I saw her notice the fear in my eyes. I saw that she understood exactly what I meant.

"Yes," I said, "I guess that's what I mean."

Katya turned away and stretched her hands down to her feet. She looked out the window at the precinct.

"Maybe it was your Russian," she said. "I thought something was different, but nothing's changed. You Americans really are all alike. Now that you've won the whole world all you can think about is losing it."

She sighed and, like a cat, climbed back on top of me. She pulled off her nightgown and threw it and all the blankets on the floor.

"Don't worry," she said in a whisper, her mouth up close against my ear. "Don't worry. I plan to sign your waiver."

Katya stayed in town until the divorce was finalized. It actually wasn't as Seymour had explained it. She could have continued on in America. As any immigrant knows, once you have your green card, it's hard to kick you out of the country. I even told her this in a half-hearted way, but when I did, she only looked at me and said, "So? And then what?"

During that last week there were so many things I wanted to clear up—so many mysteries. What had she really been doing in Utah? Did this Misha mean anything to her? But every time I asked a question of substance she looked at me incredulously. She refused to let me mark down the final period. And as the days before her flight disappeared I felt my mouth go dry and my throat tighten as if to prevent any more words from coming out.

239

Her flight was on Aeroflot—actually it was the second half of the ticket she had used to come over to America in the first place. When the day of her departure came, I borrowed Cam's car and picked her up at our apartment. We ended up making it to the airport with too much time to spare. Once I tried to speak.

"Katya, I'm sorry, I—"

"America is for the birds," she said. She was sporting all kinds of brand-new expressions now. We exchanged a glance or two. She read the last hundred pages of a mystery novel. When she finished, she closed the book and threw it in the garbage. She looked at me and spoke.

"Do you think all this was some kind of trick, Daniel?"

"No," I said, "of course I don't. Of course it wasn't."

"But it was."

"It was?"

"Yes, it was. But for another reason than you think. Maybe you think that American citizenship or a green card had something to do with all this. But believe me, it wasn't what I wanted. I wanted you. From the first moment I saw you, I wanted you."

Here she fussed with a bit of cloth that was sticking out of one of her pieces of hand luggage. She turned back to me.

"Maybe it's our national weakness—that as soon as we Russians see something we want, we're convinced that we won't be allowed to have it. We panic. We cheat. We bend the rules to win. And we get so consumed with fighting that we don't stop to ask ourselves if the fight justifies the prize. But I did want you. Once."

"And now?"

"Now it's time to go. Before I came to America, I never knew I wanted so many things. Now it's all I can do to keep myself from wanting more."

A call for boarding was made. She took up her many carry-on

items: garden utensils for her mother, a portable water pump for her father, guitar strings for her sister, and an American storybook for Dasha. I helped her on with her coat. She kissed me on the cheek, her lips just brushing me. I stayed holding the fringes of her coat looking at the floor until the last passenger had boarded.

"It's like you're waiting for some third person to say that it's okay to end this," she said.

I didn't say anything. The Aeroflot stewardess waved at Katya angrily.

"Well," she said, "some people aren't supposed to have families," and with that she slipped away down the jetway.

I stood there, perplexed that this could really be the last of it. I drew a long breath through my lips but when it started to make a whistling sound I stopped myself. I jingled the keys in my pocket and felt with my other hand how high my forehead had become. My breath grew shallow and I looked up to see the last fringes of her fur coat disappear around a corner. It wasn't the same fur coat she had brought to America. That first coat had been a fake. This new one had the ribbing and thickness of real pelts and I wanted to call out to her. I wanted to shout, "What is it? Mink? Ermine? What? Where did you get it? How much did it cost?" But both the coat and the woman who wore it were obscured by the retreating stewardesses. Boarding was closed. "St. Petersburg" was removed from the destination tablet and replaced with "Munich." I listened for something. Some last, wry remark. Some little bit of Russian folk wisdom she'd toss back to me. Some coda. But all I heard was a sucking noise and a rush of air as the crew sealed the door of the plane for the long journey ahead.

Epilogue

Nowadays newscasters and pundits like to say that Communism and the USSR have been "relegated to the dustbin of history." But for me it is not so much a dustbin as it is a filing cabinet or an illusionist's chest of which I make profitable use. Soon after Katya left, GlobeNet proposed that I become their regular consultant on Russian matters. I accepted on the condition that I'd never have to return to the former Soviet Union. This arrangement has suited us well. I am brought into meetings with investors, I make a few well-informed generalizations, and GlobeNet expands and prospers. In the last two years other multinationals—oil companies thirsty for the Caspian reserves, timber concerns out for the Siberian taiga—all of them have brought me in for a day or two. I charge an hourly rate equal to the one my father charges his patients and my business seems to grow of its own accord upward and outward, just as the big bull market jumps from crest to crest.

In fact all of the things that came during the Russia Phase have appreciated in one way or another. My apartment in Chelsea went co-op and I was offered a low buy-in price. The immigrants and old Italian families who used to flavor the corridors with stews and sauces all sold out and moved on to the Outer Boroughs. Young couples, straight and gay, have taken their places, and renovation fever has hit in full force. Our co-op board has grown in power and our lawyer is trying to move the police precinct further west, toward the river.

At the end of the workday I often walk from midtown back down to Chelsea, not because I can't afford a cab but because I enjoy looking up at the last old bits of the city. I feel light and even content during these walks, though I can't help noticing that all the slack is rapidly being taken out of our lives. Housing gets tighter, advertising crowds out the blank spaces, and the Soviet people of the world—those people who open doors for ladies and whose minds are too oblique to value simple financial transactions—they're disappearing and are being replaced by a slicker, more polished version.

Sometimes I hear a snatch of Russian spoken on the street, but when I turn my head to look, instead of seeing the angry, cheated face of a man from the USSR, it's usually a second-generation boy standing there in front of his parents' Range Rover, in from New Jersey for the weekend. Or sometimes it's the stylish progeny of the Russian quasi-mafia, decked out in Armani, heading home after a lackluster day at an expensive American private school. If their polishing goes well, they'll all find good jobs at sturdy Western investment banks.

When I get home there are usually four or five messages from friends. After the long silence they've begun calling again and, as

Katya predicted, I am the only single one among them. My old roommate Anne is married and Elizabeth is engaged to someone we all like. The two of them occasionally recommend me to one of their single women colleagues, and sometimes a group of us will make a day of it and explore the Outer Boroughs.

I had been trying to steer my friends away from Brighton Beach during our urban safaris. I'd told them that I preferred the Indian restaurants of Jackson Heights, or the Irish bars in Woodside, but eventually we ran through all the cuisines of New York, and Little Odessa and its Russian cafés became unavoidable. This past August, with the heat so intense and the city so stifling, I couldn't keep our group from the sea. We took the Q train to the Brighton stop—all the way to the end of the line.

"Which restaurant should we go to? Which one is the *real* Russian place?" my friends ask me.

All of them and none of them are the real Russian place. In this last Soviet part of the city, this enclave filled with emigrants from a country that no longer exists, every doorway has a woman with bleached-blond hair and dark roots. They carry knockoffs of designer handbags and wear wry, disgusted looks. Each one has been working the American welfare system for years but still cannot pronounce words like "the," "very," and "happy."

I take my friends to a restaurant that doesn't seem so Russian. It has the best view and it has a full menu of *zakuski,* soups, roasts, and flavored vodkas. It is poised on the boardwalk halfway between the rusted-out Cyclone at Coney Island and the new Cantonese stores that are slowly displacing the Russian markets over near Sheepshead Bay.

"Toasting, don't the Russians toast? Shouldn't we be toasting?" my friends ask, and yes, yes, I say, there is toasting at any Russian banquet. I show them how you take a pickle or a piece of herring or some dark bread in one hand and a little glass of vodka in the other. I demonstrate how you say something ridiculously ingratiating to the person across from you, how you throw back the vodka and bite down on the appetizer in two broad strokes.

"And what do you say when you clink glasses?" Anne asks, tipsy, just as Americans should be after only one glass of vodka.

"Well, you can say *za zdorovye*—to your health."

"Zazy rova?" Anne asks.

"No," I correct. *"Za zdorovye."*

"Za strosha?"

"No!" I say, this time quite loudly. *"Za zdorovye. Za zdorovye! Za-zdo-rov-ye!"* And as I say this I hear the sound of rickety wheels rattling over the boardwalk and the murmuring of a small group of Russians. And then I hear a young woman's voice rise above them, sharp and quick, like the crack of a whip in the salt air.

"Shh, tiho." Quiet.

I turn and shudder looking for her, wondering where she is, but by the time I've turned all I can see is their backs. There is a woman in her late twenties, already a little round. She's pushing a baby in a stroller and has her hand through the crook of a young man's arm. He's wearing a leather jacket. Just behind them an older couple saunters and teases their daughter for her severity. When the old people see that she isn't looking they pull close to one another and kiss. The sun setting behind the tenements puts them in silhouette, and gradually all five of them become one dark shape disappearing into the distance.

"Quiet," I hear her say one more time to the child in the stroller. "You shouldn't cry. Happy children don't behave that way."

—New York, Moscow, Sarajevo 1995–2001

Acknowledgments

Great thanks are due to my friends and family. Without them I would not have finished. Thanks first to Jeannie Campbell, who patiently sat through a reading of a very early fragment on the island of Sifnos and thereafter nudged me forward. To the playwright Cusi Cram, who helped pull my narrator out of deep space, found me an agent, and came up with a title. To David Gold, who managed, from India, to download my chapter-long dispatches and supplied me with the momentum to generate new installments. To Molly Shapiro, who applied her gracious intelligence to the work and helped do away with much of the nonsense. To Katherine Baldwin, for her excellent ear for Russian sensibilities. To my brother Matthew, for asserting his belief in my abilities. To Peter Hirsch, for his open-hearted plot surgery. To Daphne Beal, David Bearison, Mollie Boero, Rebecca Feig, Samantha Gillison, Sharon Guskin, Ademir Kenovic,

Acknowledgments

Guy Lancaster, Steve Lawrence, David McLary, Kate Mailer, Zak Othmer, Julia Pimsleur, Bray Poor, Bob and Connie Rosenblum, Marcia Sanders, Corinne Schiff, Helen Silver, Laura Straus, Elliot Thomson, Zoya Trunova, Nadya Vnoukov, Jennifer Westfeldt, and Eden Wurmfeld, all of whom were much too kind to much-too-early drafts.

On the publishing front, it is hard to judge who was more clever and kind—my agent Jack Horner or my editor Hillery Borton. It was with Jack's generous, tactful support that I was able to turn the early drafts into a professional piece of work. It was under Hillery's persistent, discerning eye and with her almost telepathic insight that *Leaving Katya* took on its final and I think best shape.

The former Soviet Union is the setting for this book and a central player in my life. Great thanks are therefore due to the people who brought me there and sustained me: my friends and colleagues at Internews International. Thanks in particular to Manana Aslamazyan, Anthony Garrett, David Hoffman, Annette Makino, Vince Malmgren, Evelyn Messinger, Persephone Miel, and Kim Spencer.

And thanks finally to Harvey, Sharon, and Nick, for their loving kindness. Thank you for helping me emerge from my Russia Phase a happier and hopefully better person.